All The Day Long

Missionaries Reaching Tribes in the Amazon

MILLIE DAWSON

WINEPRESS WP PUBLISHING

Printed in the United States of America

Packaged by WinePress Publishing, PO Box 428, Enumclaw, WA 98022. The views expressed or implied in this work do not necessarily reflect those of WinePress Publishing. Ultimate design, content, and editorial accuracy of this work are the responsibilities of the author.

Unless otherwise noted all scriptures are taken from the King James Version of the Holy Bible.

ISBN 1-57921-254-9
Library of Congress Catalog Card Number: 99-66556

All The Day Long

Missionaries Reaching Tribes in the Amazon

By Sharon Dawson (child #8)

A million memories are keeping me warm tonight. Sunny days and moonlight boat rides, laughter echoing across the waters . . . Mermaids, Flatheads, elves out in the jungle, fantasy, make-believe, life was such a wonder. I never will forget these memories.

Life was always filled with fun and good times and yes, even bad times. But it seemed like the hard times only drew us closer together. I guess it was because we saw you two uniting together, making us feel secure. It was always a good feeling lying in bed at night, hearing you two take turns praying for each of us kids by name. . . . Standing in the gap for us. Your desires were to see each of us living our lives for the Lord.

Growing up in the jungle it would seem that life was like a never-ending dream. And though the years have vanished away the memories that we made, they'll never fade. Yes, a million memories are keeping me warm tonight. Singing, laughing, having such a good time, childhood memories echoing through the years . . . Heartaches, teardrops, holding us together. . . . Yes, I love these precious memories.

Yes, life certainly did seem like a dream. A dream that has only gotten better with time. Memories that hold us and bind us together and keep us warm, in any kind of weather. And we have you both to thank for that! We surely do love you both!

This book is dedicated to my wonderful husband, Joe, who has been a big help in getting it written, and to our children: Steve, Gary, Faith, Velma, Michael, Susan, Sandra, Sharon, Joseph, and Jerald. Together we have fought dragons and conquered for Christ in seeing Yanomamö put their faith in Jesus, learn to read His Word for themselves, and grow spiritually.

Contents

ODE TO JOE AND MILLIE DAWSON

BY VELMA DAWSON GRIFFIS

It started October '53,
Many years ago.
You left your home in the USA
And headed for foreign shores.
No money and three small kids
With another on the way. . .
Your lives in the years to come
Were never quite the same.
You were there when times were hard;
You stayed when times were bad.
We've heard you say they were the
Best years you ever had.
You stayed though disappointments
Often made you low and sad.
You were there to see the gospel change
The lonely hearts to glad.
To old Platanal you first went

Through rivers and jungle trails.
From the adventures that you've had
You could write a thousand tales.
But Cosh was where you finally saw
Sin-shackled lives set free.
Changed by the power of Jesus' love
And living in victory.
Now there were times down through the years
When everything went wrong,
But better days erased the cares
And gave the heart a song,
Like when an old witchdoctor
Whispered, "Lord, I do believe."
Your trials and disappointments fade
In quiet perfect peace.
You were there when times were hard;
You stayed when times were bad.
We've heard you say they were the best
Years you ever had.
You stayed though disappointments
Often left you low and sad.
You were there to see the gospel change
The lonely hearts to glad.

I

Bautista Tells His Story

My Father wanted to know how to escape the fire; that's why we moved out to the big river," he said.

I looked up in astonishment at Bautista, our Yanomamö translation helper.

Then Joe and I looked at each other. We were working on the translation of the Yanomamö New Testament, and something we were discussing had brought the past to Bautista's mind.

His name was not always Bautista, a new name for new life. He well remembers the life he lived as a little boy growing up deep in the Amazon rain forest of Venezuela.

It is generally believed that they live an idealistic life in the interior of the rain forest, far away from civilization and all it's troubles. They seem to have an "I, Tarzan, you, Jane" existence, a life applauded by many as being the ideal, the Utopia of mankind. Still, this little band of Indians found they too had all of the problems of mankind locked within themselves.

Their lives are not so ideal as pictured, as they themselves will not hesitate to tell.

Bautista tells of fear and superstition, fleeing often in the night from one location to another to escape the "spirits" of sickness who had invaded their camp. Children were hushed as the little band quietly crept away in the darkness, hoping to escape the notice of the dreaded sickness and get to a location where they would not be discovered and would not die. They did not realize that they carried with them to their new location the very sickness they had fled to escape.

He remembers awakening often to the chanting and dancing of the shaman as he tried to expel a sickness from a suffering body. The sucking and blowing, the contortions of the sweating body glistening eerily in the campfire were scenes etched indelibly on the child mind.

How he feared the evil jecula, those spirits sent by their enemies to make his people sick. He watched with the wide-eyed wonder of childhood as his father, a noted shaman, called upon his own personal jecula to command them to protect his people and to send them against the enemy. His father had told him that the jecula called him "Father" and he called them his "children." His father had thought those jecula were his to command. He did not realize that they were the ones controlling him.

The boy was kept in fear and awe of the supernatural powers that filled the very forest around him. The dreaded words bole and boleana, which referred to the burn-blackened spirits of the dead that roamed his world and were heard often in the snapping of a tree where there was no one else around, kept him obedient to his elders and sent him shaking to his hammock if he dared to question the authority of the elders or disobey in any way. He was told of the spirits who lurked in the woods, of those spirits who lived under the streams and stole away the children. He often cast fearful eyes over his shoulder to make sure none were following him to snatch him when the watchful eyes of his parents might be turned away. From babyhood, he was taught revenge and hate. If a fellow playmate made him cry, he was given a stick and forced to return blow for blow that he might grow up fierce and able to protect himself. Fear and public opinion ruled his world. Strict taboos made life hard while he was growing up, as many foods were forbidden him.

He saw the malnourished bloated bodies of the little children, many who did not make it to adulthood. He experienced the terror of enemy raids, as the enemies of his village flooded his shabono (a large circle with roofs and poles in which all the Yanomamö live) with their arrows, leaving behind the dead and wounded. He saw the fear in the eyes of those who had been blown upon by the alowali, feared by everyone. It was supposed to have magical powers to cause loss of strength, sickness, and even death, so it was not to be taken lightly.

He saw too the brutality of his own people as they killed their enemies without mercy. He heard the cries of the stricken and the weeping of the captured women. He joined his cries and wails to the lamentations of those who mourned his dead relatives and friends.

Many baby brothers and sisters did not make it through the difficult stages of babyhood and young childhood. His father had four wives (three of them were sisters), and the children were many. At the death of each sibling, he huddled in his hammock and wept, calling upon the baby's spirit to return to the little body, but life must go on, and the body was soon committed to the bier and consumed by the flames. He covered his face and fled to escape the nauseous odor of cooking flesh.

Later the little blackened bits of burned bones were painstakingly gathered from the cooled ashes and placed in a leaf-lined basket. These would then be ground to a fine black powder and consumed in a drink made of the ripened plantains amidst the weeping, wailing, and dancing of the grieving relatives and friends.

If an older person died, the grief was more pronounced, and days were spent in the orgies of the leajou, as they drank the bones and burned the possessions of the deceased. This was a time designed to work themselves up into a frenzy of grief and rage together with other villages they had called.

To the Yanomamö, no death is happenstance or natural. Someone somewhere has worked bad magic against them and caused the death. Therefore, they must now avenge the death by going to kill someone from that village. The shaman is consulted. He goes into his doped-up trance and finds out from his spirits who the culprit is and what village he lives in.

After working themselves up emotionally to face the enemy, they paint their faces black, and the raiding party is off to bring retribution to some unsuspecting village. Of course, that only leads to more death and revenge.

Sometimes, however, their leajos are conducted for the purpose of settling old disputes and re-establishing friendships with those they had become alienated from because of inter-village squabbles. At these leajos, friends and those with whom they hoped to resolve old quarrels and become friends with again would be invited.

The chest-pounding contest in which they hoped to get rid of their ill feelings against a neighboring village often filled the child's heart with terror that his older brothers or his father would be wounded or killed.

He was especially worried when they went off on the raids. He spent many anxious hours until their return. How happy he was when peace once more reigned and the now friendly village returned home carrying away huge baskets of smoked meat that his father and the other men had spent many days killing and smoking for this purpose.

True, his belly pinched with hunger pangs. The thought of the succulent meat eaten with a tasty piece of hot plantain almost brought tears of self-pity to his eyes. However, that was life as he knew it as a Yanomamö child, and he did not think to question it.

Later his village would be invited to a leajou as a death was mourned in a neighboring village and a feast prepared for the drinking of the bones of the deceased. Then his village would carry off the baskets of meat. Then he would fill his empty stomach even as they were now.

Such was the life of the Yanomamö. These things made up his world. Of course, all was not bad. He loved to roam with his father on a hunt, killing and smoking the meat to carry home.

"Here, Son, carry this monkey on your back," his father would say handing him a limp, dead monkey. It dangled from vines made into a loop to fit down over his chest. Sometimes it was a wild turkey, a brightly colored macaw, or maybe a monkey or two.

Swinging the vines up and over his head to settle down over his chest, he would proudly stalk along behind his father, carrying the meat back to their primitive campsite. There he would clean it and throw it up on the smoke rack to be dried and blackened. This would preserve it until they could get it home. He was proud of the part he played in finding food to survive.

He liked also to accompany his mother to the jicali to bring back the large stalks of bananas that would be hung to ripen in their section of the open leaf shabono. How good they would taste as the skin ripened and he could pluck them off and fill up on the delicious soft goodness of the ripened fruit.

He loved to eat the culata, the huge plantains that his mother would peel green and place on the hot coals of the family hearth, turning them deftly so they browned evenly and cooked through. How good it was to break off the hot pieces and eat them with small pieces of smoked meat or some type of fruit that they had harvested from the forest that day! He remembers huddling around the opened package of fish with younger brothers and sisters, eating the soft tender flesh of the fish and the "bread" of the plantain—warm, content, happy. For the moment asking no more from life than a full stomach, the warmth of the fire, loved ones around him, and a feeling that all's well.

He loved to climb like a monkey up the trees in the rain forest to pluck off the ripe fruit and eat his fill. Leaves suitable for making a carrying pouch were then broken off. Fruit was pulled off the stems and packaged up in these leaves to be carried home to younger ones who had remained behind.

Yes, much of life was good. He loved the freedom, the tropical forest, the trees, the blue sky, and the trickling streams containing small fish they often shot with small arrows made of sharpened palm. These were roasted in leaves on the hot coals, the mouth-watering smells of the fish juices as they sizzled on the coals mingling with the fragrant odor of the burning leaves. True, the little black biting gnats swarming his bare body by day and the bloodthirsty mosquitoes biting at night were not pleasant. However, he knew no other life.

Always there was the fear and many times the hunger when, because of enemies camped nearby, the people of his village were afraid to leave the safety provided by their round, barricaded house in the depths of the rain forest. They were afraid to hunt for meat, going meat-hungry rather than risking an enemy arrow. They were afraid to leave the enclosure even to relieve themselves and rather did so inside against the back wall of the houses, the stench growing more unbearable with time if the enemy was particularly persistent. The children were cautioned to be quiet and forbidden to play lest their noise draw the enemy and cover the sounds of the enemies' approach.

Then too there were the many times when the gardens did not produce. Food was scarce in the forest and hunger prevailed in their whole world. Bodies grew gaunt. Resistance to sickness and disease was lowered and many died. All suffered greatly. In those times, life was very hard and little children cried themselves to sleep with hunger. This too was all part of being a Yanomamö.

So he grew to manhood, a good Yanomamö, well trained in the ways of his people, well versed in the Yanomamö folklore, and filled with the fear and superstitions of his elders. There in the forest, he followed in the footsteps of his father and began training to be a shaman.

His brother-in-law, a much older man, began Bautista's training, becoming his mentor. Bautista was taken to a special place that had been built and prepared for him in the shabono. There he remained. No one except his mentor was allowed to see or speak to him. He was given only certain types of food to eat— and very little of that. During this time, he became very skinny.

"The spirits won't come to you unless you're skinny," his mentor told him.

When he was considered skinny enough and ready to invoke the spirits who were to come and live in his chest, he was brought out. Ebena, a dope powder that they make themselves from elements of the rain forest, was placed in a long thin tube. Then the tube was placed up to his nostril. His mentor then blew on the other end of the tube and the ebena shot into Bautista's brain. He doubled over with the pain. It was excruciating. Then as the ebena began to take effect, he found himself entering into the world of the spirits. The men danced back and forth, chanting and calling for spirits to enter his chest and build their shabonos where eventually more spirits could come to live.

So he became just another Yanomamö shaman living in the great Amazon rain forest, calling upon his spirits as his forefathers had done before him.

Bautista continued his reflection to us. "Yes, many, many years ago when my father was just a young man, almost the whole world burned up. My father and his village were almost destroyed in the fire, but they managed to get out into the middle of a deep stream and were saved as the fire swept by them. My father often spoke of it. It was a dreadful time. The trees were gone. They were just blackened stubs. Blackened animal carcasses lay all around," he shook his head. "Yes, it was a bad time."

He looked at Joe with a twinkle in his eyes. "Do you remember when you foreigners first moved to Tamatama?" he asked. "You were camped on that big rock that goes down into the water. You had up a tarp for a roof to sleep under. Jacobo, Cecilio, Francisco, and Julio Jimenez were with you. We arrived from upriver in a bark canoe. We had made ourselves a bark canoe so we could come downriver to see you foreigners. We wanted to get machetes from you."

Joe nodded and chuckled. "Yes, I surely remember that all right. Millie and our four little kids were in San Fernando de Atabapo, and I was there in Tamatama building a house so I could move my family there. We had spent a year in Platanal. Then my leaders sent Millie and the kids downriver so we men could study language. But then our big chief decided that we should move out of the village to a place where there were no people, so we could study the language we had gotten written down. We wanted to learn the language well, so we could talk to you people. So, it was decided that we should move to Tamatama, build houses, and move our families there. There we would study and learn to talk well."

"Julio tried to talk to me in my language, but he didn't know it very well. He said to me, 'Later Dios [God] is going to destroy this world by fire. What are you going to do?' I was very afraid and asked him many questions, but he looked at me with no understanding in his eyes. He shook his head and showed me with his hands that he did not understand. I went back home very troubled.

"'Who is Yosi?' I asked my father. Julio had said, 'Dios,' but I thought he said 'Yosi'. 'The foreigner said Yosi is going to burn up the world. "What are you going to do when the world burns up?" he asked me.'

"My father became very excited. 'Yes!' he said. 'He tells the truth. I do not know whom he's talking about. I do not know who Yosi is. Maybe he is Ynalu [Thunder]. Maybe he is another spirit that we do not know, but I know this, he has already tested it one time to see if it would burn, and now he knows that it will burn. When did the foreigner say he was going to burn it again?'

"'They didn't say. They can't really talk.' I said. 'Nor can they understand, even though we talked very loudly in their ears. They are very tongue-tied.' I said.

"My father was very upset. 'Go back to this place where the foreigners are living,' he commanded. 'Tell them to come to our village and live here with us so they can tell us how to escape the fire,' he said."

"I remember you coming to ask us to move to your village!" Joe said excitedly. "But we didn't know that your father wanted to hear about God. We thought you all wanted us for the trade goods and medicine, just like everyone did."

"My father was very angry when you wouldn't move to our village. But then he thought and thought. 'It's because we're living so far interior,' he said. So, he moved our village out to the banks of the big river, even though the women were very afraid of the spirits that lived in that area. Then we called you again, but you still didn't come."

"We didn't understand," Joe defended himself. "We couldn't understand your language very well. We needed time to study and learn."

"Yes, you told me that you had to stay in Tamatama to study. But, my father was so angry that he moved us back interior again. But later he became sad again, and he was worried Yosi would drop the fire and we wouldn't know how to escape, so he finally moved us back to the big river again.

"'Now someone will surely come who will be able to tell us how to escape the fire that is coming,' he said.

"One day a boat carrying a priest and his people stopped at our village. As the boat pulled into the shore we saw the priest with his long white beard, and my father said, 'Look how old this one is. Surely he'll be able to tell us how to escape the fire.'

"But they could not speak to us either. They just passed out some brown sugar to us and got back in their boats and left."

"And to think," I said to Joe as Bautista finished, "that during those years we were so discouraged, thinking that nothing was being accomplished. We did not realize that there was anything at all happening in the lives of the Yanomamö. And here they themselves were searching for further light. True, they were concerned about their physical lives, but the Holy Spirit was using this to prepare their hearts. . . ."

My mind went back to January of 1960 when we had moved to Coshilowa-teli, Bautista's father's village. I remembered the interest the old man had shown from the very beginning. He had seemed to devour the words spoken to him of a God who lived in heaven. A God who loves the Yanomamö. A God who was his friend. A God who could not only save him from destruction by the fire, but also wanted to save his soul, give him eternal life, and keep him from the eternal fire. This old man, Bautista's father, believed.

Years later as the old man lay dying, Bautista had called Joe to his hammock. Joe had knelt down in the dirt of the floor, raised the old man's head, and looked deep into his eyes. "Father," he said, "Are you ready to leave us? Father, are you sure you have believed on Jesus, God's Son, to save you and carry your spirit to heaven?"

Death was near. The signs were unmistakable, and the wails and lamentations of the grieving relatives made it necessary to lean very close to catch the dying words.

"Son, as soon as I heard the message of the one who is able to save from the fire, I hung my desires on Jesus and they're still hanging there."

Shortly after that, the old man went to be with the Lord.

A few days later, Bautista came to the house again. "Pepiwa [Joe]," he said, "My sister is over in the house crying. I was witnessing to her and telling her that our Father has gone to heaven to be with Jesus and that she should believe on Jesus so she can go to be with Father some day. But she is crying and saying that she wants to go to be with Mother. She's saying, 'Where is Mother? I want to go to be with her when I die!' Pepiwa, where is Mother? She died before you got here. Where did she go?"

In relating the story to me, Joe said he could well understand the sister's desire to go to be with her mother. To a Yanomamö girl, her mother is her closest friend, the one who is there for her. Now this woman wanted to go where her mother had gone, and her mother had died before the Word of God had gotten to the village.

Joe said that the hardest thing that he has ever done was to tell Bautista that his mother had died in her sins without Christ and therefore was not in heaven. He prayed silently, fervently asking God for something to say to comfort this dear brother and to somehow meet the need in his heart. Surprisingly, the Lord brought to his mind the story of the Rich Man and Lazarus in the Gospel of Luke.

Joe related this story to him and said, "Bautista, your mother didn't know Jesus. She had not heard of Him. Your mother is in hell, but in hell the rich man's desire was for someone to go and tell his five brothers so that they would not come to that place of torment."

"Bautista," he said, "Your mother's one desire is that none of her children come to join her there in that place of torment. She is longing for someone to tell them the Good News so they too will not suffer for eternity. So go tell your sister that her mother's desire is for her to be saved and not join her there in torment."

2

GOD HAS A PLAN

It was a cold blustery day in February of 1920, the 29th to be exact, making it a leap year, when Joseph Gallians Dawson made his appearance into the world in a small house out in the country near Linden, Virginia. He was a scrawny baby weighing less than five pounds, the son of Hayward and Grace Dawson. A very unpretentious little baby, born to very humble and unpretentious parents, but God's hand was in this. He was preparing a vessel. Joe grew up in the country at a place called Hidden Valley. His father was a farmer. While there was little money, he managed to grub out a living for his family.

Joe and his brothers and sisters walked many miles to the little schoolhouse where they attended school. Many days they had to stay home from school when the harsh winter weather drove them inside. When he was about fourteen, Joe's dad became unable to work. Joe had to drop out of school, go to work, and support the family. His education suffered and Joe felt this inadequacy in his later life. But he never allowed it to interfere with what he felt God was leading him to do.

The year 1940 rolled around. Joe was 20 years old and World War II was right on the horizon. He knew he would soon be drafted, so Joe enlisted and entered the Army on October 16, 1940.

It was a hot, sultry tropical day (or night) probably around 1926 or 1927. We cannot be certain as to the exact date, but during this time, another baby boy was born. The birth of this baby was very different from the other. There was no one to assist in this birth. His mother probably slipped out to the edge of the forest and gave birth to her son. Unlike the other little boy, he was not named at his birth. He would just be called "little son" or "little brother" until someone at some future day would call him a name for something he had done to draw attention to himself.

There in the tropical rain forest of Amazonas, Venezuela, he would grow to manhood, leaving behind the toy bows and arrows of childhood to adapt to the long six-foot bow and arrows of adulthood. He never knew of the Great War that was fought to keep the world free. He only knew of the intertribal wars fought by his own people. Who was to know that this man even existed deep in the heart of the forest, far from all known civilization? God knew! Again, God was preparing a vessel.

It was another cold winter day in January of 1931 when a baby girl entered the scene. To Wilbur and Anna Mary Morris in the Shenandoah Valley, near the small town of Strasburg, Virginia, a baby girl, their second child, was born and named Mildred Lee, also of humble origin with no claim to wealth or fame. These three children, born at three different times, in three different places. Yet in God's great plan these three were to come together to work out His plan. The plan that He had for each of these lives was to be interwoven into the great plan that He had for the Yanomamö tribe hidden deep in the Amazon rain forest of Venezuela.

The year was 1943. World War II was in progress. In an army rest camp in New Guinea, a small group of war-weary soldiers sat at a rickety table playing cards. Their attention, however, was not on the cards being shuffled or even the money that had been flung carelessly in the center of the table. Their thoughts were on the war, on their buddies even now dying in battle, a battle they would soon re-enter. Would any of them make it back home? Would any of them see loved ones again?

Buddy shook his head mournfully as he studied the hand of cards he had drawn. "I just have a feeling that one of those Jap bullets' got my name on it, boys," he said. "I ain't never had much luck, and I feel what little I have is fast runnin' out."

"Yea, I know how you feel. I figure if I'm lucky enough to get back at all, some part of me'll be missin'," said Tom.

"Well, you guys may be right, but if I get through this mess alive, I'll wind up with a section eight. The things I've seen and done, guys blown to bits, bodies laying there bloody and messy. . . I tell you, I already have nightmares. I just don't think I'll be the same when this is all over." Jack's sallow face gleamed eerily in the flickering light, sweat glistening in the sultry tropical heat. A mosquito droned.

Joe looked up, his thoughts returning to the scene before him. The words of his companions rang in his ears. The horror of all he had seen and experienced washed over his memory as he pondered their words. Then, as he started to add his own dismal outlook to what was being said, he saw briefly in his mind's eye his mother kneeling in prayer. Her words came back to him.

"I'm praying for you, Son."

A peace filled his heart. His mother's God would see him through

"Well, fellows, I believe I'll be going home in one piece and in my right mind. My Mother's praying for me. . . ."

1945. The "war after the war to end all wars" was over. The soldiers were going home. Joe trudged down the shady, country dirt road that led home. As he rounded a bend in the road, the old gray country mailbox came in sight. His heart leaped within him and a feeling of great peace came into his heart. This was home. This was what it had all been about. This was why he had given five years of his life. This was why he still carried a bullet in his arm, so that he could walk down this quiet, dusty, country road in peace and safety. His eyes misted as he saw his mother coming down the path from the house. He watched as she opened the box to peer in, no doubt looking for a letter from him. Something caused her to raise her eyes and look in his direction. He saw the shock, the disbelief, the hope, and then the joy that flooded her face as they ran into each other's arms.

"Son, I've been so worried. I heard you were wounded. I have never stopped praying you would come home. God is so good."

3

JOE AND I MEET

Joe tried to pick up the pieces of his life and go on from where he had left off when the war had called him away. He found a job, and on Saturday and Sunday night, like most of the rest of the young men, he would head for town and a good show. The only theater open on Sunday night in those days was in a town about twenty-five miles away, so he and some of his friends usually headed there early every Sunday evening to be on time when the show started.

But on a certain day in April of 1945, fate stepped in on the whim of a friend and changed the course of Joe's life.

"Fellows, we've gone to the show every Saturday and Sunday night for weeks. I'm for the roller skating rink in Strasburg tonight. What do you all say?" one of the fellows spoke up hopefully.

"Not I," said Joe. "Look guys, I made it back in one piece from the war, and I'm not going to risk life and limb on roller skates," he protested.

"Don't tell me you're afraid of a pair of skates after fighting a war," one of them joked.

"You just bet I am," Joe replied. "I can't roller skate, and I've seen people falling around on them. Those things can fly out from under you, and you can really hurt yourself."

After much laughing and joking around, a couple of the boys convinced Joe that they knew how to skate.

"We'll hold on to you until you get the hang of it, and you won't get hurt," they said. "Just think about all the pretty girls that go there."

Amidst much laughing and good-natured jostling, they made their way to the skating rink in Strasburg for a Sunday night of fun.

With a buddy on each side supporting him, Joe made it around the rink once, twice, and then a third time. Yes, he seemed to be getting the "hang" of it all right.

"Well, Joe, it looks like you're doing OK now!" they said, and with a push they propelled him forward on his own into the crowd. True to his earlier foreboding, one foot went one way and one another. Then both feet went out from under him, and he found himself flat on his back on the floor with all his breath knocked out of him. As he opened his eyes, he found himself looking into what to him seemed the most beautiful face he had ever seen. Blue eyes looked down on him with pity.

"Oh boy, I'm dead, and this is heaven, and here's an angel," he said.

Then he heard a voice saying, "Let me help you up." Grasping his hand she helped him to his feet and somehow managed to get him out of the traffic and over to the sidelines, where they found a seat. From that moment, Joe knew he had met the girl of his dreams. Joe sat there on the bench and watched her skate away, never taking his eyes off her as she darted around the floor. Finally, she returned to the bench and removed her skates.

"Well, I have to go," she said. "I promised Mom I'd be home by 10:30, and I have to leave now."

"How about me walking you home?" Joe asked. "Look, I know we haven't been officially introduced, but my name is Joe Dawson. I'm a respectable guy; spent the last five years in the South Pacific and just got discharged. I live in Linden. I'd sure like to get to know you."

She smiled at him. "My name is Mildred Morris, and I live here in Strasburg. I'm sure you are very respectable and a nice guy, but no. I'm here with a couple of friends, and we walk home together."

With a slight smile and a toss of her head, she was gone. Joe fairly tore the skates from his feet. He rounded up the boys who had come with him and told them he was leaving. Some had had enough skating by that time and followed, but they had a hard time keeping up with Joe as he galloped down the hill towards the town. In the flash of the car lights that passed them by, he could see the figures of three girls ahead, walking down the hill. One of them was the girl he was rushing to keep in sight. Hearing the clatter of the fellows galloping up behind them, the girls turned to meet them. Soon they were all walking along, laughing and talking like old friends.

So it was that Joe walked me home after all, and we began a relationship that blossomed into love. From that day on there was hardly a day that we did not see each other. Joe put in an appearance, come rain or snow.

There is a standing joke in the family. Once a huge snowstorm left the roads blocked and traffic was at a standstill for hours. The mountain roads where Joe lived and where no snowplow was known to go were filled halfway up the fence posts.

"Well, I know Joe won't be able to get here tonight," my sisters teased me, so I settled myself with pen and paper to write a long letter to him. I thought I would not see him for several days at least. A knock on the door roused me from my dreams. I opened the door to find Joe bundled up to his ears but wearing a big grin on his face! His brothers still laugh at the way they say Joe hopped away over the snow like a jackrabbit in spite of their dire warnings that he would be found frozen to death in a snowdrift.

I was a sophomore in high school when I met Joe. I was a good student and liked school, even dreamed of college, but meeting him changed my plans also. I had a Math teacher in high school who was also my Bible Teacher. Yes, in those days it was still permissible and not unconstitutional to teach children Bible in the schools. He was one of my favorite teachers. He had been a missionary in Africa for three years but had given it up because of his wife's ill health. His wife later died and he remarried, but his second wife did not want to go to the mission field. His heart was still with missions, and many times he said to me, "Mildred, why don't you become a missionary? Go to college and study and become a missionary."

The idea appealed to me romantically, as I envisioned myself in a foreign land surrounded by natives that I had come there to teach. However, since I myself, at that time, was not a Christian, I am afraid my ideas of becoming a missionary were neither scriptural nor spiritual. During this time, Joe and I continued our courtship, and, amazingly, my grades did not suffer. My thoughts of college and being a missionary changed, however, to becoming a homemaker and maybe someday a mother. I graduated in June and we were married December 7, 1947.

Things did not go well for us in the beginning. Joe was suffering from bad attacks of malaria, picked up in the South Pacific. This made it hard for him to hold down a job. Jobs were scarce. His repeated missing of work made him a likely candidate when they had a lay off. Finally, we were forced to rent out the house that we were buying on the GI bill and move from Front Royal to a farm outside of Warrenton, Virginia. We did well there, and Joe soon became manager of the farm. We moved into the newly built manager's bungalow and began to furnish it with new furniture bought on the credit plan, but, nonetheless, at last my dreams of a nice home were going to be realized. I had grown up very poor. I wanted from life a nice home, a good husband, and some healthy, happy children. With the birth of our first child, Steven Douglas, on March 4, 1950 it began to look as though all my dreams were coming true.

4

SALVATION AND GOD'S CALL

"Vernie stopped by again today, Joe, to ask us to go to church with them Sunday. He never gives up does he? I keep telling him we aren't interested."

Joe was busy washing his hands at the sink after a hard day on the farm. Supper was on the table, and I was making small talk while we leisurely got ready to sit down to our meal. Nineteen-month-old Stevie was beating on the tray of his high chair while his new two-month-old brother, Gary, slept soundly in his crib in the bedroom.

We were doing well there on the farm. Things had never looked better for us. Joe was taking "on farm" training under the GI Bill. The money he received from the government plus his farm pay was sufficient to help us live well.

Then too our house was supplied to us rent-free. We received milk, eggs, and meat (chicken, pork, and beef). We raised a large vegetable garden in the spring and summer, and I preserved these in jars for the winter. With the larder full, we felt rich. I was even able to sell the cream from the milk we received. Joe gave the cream money to me. I felt as snug as a bug in a rug. I felt all of my dreams for the future were coming true.

I did not want to be bothered by Joe's brother, Vernie, inviting us to the little clapboard church in the country, where he attended. Not that I had anything against going to church. In fact, I had been thinking for sometime that it would be nice to get started going to church. Joe and I had talked about it quite at length when we were first married. We had even started out reading the Bible each night, but we would get through Genesis and Exodus, and then Leviticus would throw us every time. Then we would lay the Bible aside again deciding that probably you were not really supposed to understand the Bible anyway.

I really had every intention of going to church, but when I went, I wanted to go to that big brick church there in Warrenton. I wanted to go to a church that looked worthy of the name. That little board church, way out there in the country, was not my idea of a real church.

"Yea, well, Vernie's really wantin' us to go this Sunday. He says they're havin' a special speaker up from Washington, D.C., some radio minister. Vernie says he has a great message. He's been after me all week too. Maybe we should give it a try. It won't hurt anything, and it will make Mother and everyone happy if we go," Joe said as he seated himself at the table.

"Well, OK, I guess so." I replied, absentmindedly fixing Stevie's plate of food.

My thoughts were on the coming Sunday and just how we would like getting together with people we did not know. Stevie's impatient bangs caused me to put away my thoughts and take care of the business at hand, feeding a hungry husband and little boy.

Sunday dawned clear, sunny, and not too cold for an October day. My hopes for rain, snow, or at least severe cold that could give me a good excuse for keeping the children home were not to be realized. There was nothing to do but get ready to go. How was I to know that this was one of the most important days in my life?

The little church stood there starkly in the crisp, cold morning air. We entered hurriedly and found seats, trying to look as unobtrusive as possible. However, from the time the visiting preacher opened his Bible and began to read in Isaiah, I knew that I was in this church for a definite purpose. I knew God's hand had led me there in spite of myself.

As this man, expounding the Word of God, made it clear to me that I was a lost sinner in need of God's mercy and grace, the people around me faded into insignificance. My only thought was How could I become reconciled to a holy and just God? I knew that I was not ready to face Him.

Then Rev. Crowley told us how God Himself had made the way for me by sending His own Son to die for my sins and pay the penalty that was due me. I found myself on my feet following Joe to the front of the church to make a public confession that I wanted this Jesus, who had given so much that I could be worthy of heaven. Joe and I were both gloriously saved that night.

One month later Mr. Crowley's son, Dale Jr., came to the little country church with Elmer Rabe from New Tribes Mission. We sat on the edge of our seats as they showed the film of the first New Tribes Missionaries who had gone to Bolivia. Hostile Indians, the people the missionaries had gone to reach, had killed five of those young fellows. I sat there looking at the film of those young men and their families going out to take the gospel to people who had never heard it, laying down their lives.

I had not even realized that there were still people living like that in the world today.

I said, "Oh, Lord, I'd be willing to go tell them about Jesus and how He died to save them, but I know Joe would never want to do that. He's a farmer."

I was surprised after the service to see Joe at the back of the church talking to the two missionaries. I walked up as Joe was saying, "I sure wish I had more education. I'd really like to go to be a missionary, but I don't have enough education."

Dale Jr. smiled and said, "How much education do you reckon Peter and John had? They were simple fishermen."

Well, before we left there that night we were clutching application blanks for enrolling in New Tribes Mission. When we left the church that night we were bubbling over with what God was doing in our lives. We felt as though we were new people. Joe had been a heavy smoker all his life, cross as a bear if he was out of his cigarettes. But he came to a decision at that moment.

"Hon," he said. "How can I go to the foreign field and tell them about a Savior that can save them from their sins with a cigarette in my hand? They have to go. The Lord will have to deliver me from them."

So saying, he opened the window of the car and pitched his pack of cigarettes out into the darkness. He ate a lot of popcorn as he rode the tractor up and down the fields, throwing out feed to the cattle or running around the farm in the jeep, but never again did he ever take another puff of a cigarette. The Lord marvelously delivered him and we didn't even realize it was a big thing. We just completely expected Him to do it and He did.

We filled out the application blanks and sent them off. Joe went to work as usual. I fed and tended the kids and put them down for a nap. Then I had time to think. I walked through the little house looking at the furniture we had. I thought of the security the house, the furniture, and the job represented. I remembered the words of the missionary: "You go by faith. You trust God to meet your needs."

I began to feel sick inside wondering what we had done. Had we lost our senses? Were we being bowled over by an emotional kick that would leave us destitute when it passed by? I got down on my knees by the living room sofa. I did not know too much about praying.

My prayers had consisted of "Now I lay me down to sleep" when I was a kid and asking God not to let my mother die. She suffered badly from migraine headaches, and when I was a kid, not understanding a migraine, I had a real horror that she was going to die.

But there on my knees that day I poured out my heart to the Lord. I told Him that I was willing to do whatever He had for us. I opened my eyes and looked around. I told Him the house, the furniture, and everything we had there was not important if He wanted to use our lives to take His Word to people who had never heard.

As I poured out my heart to Him, He heard and answered. He flooded me with a peace I had never known before. The whole world looked clean and new to my eyes. It sparkled and shone on that cold November day.

Out in the fields as he worked, Joe too was going through his own time of doubt, fear, and desperation. Was he being foolhardy? Was this of God or some wild imaginings of his own? He had a wife and two small children to consider. Things were going well for him at this time on the farm. Was he throwing away his chances for a comfortable lifestyle for some pipe dream? There in the field he knelt to pray and seek the mind of the Lord. The more he prayed the more convinced he was that the Lord was leading him in this step. He arose from his knees filled with the peace that passes understanding and willing to step out by faith.

Our application was accepted. We had hoped to go in January when the new term started, but some debts we had prevented this. We found that when selling your furniture, the same pieces that had cost so much are not worth much as second-hand furniture.

Joe gave his notice at the farm. His boss was astounded and attempted to talk him out of "this foolishness."

His boss's wife said, "Joe, I just can't picture you in a long white robe!"

My older sister called me from California and wept. She was sure that we had gotten involved with some cult and were headed for disaster.

Friends and family all tried to influence us not to throw away the good things we had for a vision. But our ears were deaf to their pleas. We continued to make our plans.

We sold our furniture and moved into a small, furnished apartment. Joe went to work temporarily for the Virginia State Highway Department. We wanted to get our bills paid off and be ready to go to the Mission "boot camp" in July when a new term would start. We had received the COMMAND and we were ready.

Our every thought was on going to the mission field. Our conversation centered on that subject. We spent our evenings driving around, picking up hitchhikers, and witnessing to them, sharing with them the message that had so changed our lives.

We were finding it hard to make ends meet as every spare penny went to pay off bills, keep our rent paid, and put food on the table. One incident stands out in my mind.

We had no money to buy milk for Gary's formula. Joe's brother Wesley and his wife, Sylvia, lived in the apartment above us. Sylvia's father used to stop by every morning to see them, and he would look in on us. Stevie was a favorite of his, and he would give Stevie a dime when he left.

As soon as he was gone we would say, "Now, Stevie, let's take the dime to the store and get Gary some milk." Then we'd buy another can of milk for Gary's formula.

One day there was no dime and no milk. That night Gary cried for his bottle. We had determined from the beginning not to mention a need to anyone else. Only the Lord would know when we were in need. So we went to our knees before Him in prayer, reminding Him that our child was hungry and there was no milk in the house. Still, Gary cried. No answer came.

Finally Joe got up and went to the kitchen. I heard him puttering around. He came back into the bedroom and handed the bottle to Gary. He said, "Lord, you turned water into wine at the wedding feast, now please turn water into milk, so that this hungry baby will go to sleep."

The cries were stilled and we lay there in the darkness wondering if the water had turned to milk. Joe said one of the hardest things he ever did was lay there and not get up to look, but finally he said to himself, "The baby is quiet. Whether it is milk or not, he is peaceful, so I'll not doubt by getting up to look." With that he turned over and went to sleep.

The next day some of the men at the yard where Joe was working teased him about his faith. They asked him how he thought he would be able to make it when he left his job and stepped out on faith. "After all, God isn't going to drop money down from the sky for you to pick up," someone jested.

"Well, I don't expect Him to drop money down from the sky, but He could if he wanted to!" Joe replied, undaunted.

That day while working out in the country, on one of the country roads, following the grader, Joe happened to glance up at a bush by the side of the road. On the bush hung a five-dollar bill. He looked all around. There was no one close by. He could see no one who could have lost a five-dollar bill.

When he got into the yard at quitting time, he asked if anyone had lost any money that day. Everyone laughed and joked about who would had any money to lose this close to payday. Joe pulled the five-dollar bill from his pocket and said, "Well then, I guess the Lord did drop me down some money from the sky. He hung it up on a blackberry bush for me."

That night we had money to buy Gary's milk. It greatly encouraged our hearts to see how God could and would meet our needs.

The day finally came when in July 1952, Joe's brother Wesley loaded up his '49 Ford with his wife, Sylvia, one of Joe's sisters, Josie, and her husband, Stewart, and himself in the front seat. Joe and I were on half of the back seat. Joe had two-year-old Stevie on his lap. I held eleven-month-old Gary on my lap. Our third child was to be born in August. (She put in her appearance just one day after Gary's first birthday, which was on the ninth of August.) The remaining half of the back seat and the trunk on top of the car were filled with our household goods and personal belongings.

It was crowded and uncomfortable, but everyone was in good spirits. The car was so overloaded that it did not make it up the mountain. We had to go back down the mountain and take a longer route. Stevie's little red wagon, which was tied on top of the car, fell off.

"Don't worry about it," Joe said. "Just let it go."

"No way. We'll stop and get it," Wes said. "That boy's going to have his wagon to take along." With that announcement, he stopped the car and ran back for the wagon, which he tied on top of the car again.

When we arrived at the boot camp, the staff and other trainees met us. We went immediately to Jungle Camp. All the students had moved out of the cabins down below and had moved up on the side of the mountain. They had set up tents and makeshift dwellings where they were living. This was to prepare them for living in the jungle without all the comforts of home. This was where our missionary preparation began.

Josie told me years later how hard it was for her to leave us there at that tent, which contained nothing inside but a make-shift bed. It was a crude wooden frame made of poles with boards on top. For a mattress, there was only hay. The hay was piled up on the boards, covered by sheets. I guess the nurse in her objected strenuously to an eight-month-pregnant woman sleeping on something like that. I confess that I was not really happy about it myself as I considered my already aching back.

5

OUR MISSIONARY TRAINING

The harsh strident clang of metal striking metal awakened me from a sound sleep. Joe rolled over, stretched, and began to climb gingerly off our makeshift bed of poles and straw. He dressed hurriedly and left for the Morning Prayer meeting that took place every morning there in Jungle Camp.

I eased myself up off my knees from the ground where I had been kneeling in our tent. There was much to do. I had to dress Stevie and Gary and get breakfast ready to put on the table when Joe returned. We would have to eat hurriedly so that we could take the boys to nursery before the bell rang for classes.

My movements were hampered by the fact that it was just a matter of weeks until my next baby would be born. With Stevie just two and a half and Gary not quite a year, I had my hands full.

Then I remembered. I did not have any groceries with which to get breakfast. We had used everything the day before. It had been our week to go to town for groceries, but we had no money and so had not gone. We had diligently prayed and watched our mailbox for an envelope containing money, so we could go to town. None had appeared.

In those days in boot camp in Jersey Shore, Pennsylvania, you were only allowed to go to town every other week. Since we had not gone on our week, then it would be two weeks before we would have another opportunity. Thank the Lord, I did have some milk for Gary's bottle, and a glass of milk for Stevie kept him happy as I tried to figure out what to fix for Joe.

While I was still dejectedly looking in the wooden box nailed up on a pole that we used for a cupboard, Joe came in all smiles. Well, when he remembers that we don't have anything here to eat, that'll take away his smile! I thought bitterly, feeling sorry for myself.

"Hi, Hon. Havin' trouble finding something to fix for breakfast?" he asked cheerily. "Here, let me look." With a flourish he pulled out a dilapidated box of some kind of hot cereal made of wheat, bran, or something similar. I had stuck the box away, as it was not a cereal that appealed to any of us.

A fellow in camp who had a large family of small children had brought us a small box of food when we first arrived in camp and this box of cereal had been in it. At that time, we had food in the tent, and I remember Joe saying, "People really ought to pray about what they give. I know that fellow with all those little children probably needed this food himself more than we do. I don't think the Lord was leading him."

Well, we had had to eat those words many times. Our food gave out. No more money came in, and we had to keep dipping into the little box of food we had previously questioned. This one little dilapidated box of cereal was left.

"What can we do with that?" I asked dubiously.

"You'll see what a tasty batch of pancakes this old box of cereal is going to make!" Joe grinned. He dumped the contents of the box into a bowl, added salt, baking powder and some water. Soon, we were outside making pancakes on our jungle camp wood stove. We bowed our heads over the thin, straggly-looking pancakes. Joe remembered to ask the Lord to forgive us for the remarks we had made concerning the gift given by a brother. The Lord had known we would have need of this little box of food.

After morning classes, we picked up the boys from nursery and headed back to our tent. Everyone lived out doors in the mountain above the New Tribes Mission Institute, where candidates were taking instruction, preparing themselves for the mission field. This property had originally been the Indian Park Bible Conference Grounds and had been donated to NTM for a training camp.

During the summer months, the grounds were still used for a Bible Conference, so the students moved up into the mountain. There we built shelters and set up camp. This was to help us learn how to live out in the jungles away from civilization. It was also to test us to find out how we would stand up under the strain of living without the modern conveniences.

We had classes all morning. Then the men had work detail in the afternoons while we women with small children did our housework and cared for our children. Each night we walked down the mountain and attended the conference meetings. After the meeting we once more climbed the mountain back to our little camp home. As I looked around at all the people preparing their noon meals, I realized that we were once more facing the preparation of a meal with no groceries. Realizing that for us not to be at our outside table would signify to all that we had no food, pride made me say, "Let's sit here at the table and talk. That way the other people won't know that we don't have any food."

In spite of my pride, the Lord was good to us. We had not been sitting there long when a lady came over who lived not too far from our tent. She was carrying a big bowl of prunes. "Could you folks use some prunes?" she asked. "I don't know what in the world made me cook so many prunes. Forrest and I will never be able to eat them all by ourselves," she said.

We thanked her and assured her we would enjoy the prunes very much. After she left we thanked the Lord for his provision and gratefully devoured the prunes. Neither before nor since have prunes tasted so good to me.

Many years later when we met out neighbor again, we mentioned the prunes and how grateful we had been, as it was all we had to eat. She was very shocked and surprised to learn that at that time we had only those prunes to eat. She assured us that she had had no idea she was meeting a need. She had thought we were doing her a favor by keeping the prunes from being wasted. It was through many experiences such as this that the Lord saw us through our training. He taught us things that we could have learned no other way. He taught us to trust Him for our every need.

Steve was just a little fellow not yet three years old when he taught us the power of a little child's faith. He had been running around the floor pretending that he was an airplane. With arms outspread he ran around the room. Busy working, I had not noticed that he had a comb in his mouth. In his antics he accidentally ran into the side of a cupboard and drove the large comb down into his throat.

His screams brought me running to his side. Looking down his throat, I saw a cut on the side of his throat that the comb had made. By that evening, when Joe came in from his job on work detail, Stevie's throat was very sore. He was crying and refused to try to eat his supper. We tried to coax him into drinking his chocolate milk. Bravely, he tried to swallow it but could not. He looked up at his dad with tear-filled eyes.

"Pray, Daddy," he said. We bowed our heads. Joe prayed a fervent prayer asking our God to heal his little boy. We had no money. There was no one else to turn to.

"Try again," Joe said, as he held the cup to Stevie's lips. But still the little fellow could not swallow the chocolate milk. Once again, we bowed as Joe prayed. Once again, he held the cup up for a trial drink only to have Stevie cry and push the cup away. "You pray, Stevie," said his dad wearily. Stevie bowed his head and asked the Lord to take away the pain in his throat so that he could drink his chocolate milk. He raised his head, reached for the cup, and downed the drink in just a few gulps, as we looked on astonished.

"Does it hurt you now, Son?" Joe asked.

Stevie solemnly shook his head "No."

Astounded, Joe called for a flashlight. We looked down his throat by means of the light. To our amazement, the cut was gone. There was no sign of it. We knelt in grateful thanksgiving and praise, knowing that we could go forth trusting in this One who so graciously answered prayer.

A few months later when snow fell there in the Pennsylvania Mountains, it found us unprepared. Stevie had no boots to wear in the snow. He had to be carried each morning to toddler's class on our way to our classes. That night he fervently prayed for boots. The next day, one of the ladies in the camp came bringing him a little pair of red boots, which he proudly wore as he trudged through the snow.

Then one day, having watched some of the bigger kids in camp coasting downhill on a sled, he decided that he would take a ride also. He climbed up on the sled that had been left sitting there. He was too young to realize that the sled required snow to coast downhill. The snow had melted away and the sled runners sat on the muddy ground.

"Stevie, you have to have snow to ride a sled," said a lady as she came by and saw him sitting there crying. "You'll have to pray for more snow so that the sled will be able to coast downhill," she said.

That night as Stevie said his prayers before I tucked him in, I heard him pray, ". . . and dear God, please send some more snow here, so I can ride downhill on the sled tomorrow."

The next morning before daybreak he stumbled sleepily out of the little bedroom, ran over to the kitchen table, and pulled out a chair. Using the chair, he climbed up on the table, kneeled before the window, and pulled back the curtains.

He fairly leaped to his feet on the table and clapped his hands with glee. "It really did snow!" he exclaimed.

It was the biggest snow that we had that year. Stevie got his sled rides. People jokingly said, "Please don't let Stevie pray for any more snow!"

One incident that I remember very well was a time that we had no money to go grocery shopping and our cupboards were as bare as Old Mother Hubbard's. We were standing at our little cabin window looking at the cars streaming in with people who had gone shopping. We watched as they unloaded their cars and carried large boxes and bags to their own cabins. For me it was a really low time. I remember sighing and saying to Joe, "I just don't understand it. If we are all God's children, why does He give to some and let others be in need? I could never do that with my children."

Joe looked at me and sort of grinned. "Well," he said, "Can you be just as thankful for your nothing as they are for their plenty?"

"No, I can't," I said angrily and turned away. Why did he have to be so spiritual when I felt so carnal!

It was our habit at that time to get together for fellowship with the boot camp director in the evenings, study the Scriptures, and talk about the Lord. I always served coffee. This night I had no coffee to serve and did not wish to explain why. I told Joe, "Let's go to bed early and turn out all the lights so that the director will see that we are in bed and not come by to fellowship tonight as I don't have any coffee to serve."

So that is what we did. After quickly having our nightly devotions, we turned out the lights and went to bed.

We had not been in bed long, however, when we heard a knock on the door. "That must be John," I hissed from under the covers. "I'm not going to get up. You'll have to see to him." I turned over and burrowed my head deeper under the covers.

Joe went out to answer the door. I stuck my head out from under the blanket to listen, but I did not hear him talking to anyone. After a long pause he called, "Come here and look. You won't believe this!"

Joe was standing over a large cardboard box that he had lugged from the front stoop into the kitchen. As I peered into it, imagine my surprise to find it full to the brim with all kinds of good food to eat. I could not believe my eyes. There were foods that we would not have bought if we had the money. We would have felt guilty to buy them. Little canned hams, canned fruits, coffee, tea, sugar, flour, and so much good nourishing food. We felt as rich as kings.

My eyes flooded with tears at God's goodness to us. I had been feeling so bitter and so resentful, when all the time my heavenly Father was preparing these goodies for us. I had to stop and confess my sin to Him and ask Him to forgive me and to bless the bearer of these things.

The Lord had already taught me one lesson in humility when our daughter Faith Eileen was born on August 10, 1952. The mission had moved our family down from the mountains a few days before. They did not want me to be up in the mountains with no way to get down when the time came to go to the hospital.

New Tribes Mission was very new in the Jersey Shore area, and folk around were very skeptical of their intentions. I had seen a doctor upon my arrival in July. When he found out that I was from the camp and that we were without insurance and living by faith, he suggested that I enter the hospital under the county welfare plan. Joe and I both were, of course, horrified at the idea and declined the offer.

After Faith was born and I had spent six days in the hospital, the time came for me to go home. (Since I had three children under three years old, the doctor insisted that I spend an extra three days in the hospital to recuperate before taking on the load at home.) Every day Joe had come in at visiting hour, and I had eagerly asked him if the Lord had sent in the money for the hospital bill. Every day he had met my question with a negative shake of his head.

We had prayed earnestly and fervently that God would supply the money for the bill. We reminded God that it would be a bad testimony if we were unable to pay when we had said that we trusted the Lord and lived by faith. I was so sure that God was going to send in the money. I just knew that He could not fail us! Wasn't this what our whole life was going to be about? Trusting Him to meet our every need?

The day to go home arrived. We were ready to leave. Faith looked beautiful in her nice yellow outfit and receiving blanket. I was anxious to get home to my two little boys, Stevie, two years old, and Gary, who had just turned one year old the day before Faith was born, just babies themselves. I had missed them so! But when Joe came in for us, his face told me that all was not as I had expected it to be.

Joe had eagerly gone to our mailbox that morning fully expecting to miraculously find a check to pay my hospital bill. Imagine his dismay to discover the box empty. When he got to the hospital he went up to the desk and presented himself to have his wife and baby released from the hospital.

"I don't have the money to pay all the bill," he said. "Would it be all right to give you what I have and pay by the week until it's all paid?"

The lady was very friendly and smiled kindly. "That'll be fine," she said. "How much do you have to pay on the bill?"

Joe blushed in embarrassment. "Two dollars and eighty cents," he said.

The lady's eyebrows raised in astonishment. "Well, that's not very much!" she said. But the Lord was with him, and without any further censure, she passed the papers to Joe and he signed them.

Joe had come for me in a pickup truck that he had borrowed from someone at the camp. After he had helped me into the truck, I turned ready to hear how the Lord had answered our prayers and how he had sent in the money to pay the hospital bill. Joe had a very funny expression on his face.

"Well, actually the money never came in," he said. "I went up to that desk feeling like a convicted man. I told the girl at the desk, 'I don't have all the money to pay my wife's bill. Will it be OK if I give you what I have and pay the rest off each week?'"

When I heard the rest of his story, I shed bitter tears. I felt so ashamed. I felt that somehow the Lord had not heard our prayers. In fact, I felt that we had ruined our testimony. We had wanted to present to the hospital a testimony of how the Lord was with us in what we had set out to do. We had wanted to prove to them that He would meet our needs.

Every week thereafter, during our time at boot camp, we took in all we could scrape together and paid on our bill. When we left, it was completely paid off. One of the office personnel in the hospital mentioned that it had been good to see someone so faithfully pay off their bill, as they had overdue bills in their files by people who could pay them if they chose, but who made no effort to do so. God used our steadfastness in meeting an obligation to speak to hearts. This was not the way I would have chosen. I would have preferred to see it paid off in the beginning, but I realize that God was dealing with a proud and haughty spirit. I needed to see this in my life and deal with it.

6

OFF TO THE MISSION FIELD BY FAITH

We had spent our year in boot camp. July had rolled around again. The Lord had taught us many, many lessons. Now it was time to see if we would be set apart for serving the Lord on the field and sent out with the blessing of our leaders.

Yes! Praise the Lord! We were set apart in a "laying on of hands" ceremony by the leaders. Others of our class, who had been in our group, were also set apart. We were elated. Now we could be on our way to those who had never heard.

During World War II, Joe had served in the Philippines. During our year in boot camp, we had done our Maps and Gaps study on the Philippines. We had thought that the Philippines was the place we would serve the Lord, giving forth the gospel to tribes that he had seen while stationed there. However, the Lord had other ideas for us.

During the last months of our training, the leadership had been receiving news flashes from the field chairman in Venezuela telling of their trials in getting permits to reside in the interior where the tribes were located. This was the Amazon territory and strictly off limits to Protestant missionaries.

Just about the time we were being set apart for the field, word was received from Venezuela that they had received their permit. Missionaries there were all overdue for furlough, and they wanted new missionaries as soon as possible. Joe had been in the Morning Prayer meetings when they were praying long and hard for just this permit. His heart was challenged to answer the call.

Together we prayed about it and sought the mind of the Lord for our next move. The mission director had already told Joe, "You've been set apart for the field, but no one knows you. You have no support. We feel that Millie and the three children should stay here in the camp, and you should go on deputation, taking the mission film and presenting it in the churches. You'll be able to raise your support for the field."

Joe had agreed to do this and that was the way our plans were going, but suddenly we knew that the Lord wanted us to go ahead and make the step of faith, trusting Him for every step of the way. Joe went up to the office to talk to the director, who was not so sure that this was God's plan for us. He tried to talk Joe out of his belief that this was God leading.

Finally, Joe said, "John, what would it take to convince you that the Lord wants us in Venezuela right now? What would the Lord have to do to get you to give us your approval to go to Venezuela and not stop to take time to go on deputation?"

John stared at him for a long moment and then said, "If God sends in your passage, then that should be evidence that He wants you to go right away. If God sends in your passage, then I'll approve of your going right away."

"How much do you figure it'll take for our passage?" Joe asked.

John did some figuring on his note pad and said, "I figure five hundred dollars should get you and your family there."

Joe left the office exhilarated, filled with hope. He burst into the little cabin by the river where we were living and told me, "Millie, let's pray! John has told me that if the Lord sends in five hundred dollars for our passage, he will release us to go right away without doing deputation. Come on, let's pray."

We went into the tiny bedroom and fell to our knees by the bed, calling on the Lord to send in the five hundred dollars if it truly was His will for us to go at that time. We were still praying when we heard a knock at the door. We arose and answered it.

As we opened the door, we saw one of the ladies of the camp, whom we knew well and for whom we had great affection. She and her husband were an older couple with a grown daughter. They had sort of looked after us as their children during our time there, and our children loved them. We invited her in, and she chatted with us for awhile. Then as she rose to leave, she pulled an envelope from her pocket.

"You've been set apart to go to the field, so my husband and I wanted to help you out a little to get you on your way," she said with a smile.

We thanked her politely and saw her out. "Well, hurry and open it!" I said excitedly. "Let's see what it is!"

Joe casually opened the envelope. "Probably five or ten dollars," he said. Oh, ye of little faith. We were asking the Lord for five hundred dollars but expecting five or ten.

Well, the Lord was gracious anyway. When Joe pulled the enclosed check from the envelope, it was for five hundred dollars! To say we almost passed out from sheer excitement and joy is putting it mildly.

Joe ran out the door and took off for the office as fast as he could run. He had talked to the director less than an hour before. Now here he was with five hundred dollars in his hand, and we had not mentioned it to anyone, but the Lord.

Joe burst into the office and confronted a surprised John. "Did you REALLY mean it when you said we could go if the Lord provided our passage?" he gasped breathlessly.

John, a little taken aback at this abruptness, said slowly, "Yes, that's what I said."

Joe plopped the check down on the desk in front of John and grinned as John did a double take. He shook his head and rubbed the back of his neck in astonishment.

"Well, I'll be as good as my word," he said. "I told you that you could go if the Lord gave you five hundred dollars for passage, so I have to stick with it, but the honest truth is that I told you that to get you off my back. I had no idea you'd get that much together for a long time."

This changed all our plans. Joe left right away. Since we had no car, he hitchhiked to Virginia to make plans with his brother to bring him back for the kids and me.

There in Virginia we applied for our passports and visas for Venezuela. Then we got our necessary shots for international travel. We felt that there in Virginia we hardly knew anyone that called themselves Christian much less anyone interested in foreign missions enough to pledge us support. However, our faith was undaunted. Although we had three small children and were expecting a fourth in November, we never once even thought of turning aside from the course we had set for ourselves.

September came. Since my baby was due in November, our families began to try to discourage us.

"They'll never let you on the plane this close to your due date," they warned me.

We waited impatiently for our visas to arrive. When they finally arrived in September, we left right away for Jersey Shore,

Pennsylvania once again to pick up the check we had left in the office there and to make our final arrangements to leave from there. We went into the office and picked up the check.

Shortly afterward the same lady approached us and said, "Joe, do you still have that check I gave you? I need to change it a little. Could I have it for a few minutes?"

Joe got the check and handed it over to her. After she left we looked at each other and wondered what she was going to change. Maybe she had meant to make the check for fifty dollars or maybe even five dollars, we both thought, afraid to voice it to one another.

Imagine our elation when she returned a few minutes later with a new check. She had made this one was for $700! How happy we were to have a little something extra for traveling!

A young couple there in camp very graciously took us into town and purchased dishes, pots and pans, a small Coleman stove and lantern, and some other necessities which we packed along with our clothes and personal items in duffel bags. We were ready to go.

We traveled by bus to Miami, and the one thing that sticks in my mind from that trip was the foul smelling sulfur water that I had made Faith's bottles with at the NTM Florida boot camp. She cried and refused to drink the milk, so each time the bus stopped at a station, I would get off and dash into the restroom, pour out the milk and rinse the bottle under the hot water. Then I would dash out to the lunch counter, buy a glass of milk, and pour it into her bottle.

We left by plane from Miami in spite of all the dire warnings our family had given. The authorities in Miami did not refuse us passage on the plane due to my condition. They didn't even mention it.

I, being thin at the time, did not look as though delivery time was imminent. Plus I was carrying Faith in my arms. She was only thirteen months old and very small. So they never questioned us. We were in God's will, and He was taking care of all these minor details. The date was October 11, 1953.

We arrived in Maiquetia, Venezuela at the airport and were met by the mission field representative, Bob, who helped us through customs. We spent several days at his house while he helped us get all our paperwork done.

We received our resident visas immediately. . . now an unheard of thing. It takes years, much paperwork, and much money to get a resident visa now, but then it was different, thank God!

One thing I remember was plodding wearily up a number of flights of stairs to the office of some high official where he looked at our passport pictures, then scrutinized our features to be sure the pictures were truly of us.

Bob told us later that we had arrived so soon after the visas had been issued in the United States, that they did not think we could get there that fast.

On October 15, 1953, we traveled by the old DC-3 to Puerto Ayacucho. As the old plane roared and shuddered and shook, I began to wonder if we would really make it, but then I was assured that underneath were the "everlasting arms."

Gary was sick and vomited. All were crying with ears hurting, but in spite of all the discomfort, there was a feeling of extreme peace. We knew we were where God wanted us, doing what God wanted us to do. In spite of the unknown in the future that lay ahead of us, all was right with our world.

The plane landed and taxied to the small terminal. As we descended the stairs, we glanced around us with wide eyes. We were really out in the boonies. It was very hot and humid.

The missionary standing to the side at the foot of the stairs watched us descending. He saw a short, dark-haired man in his early thirties carrying a small boy of two and holding the hand of another little boy of three. By his side was a blond-haired woman carrying a baby of about a year, he surmised, who was obviously going to have another before too long.

As we reached the bottom of the stairs and stepped to the side, he took Joe's hand, looked him in the eye, and said, "You're the biggest fool I've ever met."

That shook us up to say the least, but Joe shook his hand warmly and greeted him as though he had not just been badly insulted. My insides were quivering with the first tinge of doubt that I had heretofore experienced.

It was one thing when the world kept telling us that we were fools and making a dreadful mistake, but here was a full-fledged missionary looking us in the eyes and calling us fools. Weren't the missionaries supposed to be happy to see us? Weren't we supposed to go by faith, trusting the Lord every inch of the way? Why then should we be called fools by the very ones we had come to work with? My heart sagged!

7

LORD, WAS IT YOU WHO CALLED US?

As the missionary drove us from the airport at Puerto Ayacucho along the dusty dirt road that shook us up with a washboard effect, we gazed around us in wonder. Truly we had never seen anything like this. We were in a different world, one that was very hot and humid, but one that was also beautiful. Our children were quiet and subdued, lethargic with the heat and the long trip.

We reached the town and found it very primitive. There were no paved roads or streets. There were no streetlights. Most of the houses were roofed with palm. There were a few that had tin roofs. We were told that they had just passed a law that no more palm roofs could be put on future houses. From then on when an existing house was re-roofed or a new house built, it had to be of tin. There were enough houses there for them to begin to realize the danger a fire would wreak. There was one store in that town at the time, owned by a man who owned most of the town.

"The mission house is just ahead," our companion said, and we craned our necks to see it.

I saw some large buildings. One on one side of the road, surrounded by a fence and another on the other side, sitting up on a hill, back from the road. I imagined the one with the fence must be the mission house, as I had read in books about mission compounds. They always sounded like large establishments within the security and privacy of their own gates. But, no, we went on past the large building and came to a flourishing halt in front of a dilapidated little old mud house. One part, obviously older than the rest, was still covered with a palm roof; the rest had tin on it. There was no fence, no gate, and no compound!

As I looked at this nondescript little house that was the headquarters of what we were representing here in this foreign land, I tasted the bitterness of disappointment, and, yes, some apprehension. This place, which I was unprepared for, along with the meeting we had experienced with the missionary, did not make me feel enthusiastic for all I had to face.

I found out later that the building I had mistaken for the mission house was the living facilities used by the doctors who worked in the building I had seen on the hill, which was the town hospital, such as it was. The unknown loomed before me and with it a fear of the future.

What would become of our children and us here in these hostile surroundings? The verse that the Lord gave me was, "Perfect love casteth out fear. . . ." Truly His love for me was perfect, and just as I was prepared to protect and care for my children here in this place, God would be protecting and caring for me.

Joe had his testing also. He had not found favor, and the job assigned to him right away was to push a wheelbarrow up and down the streets there in the town and pick up the new fresh cow manure that was dropped by the cows that wandered the streets night and day. This he in turn mixed with a mud and sand mixture and smeared with his hands onto the surface of the mud walls of the mission house. A section had fallen out and had to be replaced, and Joe was put to the task.

However, as we assured ourselves at night in the privacy of our bed, the Lord had sent us here, and He was the One who was in control. This was where He wanted us, and this is what He wanted us to do right now.

Our fourth child, Velma Dolores, was born at the hospital in Puerto Ayacucho on November 6, 1953. It was of course nothing more than a home delivery, except that I was not at home, where I would rather have been.

Another missionary lady, who lived with her family in the side with the tin roof, went to the hospital with me, as she spoke Spanish fluently and could help me understand what was being said to me. I had my first shock when the doctor put in his appearance. He announced to me through the haze of pain I was in that he would not be attending the delivery. He said that he always left that kind of thing—here I presumed he meant minor thing—to the head nurse.

"Oh, yes, and another thing. . . ." He casually mentioned that they did not give any kind of anesthesia. "We only have ether here, and that's not good in a delivery, but then I know that you American women are brave," he said and left.

The town electricity was very poor and erratic. The town generator was turned on at dark and off at about 10:00 p.m. Just as I was put on the delivery table, the lights went out, and I could hear everyone frantically scurrying about in the dark, jabbering to each other in Spanish, while I, of course, was taken up only with my own misery. Finally, they coaxed light out of an old Coleman lantern and proceeded with the job at hand.

When it was over and I was in my bed with Velma in a baby hospital crib in the room with me, Billie, my friend, left me to go down the hill to the mission house. I was all alone with my pain, my fears, and my dreads.

One of the hospital aides came in with a huge, continuous-action bug sprayer and began spraying vigorously all over the room. When she sprayed all under, over, and around the baby crib, I was almost crying with frustration. I just knew she was going to kill my baby, and I did not even know how to ask her to stop. Not that she would have, I'm sure. I had never in my life heard of a newborn baby being subjected to that kind of treatment.

She lay there in the little bed, naked except for a band around her middle. I just knew she would catch pneumonia. Then to make matters worse, she began to cry and wave her arms and feet in the air. I had been warned not to move about or even move off my back, which was aching abominably, so I lay there helplessly watching her. I saw that her feet were purple and felt that my fears of her freezing were justified. (I found out the next day it was from the dye with which they had taken her footprints.)

I began to talk to the Lord and to ask myself if I really believed what I had been telling everyone else, what I had come to this place at the end of nowhere to tell other people.

Did I believe that I was in God's hands and that if I didn't make it through this haze of pain and the horror that I found myself in that I would go on to heaven to be with Him? Or was that just some pipe dream that I had thought true when there was no testing fire devouring me?

Finally I had to cling to my verse that "perfect love casts out fear." Finally I was able to give my fears to Him, and He helped me make it through that night. The next day things looked much brighter, and I decided that both of us, my new baby and I, were going to make it after all. Now with this behind us we could go. Where were those tribal people we had come to reach?

8

UPRIVER TO THE YANOMAMÖ

We left Puerto Ayacucho early in December. Our mission director, Karl, had come down from San Fernando de Atabapo where he lived with his family at this time. He and a veteran missionary, Harold, who also lived with his family in San Fernando were to help us prepare for our trip upriver to the tribe we would be working with. Since we had no money with which to buy supplies, we had to wait several days until the plane arrived from Caracas. In those days, it came only once a week on Thursday.

We were discussing with these two men our plans for our trip upriver.

"When the plane gets here and the checks arrive, we'll buy your supplies that afternoon, pack them up, and we can be on our way upriver the next morning," they said.

"What if the checks are not on the plane?" I asked. "Then the plane won't come again until the next Thursday."

Everyone looked at me in astonishment.

"Woman, where is your faith?" Karl demanded. I felt about two inches high.

So on Thursday when the plane arrived and, sure enough, the checks did not come, I was not sure but that it was my lack of faith and my questioning spirit that had caused them to be held up.

Be that as it may, one of the missionaries—Jim Barker, a single man who was working with the Yanomamö in the tribe where we would be going—had told the director that if a family came in without the money to make the trip, then their trip could be financed from his account. He said we could pay it back when our money came in. So we bought our supplies as he had directed and packed to go upriver the next day.

Since we had no pledged support and no idea what might come in for our support, we were very careful about what we bought. Everything was so expensive, and we knew so little about buying for an extended time.

"Plan to buy enough to last you for three to four months," Karl said. "The supply boat won't be able to bring you more supplies until around that time."

As we looked at the food and the prices, we decided to get a lot of macaroni, as that seemed to be about the cheapest thing one could get. We bought twenty kilos of macaroni.

This was a mistake we were to regret during our first months in the village. We had no idea how to keep it from getting buggy. Later we learned that the missionaries toasted it in the oven to kill all the bug eggs. This made the macaroni slightly mushy when cooked later, but at least it kept the bugs and worms from eating it before we could.

Not knowing this, we poured it into large tin cracker cans we had bought in town. At our destination, we set the cans on shelves in the crude little pantry Joe had fashioned from poles.

The first can of macaroni was fine, and we enjoyed it. Then as I opened the cans, some sort of moths flew out. The macaroni was definitely getting worms and bugs.

In order to cook it, I spent hours breaking out all the buggy and wormy pieces and piling them to one side. At first, the pile of buggy macaroni was far larger than the pile I had managed to salvage to cook. Joe was forced to dump can after can in our garbage pit.

Later my piles for cooking got larger and the piles for garbage got smaller as I was forced to turn a blind eye to many bugs and worms, realizing we were not going to have food to last. One day as Joe dumped a can of wormy macaroni into the pit he said gloomily, "Now I know how the children of Israel felt when they gathered too much manna."

But I am getting ahead of my story. . . .

After buying and packing our supplies, we left the next morning to drive the forty-five miles to Samariapo to the river port where the boat was tied. Our director had talked at length about the boat we would use to travel upriver. In my mind's eye I pictured what I thought would be an ordinary boat, possibly some sort of river steamer. When we arrived at the port, though, I saw nothing like the boat I had imagined.

"Where is the boat?" I asked. I was shocked and slightly horrified when they pointed to a large dugout canoe with a palm awning woven across the center for keeping the supplies dry and a tin roof in the back where the men would sit. I looked at the amount of stuff piled on the bank and the people who were going in that boat and thought, "No way! We'll never get it all on that thing!" I held my tongue and was glad I had when the men managed to get all the supplies under the small roof, including Velma's tiny screened-in crib, which fit right across the opening so that I could tend to her without too much trouble.

It took eleven days on the river from Puerto Ayacucho to the village of Majecodo-teli. Each evening just before dusk, the men would clear out a place large enough to hang hammocks for everyone near the riverbank.

There were two Venezuelans with us who were a big help. One was the motorista and the other the practico who watched the river for rocks and such. Supper was cooked over an open fire. Traveling in the open air on the river makes one hungry, and we ate with good appetites.

After getting the children bedded down in their hammocks, we would start our little Coleman stove, boil water, and pour it into the baby bottles we had first sterilized so that I could use them the following day as we traveled.

Velma had an inflamed navel, and the doctor had told me that it was very important for her to have a bath every day, after which I was to sprinkle her navel with a sterile powder he had given. Every night after everything else was done, Joe heated water, then I bathed Velma. By the time we reached our destination, her inflammation was healed.

We experienced a near tragedy as we traveled. One day when the sun was first coming up with its tropical brightness, the motorista found his eyes blinded by the rays. The practico tried to hang a shirt along the side to hide the rays, and in doing so, he obscured the motorista's view of the riverbank.

When the motorista was finally able to see clearly again, he found himself about to run the boat into a huge tree limb that was jutting out over the water. He quickly cut the motor, but the prow of the boat was still jammed into the tree branch and pushed itself up into the thatch awning covering the center of the boat.

Our family rode in the front of the boat. Joe had been sitting in the very prow with his back to the river, facing the family, with his Bible in his hand and Gary on his lap, as we were having family devotions. As we realized what was happening, we all ducked and crowded backward to miss the limb. As the momentum pushed the boat under the limb, Gary was caught between the limb and the thatch roof of the boat.

Only the mercies of the Lord and the fact that the thatch gave as Gary was pressed into it saved him from great physical harm or even death. We thanked and praised the Lord before starting the motor and continuing on our journey, happy that we were all still safe and well.

On the eleventh day, we were told that we were near the place where they would pull in to shore for us to unload. From there it was about a half-mile walk in to the village. Finally we saw two men standing on the shore waving to us. As our boat approached the shore and we were in clear view of those standing on shore, one said, "The Dawsons! Oh, no!"

As you can imagine, that did not make our day. We knew the speaker, Dave, from NTM boot camp. He had been our linguistics teacher. He had also talked to us about birth control, and we had obviously since added another member to the family. He possibly thought, "Why me, Lord?" with good reason. We never asked.

"Only the scrubs make it," he told us later, so we realized where we stood in his estimation.

As we told ourselves later, we had not come all this way to be deterred by the lack of approval of man. It was the Lord we wanted to serve. He was the One we wanted to please, and to do that, there would be many obstacles in our way.

9

MEETING THE YANOMAMÖ

Our director, Karl, and one of the two single missionary men went downriver, taking the older missionary couple who had been working in that village. The men would help to get the couple settled in another village. This village was located on the Ocamo River, a tributary that flowed into the Orinoco further downriver. The couple was to remain there until their term of service was up. Then they would go home on furlough. Karl and the single man would return in a week. Then Harold, the missionary from San Fernando who was staying at this village with us temporarily, would return to San Fernando with Karl.

That same day after the boat left with the older couple, the other single missionary left by trail to spend time at another village inland. That left our family alone with only Harold for company.

Harold had made trips to this village before and had in fact built the little two-room mud house we were to live in. We appreciated his efforts as it gave us a shelter for our family. While he was waiting for Karl's return, he built us a table and a couple of benches. He also split open a long palm tree, hollowing it out. He made drains for our roof and many other improvements to help us get settled in comfortably.

The Indians living out in the forest did not know as yet that we were there. The Yanomamö are a nomadic tribe who often live out in the rain forest for months at a time, coming back to their gardens periodically to check for food. We wanted to get as well set up as possible before their return.

Harold had an old metal boat tied at the riverbank that he had used as sleeping quarters when he had built the house.

"If you want me to eat supper with you, then you'll have to fix an early meal because I'll be leaving here promptly at five o'clock each evening," he told us.

Every evening at five, he walked to the riverbank, got in his metal boat, pushed out into midstream, and anchored there. He did not want to be on shore at night, as he feared the Yanomamö.

On one of his earlier trips he had seen a warrior draw back his bow and shoot an arrow at the back of one of his missionary companions. The fact that the warrior had removed the point and just shot the blunt arrow showed that he was only expressing his contempt and displaying what he could do if he wished. He had not intended to kill or even wound, just to scare. This had made quite an impression on Harold. He told us often to be very careful of what we said or did with these excitable and extremely dangerous people.

Before going off with the older couple, the single missionary Jim had told us, "When you are fixing up your house, put a long pole down the length of the room to make a barrier that the Yanomamö are not to cross over. That will help you control them."

Joe and I considered the pole as we arranged our main room later that night.

"I can't put a pole down the length of the room to herd them back," Joe said. "It would hurt their feelings."

"Sholi, noji."

Startled, I looked up at the open screen window. The face I saw framed there shocked me. The red ochre paint smeared over the face glistened with sweat brought out by the hot tropical sun. The lower lip protruded grotesquely by a large cud of tobacco, which shone moistly as the lips were widened in a huge grin. Short arrow shafts stuck through the ear lobes. The hair was black, coarse, and straight, cut straight across just below the ears. The whole picture was like something out of a bad dream.

My thoughts flew back to my reason for being in this place at the backside of nowhere. These were the people we had come to reach with the gospel of Christ. In the Yanomamö's absence, we had been able to get somewhat set up before they returned from the rain forest.

Now they were here. Suddenly the room was alive with naked, dirty, sweating bodies lavishly smeared with red paint that was fast being deposited onto everything they touched, sat on, or rubbed against.

I had not expected them. I had been peeling the last of the few kilos of our precious potatoes that we had so carefully guarded on the trip upriver. Quickly I slipped the last one into the pressure cooker, fitted on the lid, and placed it on the burner of the small Coleman camp stove.

"Be nonchalant. Act as though nothing is out of the ordinary," Joe said, so I tried to appear calm.

I had a big pan of yeast bread rising under a clean tea towel on the table. One of the Indians pulled the cloth off and threw it around himself to see if it was large enough to be of use as a shirt. So much for that tea towel. In a matter of seconds, it was all red as well as dirty. But it was almost more than I could stand when the Indians, seeing the strange mass in the pan, began poking their dirty fingers into my bread. We did not know one word of their language to ask them to stop. Neither were we sure of what their reaction would be if we tried to stop them. So we stood helplessly by while some poked in the bread and others began trying on the clothes from the piles of dirty clothes that were lying on the floor.

The wash tub with the old washboard was sitting on a cut tree stump. I had planned to start a wash as soon as the potatoes were on. Stevie and Gary, both very small at the time, clung to Joe's legs in fear. Faithie, about sixteen months, was fast asleep in a hammock, and Velma, one month old, was asleep in her tiny, screened-in crib.

We had left Miami for Venezuela scarcely two months before. We were getting initiated in a hurry to our life among the Yanomamö.

The Indians continued their inspection of everything in sight, all the while talking and gesturing, laughing and prancing around. I had been aware for some time of a crackling sound, but with all the commotion I did not realize just what the significance was until, with a terrible hiss, the safety gauge blew out of the pressure cooker, sending a fountain of steam hissing up into the air.

The Yanomamö darted in every direction. They pushed and shoved in their efforts to get out the door first and were soon running down the trail towards their shabono. Joe rushed over and turned the burner off under the potatoes. Imagine my chagrin to realize that in my agitation I had put the lid on the pressure cooker without putting in any water. My potatoes were ruined. The gasket to the pressure cooker would never be the same.

Joe and I looked at each other, first in amazement, then in disbelief. Then as the humor of the situation hit us, we collapsed in each other's arms in helpless laughter. I gave a tiny shriek as I suddenly felt a hand grab me around the ankle. We heard a grunt and looked down to see one of the fierce warriors crawling out from under the table where he had dodged to escape the hissing monster.

Seeing that we were still alive and able to laugh, I suppose gave him the courage to show himself. He danced up and down, first on one foot and then on the other, all the while waving one arm over his head and delivering a speech which I wonder about to this day. Then, with a grave dignity, he sauntered out the door and down the path.

After that first visit, you can believe that Joe quickly put a pole down the length of our room and instructed the Yanomamö to stay on the far side to visit us. Many were rascals who would perch, stark naked, on the pole and stare at everything we did. Others would reach across as far as they could and try to get a cup or plate off the table if they thought we were not looking. That side of the room was always full. As one group left, another came in to take their place.

The Yanomamö have many taboos. A man and his mother-in-law cannot be in the same room together. So, someone would peer in the door and see if the coast was clear and if so, the ones wanting to visit would enter.

The little black blood-sucking gnats were terrible and were really giving the kids and me a rough time, as we were blond and fair-skinned. We were soon covered with ulcers. So, it was a real torment for me when they would run in and out, holding open the door. The first Yanomamö phrase that I learned was Täca da lac! "Shut the door!"

Pretty soon, they caught on that this bothered me and so they would stand and deliberately hold the door open.

Finally, "Just ignore them," Joe said, "And they'll get tired of worrying you."

It took all of my willpower, but I managed to ignore them and not call Täca da lac. They couldn't understand why I suddenly had no interest in telling them to shut the door and they would yell, "Milimi, say Täca da lac!"

Several weeks after our first encounter with the Yanomamö, the Indian who had hid under our table in response to the pressure cooker explosion sauntered into my kitchen one hot day. Without one word of greeting, he walked over to the little crib where two-month-old Velma lay sleeping. Before I had any idea of what he was about to do, he reached down into the crib, scooped the sleeping baby up in his arms, and sauntered back out the kitchen door.

I was transfixed for an instant with horror. I knew these people were women stealers. My mind envisioned the worst as mentally I saw him go off into the rain forest with my baby, never to be seen again. I came out of my stupor and ran frantically down the trail after him.

Catching up to him, I began to pound him in the back with my fists, screaming in English, "Give me back my baby!"

He marched on, seemingly impervious to my fists and my shrieks. By this time, I was weeping in despair. Just as he reached the edge of the rain forest, he stopped and turned around to face me. Then he grinned, reached down, and placed Velma in my arms. I could only stare at him in bewilderment. Clutching Velma to my breast, I smiled back weakly.

Without a word, he walked on off into the rain forest. I never knew whether he was paying me back for the scare I had given him earlier and the loss of dignity I had caused him or if he had a more ulterior motive in the beginning. I was only too happy to have my baby safe in my arms again. I returned to the house thanking God that He had taken care of that situation for me too.

We had a little wooden Gospel Recordings record player in those days. Someone had given it to us with a few gospel records in Spanish. Since the language of the Yanomamö had not been written yet, they had no alphabet, no literacy and, of course, no records made in their language.

Still, we played the Spanish records for them. One day, they got very excited. We could not understand what they were saying, so they ran to get Jim. He said that they were excited because the box had said something about a murderer. We, of course, had no idea what they were talking about as the recording was not even in their language. Finally, we decided they were talking about the song "Uno Hay" or "There Is One" (Jesus). The Yanomamö word for murderer is unocai.

I went around the house singing as I did my work. Stevie and Gary especially liked me to sing "Heavenly Sunshine." There was one Yanomamö teenager named Iwawä (Alligator) who really liked to hear me sing that song and asked for it constantly.

"Sing 'Heavenly Sunny Shiny'," he would say. He would try to sing it too. However, one day Jim heard Iwawä trying to sing it with me and told me not to teach them anything in English.

"If you want to teach him the song, teach it to him in Spanish," he said. Jim gave me a copy of the Spanish words, and I tried to sing them with him, but as far as he was concerned that was a completely different song. He did not want to hear or sing that song and never understood why I stopped singing "Heavenly Sunny Shiny."

10

Separation

Before the first supply boat arrived, we found ourselves out of food. We had no milk for Velma who was still just a few months old. Not having enough milk to feed her myself, I was unable to satisfy her needs and had to supplement with the bottle. After our milk ran out, I took large green plantains we could get from the Indians, peeled them, sliced them thinly, and put them out to dry in the hot tropical sun. Then I grated the dried plantains, mixed them with a little sugar and water, and fed it to Velma like pabulum. Needless to say, she was not completely satisfied and cried for her bottle too. But the Lord was good to us, and she never became ill. Before too long, the supply boat arrived and we had milk for her once again.

During this time of want, I remember many times when two-and-a-half-year-old Gary cried for a piece of bread. Since I had no bread, I would peel a banana and put it in his hand. To this day he says, "I remember when I used to ask Mom for bread, and she would stick a banana in my hand."

After we had been there about six months, the leaders of the Venezuelan field decided that the children and I should move back downriver to San Fernando de Atabapo, a national settlement at the mouth of the Atabapo River. Some other missionaries, who were single, had joined the work in Platanal. The one other married man had left his wife and children downriver in San Fernando. So, it was decided for us to go back with the supply boat that had brought the men upriver. They felt this would give the men opportunity to study the language unhindered by the daily necessities of caring for a family.

With much trepidation I found myself with my four very small children back on the boat and heading back the way I had come just six months earlier. It was a very hard move for both Joe and me. He felt the loss of his family greatly, and I felt desolated at being so far away from him. We were to spend six months apart with very little communication. That was in the days before we had radios on the bases or airplanes landing with mail. Much of the time as day faded away and I lay in the darkness in the little one-room house where we lived in San Fernando that they called the "bug house," I was consumed by loneliness for Joe and a fear that I might never see him again. I truly did not know if he was still alive or if he had been killed by the Indians or succumbed to some disease or poisonous reptile bite. I would know absolutely nothing until the supply boat had returned from making its torturous way into the upper Orinoco and into another world.

During this time, I was plagued with a severe rash on my hands. This was probably caused by the fact that I was washing our towels and washcloths in a solution of creolina water. We had come down from the upper Orinoco with a bad case of pink eye, which Stevie and I were finding hard to get rid of. One of the other missionaries had suggested that we were re-infecting ourselves and that I should wash all towels and clothes in the strong disinfectant. My rash steadily grew worse.

About that time, Faithie, who was about two years old, developed a large painful blood blister on her foot. I took her to the doctor in San Fernando de Atabapo. He was a Polish displaced person who was married to a German woman. She had been a member of the Nazi youth during the late war. They both spoke fluent English. I had met him before and had found him to be very antagonistic to the gospel. Once he had told me emphatically that he did not believe the Bible and that he did not believe in a bodily resurrection.

"I've seen too many bodies cut asunder to ever believe they'll be whole again, and anyway, if you have a body, you'll be subject to the same sicknesses you have now," he had insisted.

During Faithie's examination, he noticed my hands were raw and cracked open with the rash.

"Sit right down here in this chair," he said. I sat in the somewhat rickety chair, and he began to examine my hands. They were very painful, and he was not trying especially to be gentle. It was excruciating when he began to straighten out the fingers, cracking open the raw swollen places.

The next thing I knew I was opening my eyes and looking up into the faces of the doctor, his wife, and my missionary friend, Allie Lee, who had accompanied Faithie and me to the doctor's office. I had passed out and was lying on the examining table.

"Well, where were you? In Paradise?" the doctor asked sarcastically. But I noticed that he was gentler after that. His wife had scolded him.

"I know just how painful that rash can be," she told me. "I had the very same kind of rash on my hands from using a laundry soap that was too strong," she said, smiling sympathetically. They became quite friendly with us after that incident.

Later that year, it was decided that the men would go downriver from the Majecodo village to a place called Tamatama and build small houses for their families. We would all regroup there and study the language materials that had been gathered. It was thought that their studies would profit more by the men being away from the constant distractions of the villagers.

Also, the demands of the Yanomamö were becoming ever more pressing; they constantly wanted more and more material things—axes, machetes, etc. The NTM leaders felt it might be more spiritually harmful to the Yanomamö for the missionaries to stay while not being able to communicate well.

It was during this time in Tamatama that Bautista heard about "Yosi" and the big fire that was coming to burn up the world. Joe had no way of knowing that his meeting with this little Yanomamö man was a milestone for the gospel penetrating into the spiritual darkness that had held these people for so long.

The men arrived in San Fernando de Atabapo in December of 1954. Needless to say, it was so good to see all of them again. The Lord had truly been good to them. All were alive and in good health. It was a happy reunion there on the banks of the Atabapo.

II

MOVING TO TAMATAMA

It was February of 1955. I was almost two months pregnant with child number five. The men were preparing the supply boat to return to the work upriver. We had hoped to be on this boat, but had just been told by the field director that we would have to stay downriver until after the birth of the baby. Seven long months. What could we do in all that time that might be profitable towards reaching the Yanomamö for Christ? We discussed this at length with the director.

"I've never had any problems in childbirth," I told the director. "And I feel that we can go trusting ourselves to God to meet our needs when that time comes. We are willing to go by faith and trust Him all the way. We won't expect the help of others who might feel 'put upon' in some way" I told Karl.

"We'll just be happy to be allowed to go," Joe said.

But Karl was adamant. We must stay behind in San Fernando.

During those days while the boat was preparing to leave and we were sadly contemplating being left behind, one of the believers in San Fernando gave birth. She was a member in the local church founded by some of our missionaries. They discovered that the baby was one of twins, but the other twin was not cooperating. The mother was in trouble. The local midwife was working in another area at her conuco (garden site) and was not available.

What could be done to help this poor woman? There was talk of trying to take her by boat down to Puerto Ayacucho. But would she make the long trip in time to save her life? When they went to talk to her about it, she said she would not go.

"I will stay right here in my own home and trust the Lord for the baby to be born. If I am unable to give birth, then I will die right here in my own home, still trusting the Lord," she said.

Shortly after this, the second baby was born; mother and baby were doing fine. At the men's Morning Prayer meeting the next day, Karl spoke on faith. He mentioned the lady's faith to trust the Lord and how the Lord had met her need.

"I just wish we had missionaries who had that kind of faith, who could go out trusting the Lord for everything," he said.

Joe stood. "I am happy to hear you say that, Karl," he said. "Millie and I want to go upriver by faith, trusting the Lord for everything."

Karl looked at him, astounded, not knowing what to say. What could he say? After a pep talk like that and a legitimate response what more was there to say?

Praise the Lord! We were on our way upriver. We were on our way to Tamatama to prepare ourselves for work with the Yanomamö. We would have to learn their language so we could tell them there is a God in Heaven. He is the Creator of the universe. He is the God who loves the Yanomamö. He gave His

Son to save their souls and deliver them from sin. He was the God who had sent us with the message of the Cross. Michael Eugene was born in Tamatama, August 2, 1955.

We arrived in Tamatama early in 1955. Right away, we noticed something strange. Some mornings we found tied to the door what seemed to be gifts. Occasionally we'd receive a bunch of ripe eating bananas, other times a small basket or a bunch of beautiful bird feathers. Talking to our missionary neighbors, we discovered that we were not the only ones receiving these gifts. They were being left at the doors of other houses also. Puzzled, we had no idea who were the gift-givers.

"Well, I've heard of missionaries leaving gifts to make contact with the tribal peoples, but I've never heard of the tribal people trying to make contact with the missionaries in this fashion," I told Joe.

Soon the puzzle fell into place. A family of Ye'cuana (also known as Maiquiritari) came out in the open and made themselves known to us. An old Ye'cuana mother, two adult daughters, and one adult son walked out of the rain forest. They came hesitantly, very shy and fearful. They told us that years ago they had lived in Tamatama with their tribal people who were held as slaves by a man known as Noguera.

They had escaped along with their father twenty years before and had been living in the rain forest every since. The father had died and they now wanted to get back to their own kind of people. The women wore dresses made from the beaten bark of a certain tree. This is the same bark that the Yanomamö use for making their carrying slings for their babies. The man carried a Spanish shotgun, beautifully inlaid with silver. His father had stolen it when they had escaped from the slave master who had fearfully abused them for so long.

They had been watching us for months, trying to see if we looked friendly or if we were an angry people who would do them harm. They greatly desired to return to their own people, but they were afraid to show themselves because of the bad treatment they had received by Noguera, who had also run Tamatama twenty years ago. Noguera had detained many Ye'cuana people as slaves. He had beat and killed them if they resisted him in any way. This family had seen people killed in front of their eyes and had lived in constant fear that Noguera would find them again. They happily received the word that he was long since dead and that there were no longer Ye'cuana slaves in Tamatama. In fact, no one had been living in Tamatama for years.

Not long after this gift-bearing family came back out of the forest, desiring to find their own people and resume their lives, a boat pulled into Tamatama. The man who owned the boat was a son of the cruel man who had lived there many years ago. The gun the Ye'cuana carried had belonged to his father, and he recognized it. Much to our sorrow, he persuaded these people aboard his boat and took them downriver with him.

We later heard that the Ye'cuana man (who had come to be known as Pedro) was hit in the back of the head with a shovel and killed while digging ditches in Puerto Ayacucho. We were grieved that after all they had suffered he never had the chance to hear God's Word in his language. The three women eventually arrived in Aacanana, a Ye'cuana village on the Cunucunuma River. Years later, they came to know the Lord through the gospel being preached to them there.

12

JOE'S UNFORGETTABLE TRIP

Joe says that he well remembers and yea, will never forget his first trip up the Padamo River and into the headwaters of the Cuntinamo River area. It was 1955. Joe and three single fellows, Jim, Jake, and Frank, decided that they would try to make a contact with the Yanomamö who live in that region. Jim Bou, just about twenty years of age at the time, planned to work with the Ye'cuana (Maiquiritari) tribe, which, we had heard, lived with the Yanomamö in that area.

After much talking and planning, they decided to go like Sophie Mueller had gone to the tribes of Colombia. Sophie took no food or trade goods with her but lived off the tribal peoples. The Yanomamö we had worked with up the Orinoco River had been interested in us only for our trade goods. The men reasoned that if they went completely without trade goods, the Indians would not be distracted by materials things, which they would immediately covet, and would listen when the men explained that their reason for coming was to tell them about God.

When they arrived at that first Yanomamö village with nothing in their possession but an old machete with no handle, the Yanomamö greeted them with downright hostility.

"Don't you have any possessions to trade with us?" they asked.

"No, we haven't come to trade with you," our men said. "We've come to talk to you. We want to tell you about Dios [God]."

This did not thrill to say the least. They told the men to just keep on going; they had no room for the men there. If the missionaries had no trade goods, the Indians did not want them to stay. Our men asked if the people would supply a guide to show them the way to the next village. After much ado, the tribesmen grudgingly agreed to send a guide with the men, probably figuring that was the quickest way to be rid of unwanted guests.

Huecito ("little bone"), who was a Ye'cuana Indian, a Spanish national named Juan Gomez, and another missionary had brought them to the big falls at the mouth of the Cuntinamo River where it empties into the Padamo. To reach that spot, they had gone through some white water that would make your hair stand on end.

At the first rapids, where the water boiled over the rocks and which seemed to stretch clear across the river with no channel, Juan Gomez had panicked and declared he would go no further. He thought there was no channel and the boat would come to disaster, although Huecito, who had traveled that water before, assured him there was a way through. Finally, Juan had grabbed his little bag out of the canoe, climbed out on a rock, and refused to go further. The men found the channel, made it through, and then circled back to the rock to pick up a shamefaced Juan and continue their trip.

By the time they reached the mouth of the Cuntinamo, they had eaten up most of the meager supply of food that they brought with them. Juan Gomez, deciding to make a pot of tea and not knowing the first thing about it, poured the whole can of tealeaves into the boiling water. So that was the last of the tealeaves.

Cecil (the other missionary), Juan, and Huecito left in the boat and motored the next morning for Tamatama. Our men were on their own. They walked to the village of Cuaisi-teli, which was not far away, but now they were being told to "Just keep on going."

Their trip was not working out as they had planned. There was nothing to do but continue on by trail with their two unwilling guides. These guides walked with them to a place called "The Port." So named as that was as far as it was possible for one to go by boat and motor. Their guides pointed out the trail that led on into the jungle and assured them that the village they were seeking was just a short way down the trail and that they could not miss it.

"Those people in that village are enemies to us," they said. "We can't go any farther with you, but the village is not far. Just follow that trail," they said, pointing to a half-visible trail leading off into the dense rain forest.

On their way to the Port, the men got a big fish. Jake saw it in the water and pointed it out to one of the Yanomamö guides who quickly shot it with his arrow. However, they were all so tired when they arrived at the Port that they decided to put it on a smoke rack and let it cook slowly. They were too tired to enjoy it and thought they'd feel more like eating it in the morning. However, the guides from Cuaisi-teli got up before daylight, ate the fish, and left for home. The men awoke hungry with no food in sight.

They decided for Jim Bou and Joe to go down the trail to the village and persuade some of the natives to come back with them and help them carry the bedding packs to the village. Jake and Frank remained with their few possessions and tried their luck at catching a fish for their noonday meal.

13

WHERE IS THAT VILLAGE?

Joe and Jim trudged up one mountain and down another; always hopefully expecting to see the village for which they were looking. Unaccustomed to traveling through the jungle as they were, they were tired, footsore, and very hungry. Yet there was nothing to do but keep on trudging. With no one to guide them, they had missed the trail and were trudging off in another direction. The trail was not clear, to say the least, and often other paths seemed to lead off from it. The natives had assured them the path was very clear, but a path that is clear to a native is not necessarily clear to two Americans who know nothing of jungle travel.

The day was swiftly passing by. They did not want to turn back, as they were afraid that over the next hill or around the next bend the village would come into view. To turn back would be to miss it when they were so near, so on they went. To their disappointment, they came to the banks of a river.

The guides had mentioned no river, so they felt that without a doubt they had followed the wrong trail.

Who knows how far we are from the village we are looking for? they wondered.

Two tired, hungry, and discouraged missionaries looked at each other. Now what should they do? Shrugging wearily, they decided there was nothing to do but start back for the Port, where they had left the other fellows. Maybe tomorrow they could get another start and try once more to find the village of Shawalawa-teli.

They retraced their steps along the trail and began their climb back up the mountains, up one side and down the other, their steps much slower than when they had started out so sprightly that morning. They had not covered much territory, however, when it became obvious that the sun was gone and darkness had fallen in the rain forest. Is there anything so black as a dense rain forest in the night? They had neither hammocks nor blankets with them, having fully expected to reach their destination well before nightfall.

Joe did not know about Jim, but his mind was filled with fears of snakes, scorpions, and all kinds of creeping, crawling creatures, not to mention jaguars and other dangerous animals. Still, he was unable to go any further. He fell to the ground there on the trail.

"I just can't go another step, Jim," he said. "We'll just have to sleep right here."

Jim did not want to stop; he had wanted to keep going. Knowing how easy it is to get lost or to step on a snake in the darkness, as well as just being too exhausted to go any farther, Joe insisted that they sleep right there and go on in the morning.

They stretched out wearily on the rain forest floor, too tired to be mindful of all that lurked and crawled around and over them. Jim Bou's little dog, Tanusi, was with them, and they were thankful for his presence there in the darkness.

In spite of the hunger pangs in his stomach, Joe soon fell into an exhausted sleep. Sometime in the night, he awoke to find that Jim was gone.

"That fellow has gone off and left me to die, all by myself, here in this jungle!" Joe said aloud.

Beside him the dog whimpered and stirred. Quickly, Joe grabbed him and held him close. "Oh, no you don't!" he said. "Your master may have left me, but you're staying right here with me!"

Soon after, Joe heard a crashing around in the brush close by and Jim came into view, or rather, the small glowing eye of his flashlight did.

Jim dropped down onto the ground beside Joe, panting with exhaustion. "I was so thirsty I just had to go and try to find some water," he said. "I figured that there would be water downhill somewhere, and I did manage to find some and got a drink, but now I'm thirsty again, after the climb back uphill," he panted.

"Jim, do you realize how easy it would have been to have gotten yourself lost out there in the jungle in the night? The Lord was surely looking out for you," Joe said. "Promise me you won't try that again." Once more Joe dropped off in a troubled sleep.

When the rays of the morning sun finally filtered into the gloomy forest, giving them enough light to see by, Joe roused himself. He spent a little time giving thanks to the Lord for seeing them safely through the night in that place. He shook Jim and tried to rouse him. Tanusi was up and ready for the trail, but Jim just groaned and shook off his hand.

"I can't make it, Joe," he said. "Just go on back and tell the other fellows that I died out here on the trail."

Sleep had revived Joe. He was anxious to be off. However, Jim, who had been willing to keep going the night before, was now feeling the effects of their all-day hike on an empty stomach.

"Come on, Jim," Joe said. "You know what a good fisherman Jake is. He is sure to have some fish cooked for us back in camp. The sooner we get started, the quicker we can eat."

Joe finally got Jim on his feet, and they made their long, weary way back to the camp they had left in such high spirits the day before. They pulled their weary bodies into camp but found Jake and Frank just as hungry as they were themselves.

"This is the poorest place I've ever seen," Jake complained. "I haven't even been able to find a fishing worm."

After two whole days with nothing to eat, they were beginning to feel the effect of it. They lay in their hammocks wearily contemplating their desperate situation, each one lost in his own thoughts. Jim's Tanusi seemed to be the only one with strength or ambition to move. He sniffed around the area as the men's eyes followed his pursuits. Jim too watched Tanusi's antics when suddenly a look of horror crossed his face. He leaped from his hammock, grabbed up his dog, and crawled back into his hammock with the struggling dog tightly clasped in his arms.

"Oh no you don't, fellows!" he panted. "You're not eating my dog!"

The next morning, day three of their fasting, Joe opened his eyes to another day in the jungle. Nothing had changed. They were still there, still hungry, and still with nothing to eat in sight. Joe looked at the green, tender-looking grass growing on the bank of the river.

"Fellows," he said, "Old King Nebuchadnezzar ate grass. If he could eat grass, why can't we? There must be some nourishment in it."

So they pulled some grass, cleaned it well, and put it on to cook in a tin can that had once contained milk powder. They hungrily awaited it. But hungry as they were, it was still a hard meal to get down. There is just nothing tasty about cooked grass, no salt, nothing! To make matters worse, they had discovered a sure cure for constipation, if they had been constipated that is, which none of them were! That ordeal left them weaker and more spent than ever.

On one of the hurried trips to the bush, someone discovered a palm tree of the kind with an edible heart. They decided they would take turns cutting down the tree with the old machete that had no handle and extract the heart. One person, they decided, should stay in the camp to watch for any possible passersby. Frank was elected. The rest started cutting down the tree. It was hard wood and very hard to cut with an old dull machete, but they doggedly kept at it. By now they all had blistering hands. Still hunger drove them on. While they were in the process of getting the tree down, Frank strolled up to them.

"Fellows," he said, "I just thought I'd better tell you that a Guaica (another name for the Yanomamö) just passed through our camp."

"What! A Guaica passed through and you didn't stop him?" Jim Bou screamed and took off running down the trail, yelling at the top of his lungs, "Sholi! Sholi! Noji! Noji [Friend]!"

Well, they never saw that Guaica. Joe said he could imagine that after getting a glimpse of Frank, who had grown a bushy beard to protect his face from the little bloodthirsty gnats, the Guaica or Yanomamö, that is, thought he had seen some sort of spirit and took to his heels. Then, if he was still close enough to hear Jim Bou crashing down the trail behind him, yelling like someone possessed, this no doubt put wings to his heels.

Jim dispiritedly returned to help them chop out the heart of the palm tree that they had worried to the ground. Having finally battered it down, they began to hack at the large bulge in the trunk where the heart was located. Getting the heart out of the trunk proved to be several more hours of work, but finally it lay exposed to where they could get to it and begin to tear off strips. After heartily thanking the Lord for this food, they started to bite into the crisp, tender, cabbage-like palm heart, and Frank said, "Fellows, I think I'll fast."

"Man," Jim said, "what do you think you've been doing? It's time to quit fasting and get some food inside you so you'll have strength to get across that trail!"

They tore into the palm heart and devoured it. This food put new strength in their bodies and hope in their hearts.

The next day, Jake and Jim decided to walk back across the trail and see if they would be able to find the village. Frank and Joe stayed in camp. Jake and Jim took a different branch off the trail than the one he and Joe had taken before and found the village of Nakishima up in the hills. There they soon found themselves resting in hammocks and drinking some delicious hot plantain soup. The villagers told them that the village they had been looking for was located across the river. When Jim and Joe had come to the river, they had turned back as they did not know it was on the other side.

"If you had yelled, they would have heard you and come for you in a canoe," they told Jim.

They provided a guide to go with Jim and Jake who showed them the way to the village of Shawalawa-teli, where they had been planning to visit from the start. Meanwhile, back in the camp, the Guaica who had passed through previously came back, bringing them some plantains. They were never happier to see anyone in their lives. This was the man who later came to be known as Pajarito.

The next day Jim and Jake arrived with the porters from the other village to carry their packs, and they all took off for Shawalawa village.

14

OUR CALIJOCO VILLAGE MINISTRY

We made many trips into that area during our first six years on the mission field. Each one was different than the one before. We experienced the terror of traveling through the white water in a dugout canoe. The canoe was being powered by an old clunker of a motor owned and driven by a Ye'cuana native whom we called Velasquez. We had our six small children in the canoe with us; our oldest was only eight when we finally made our last trip to that area.

We knew the exhaustion of the trip from the Port where we left the boat and went by trail to the village. We plodded up the mountains, up one side and down the other. We waded through the streams, shoes and all, our feet wet and uncomfortable as we sloshed along. There were just too many creeks to stop each time and remove our shoes. Those without shoes constantly suffered from thorns and briars in their feet.

I remember our first trip as a family. Mike was the baby. He had been crabby before we left Tamatama with what I thought was a bad diaper rash, and I doctored him for a couple of weeks with everything that I could think to use. We spent the night at the big falls at the mouth of the Cuntinamo River. The next day, the large dugout canoe would have to be taken out of the river and pulled up the mountain on skids to get it round the falls and into the river at the top. Then we could continue on our way to the village that we planned to visit.

Mike cried most of the night. The first rays of dawn found us heating some water and pouring it into in a large aluminum pot so that I could give him a bath and try to sooth his rash, which had now turned into big open sores. Our Ye'cuana motorista came over to where I was bathing the crying baby. Squatting down on his haunches, he peered at Mike sitting in the big pot.

"What's the matter with your baby?" he inquired. "What seems to be the trouble? I heard him crying most of the night. Is he ill?" he questioned.

I told him about the sores and how they were affecting Mike with fever and much pain. He looked at them closely and then said, "Those aren't sores. Those are guasanos del monte [the larvae of a type of blowfly that lays its eggs in the flesh]."

This news horrified us, of course, and we could hardly imagine the pain the baby had suffered for weeks with nineteen of these creatures eating his flesh. There was nothing to do at that point but to dry him off and dress him, as preparations were being made to haul the dugout up the side of the mountain. We had to follow.

They put the dugout back in the water at the top. We all piled in again and were once more on our way, this time heading up the Cuntinamo River, where we would arrive at the place called the Port. There we would leave the dugout and continue on by foot.

When we reached the Port and left the dugout, some of the Yanomamö appeared out of the forest to carry baggage and kids for us. An old Yanomamö woman was carrying Mike. Sitting in her carrying strap in his condition was making him miserable. When we stopped to rest, I showed her the open holes and told her what Velasquez had said.

"Don't worry," she said. "Wait until we get a little farther along, and I will get them out for you." I was so happy to hear that. I could have hugged her—dirt, sweat, tobacco cud, and all!

True to her word, at our next stopping place, farther up the mountain, she went off into the forest and returned with some leaves that dripped white sap from their broken stems. Taking the baby from my arms, she began dripping the sap into the open holes. Then she told me to wait a little while until the poison took effect. Soon, she was squeezing the large ugly worms out of the writhing, screaming baby as I held him tight. In the end, I don't know which one of us was the most limp and faint with the ordeal, the poor baby or me, as I suffered with him.

After spending about six weeks in the village, preaching and teaching God's Word, our supplies ran low. The rains were starting in the headwaters. The people told us that we would not be able to cross the small creeks if we did not soon leave. Since all our children were still small, we hired some of the Yanomamö to carry them across the trail for us.

We started the long trek back out to the Port, where we had left our dugout. A young Yanomamö woman carried Faithie, who was about four years old. She sat piggyback on a carrying strap that went around the woman's forehead. This meant that she faced forward on the trail.

Since the woman was in front of me, Faithie could not see me and began to cry. At first the young women pushed me to the front so Faithie would stop crying. However, the woman soon discovered that this foreigner could not read the trail well enough to make any time as we went along, so she relegated me to the back again. At this, Faithie began to cry in earnest. This so infuriated the woman that she began to run off down the trail, quickly leaving me far behind. Joe was with some of the men and some of our children, behind us somewhere on the trail. When the woman carrying Faithie ran off and left me, I kept on going, on what I deduced to be the trail she traveled. Sometime later, I heard Joe, Calijoco, and some of the other men talking as they passed on a trail which seemed to be far above me to my right.

Am I on the right trail? I wondered. Or have I wondered off on some other trail, going who knows where?

I almost did not call out, feeling ashamed that I was probably off the trail and not wanting to appear so stupid that I could not follow a trail. Then, I remembered stories of people lost in the jungle, and I began to call at the top of my voice.

Calijoco came plunging down the hill, plowing through the underbrush. "What in the world are you doing way down here?" he asked in amazement. "We almost lost you in the jungle. Come on and stay close to us," he said, which I was glad to do.

We arrived at the Port footsore and very tired after a long trek. We set up camp in an old shack left by some Venezuelan lumber workers in times past. It was sadly in need of repairs, but we felt better than being out in the open. The Indians hung their hammocks in the trees under the stars. Things went well until the middle of the night. Rain began to pour down in sheets. Of course, the Indians all pushed into the shack with us. Since they were pushing in from the front that meant that we had to keep moving toward the back.

Well, guess what? Since the roof had obviously leaked for some time, the former occupants had stuck leaves in such a way as to funnel the water to the back of the shack. We were at the back of the shack under the funneling waterspouts. Joe and I spent the rest of the night standing up, holding a large piece of plastic over the hammocks of our sleeping children so they would not get wet. The Indians who had moved into the front of the shack had all moved their fires in with them to keep warm in the dampness and cool night air. That meant that Joe and I, with our heads up close to the roof where we stood holding the plastic, found ourselves with runny eyes and noses from the smoke of the fires. A very unpleasant way to spend the night! We were happy to see morning come, and we were once more on our way downstream.

Susan Joann, our sixth child, was born October 16, 1956. When she was about two months old, we made the trip once again as a family into that area. It was getting late as we arrived at the Port, so we did not attempt to go across the treacherous mountain trails. We made camp and spent the night in a place near the trail that the men had chopped out in the underbrush.

Susan, in an infant basket, was just to the side of my hammock, well wrapped in blankets against the damp coolness of the forest. During the night, I awoke to check on her. I shined my flashlight down into the basket. Imagine my shock and terror to find her basket alive with large ants. I quickly awakened Joe, and he gingerly reached into the depths of the pile of blankets and pulled Susan out of the swarming ants, handing her to me. They were having a feast on her blankets and had not reached her; thus, she was sleeping peacefully through the siege.

These were bachaco ants, which can completely strip the leaves from a tree during the night and haul them away on their heads like umbrellas. In fact, they are often called "umbrella ants." Susan's blankets were well riddled with holes, but we gave thanks to the Lord that He had awakened me before they got through the blankets. Another instance where He made His watch care over us so very real.

Once when we were in the village, which we called Calijoco-teli, as Calijoco was the name of the headman of that village, we discovered that vampire bats truly exist.

Before this we had always thought they were just something in a fictional horror story. The Indians had been having trouble with the bats killing their chickens, so they made little leaf enclosures like tepees and shut the chickens up inside. That night, the bats, looking for some other creature to feast on, found Gary's big toe. Gary was about five years old. We awoke in the morning to find Gary's foot, his hammock, and his blanket full of blood. These bloodthirsty creatures will slice a piece right off where they intend to lap your blood. They inject something into the blood to keep the blood from coagulating, and as the blood runs freely they sit there and lap it up. They fan with their wings to produce a no-pain state in their victims. When they are full and flyaway, the blood keeps on flowing; you can lose a good bit of blood before it begins to coagulate again.

On this morning, when we found Gary with his foot encased in a bloody blanket, we determined that they would not get Gary again, or any of the children, or us for that matter. We took turns sitting up through the night. Joe and I each took a watch to make sure that no bat was going to attack in the night. We were living in an open shack of a house, which consisted of a leaf roof on some poles with jungle vines stretched around and leaves folded over these vines halfway up the walls. No protection from bats at all.

I do not remember who was on watch, but whoever it was fell asleep just before daybreak. At that point, the bat returned and got Gary on his other big toe. We were feeling so bad about it that the Indians wondered about it.

"Why do you have such long faces?" they asked us. "What's wrong?" they wanted to know.

We explained it all to them.

"Well, you must burn your kerosene flares all night," they told us. "Bats will not come where there is light." That solved our bat problem somewhat.

On that particular trip, when we left the village and started on our journey back downriver to our base at Tamatama, we once again encountered the vampire bats when we camped at the Port. Not realizing that they would be there also, we had given our kerosene flare to the headman, Calijoco, when we had left. That night while we were all sleeping, a bat bit Faithie on the wrist leaving a wicked-looking cut and leaving her arm all bloody.

We left that morning by boat for downriver. That night we slept on a sandbar on the edge of the jungle. We spread a tarp on the ground for a ground sheet with our blankets on top and placed all of the children on the tarp while Joe lay on one side of them and I on the other. We felt that in that way we could protect them from bats or other dangers. To our chagrin, a bat visited us in the night and bit Mike right in the top of his little exposed head. The blood was still running when we awoke. After that, we always kept a kerosene flare with us to ward off bats.

Another trip into that area that I will never forget was the time when other missionaries, who walked in to the village with us, just left us there at the village. They, including our Ye'cuana guides, returned downriver after taking us in there. We spent almost two months in there. Then, as food was getting scarce, including milk for baby Susan, we decided it was time to go back downriver. We asked some of the Yanomamö if they knew the river. Did they know how to navigate it to get us safely back down through the rapids? They assured us that they did, so we left with Calijoco and his younger brother Shani (a corruption of the name "Johnny") as our guides back to the downriver base.

We soon discovered that their knowledge of the river consisted of using a paddle canoe, skirting the edges of the river, and keeping well away from the rough and tumble of the boiling rapids. We did not discover this, however, until they took us down through some places that we got through only by the grace of God. They would motion Joe down through a section of river, and then after we had gotten well into the current of the rapid, they would spot all the rocks and yell, "Go back! Go back! We can't make it through here!"

Once committed to the current, with a three horsepower motor, there was absolutely no turning back, so down and through we would go. We had some harrowing experiences.

They obviously did not know the channel. Once we found ourselves in the big, old, clumsy dugout canoe perched right on top of a rock hidden just under the water. It balanced there precariously. All the men's pushing and shoving efforts could not seem to budge it off.

After a couple hours of standing out in the river as they maneuvered the boat from side to side, they finally managed to slide it off, and we were on our way once more. Not too much farther down the river at another large rapid, we had to stop and pull into the bank so that everyone could get out. The children and I were to be guided by trail around the rapids. Then the men were to let the empty canoe down through the rapids with ropes to a place where we would get on board again and continue our journey.

Joe had been insisting that the trail was located on the other side of the river. He told them that we were on the wrong side, but they assured him that they knew the trail well.

"Everything's just fine. We know the trail well," they said. "Just don't worry about it."

When we pulled onto the bank of the river, there was a huge nest of hornets in the tree above my head, and they immediately descended on me in a cloud. I was sitting on a wooden box in the middle of the canoe with all the children sitting on the floor around me. Therefore, I was the highest object in the boat. The bees directed all their attack on me. Everything exploded in chaos. I was screaming in pain, desperately trying to keep the bees off the kids. The kids were screaming in fright because their mother was quite hysterical. Calijoco, the Yanomamö in the front of the canoe, panicked. He grabbed Faithie, who was sitting nearest, and dashed off the boat.

"No, no! Don't run! Tie up the canoe!" Joe screamed. That stopped Calijoco's wild dash.

He came back and tied the canoe so it would not drift back into the current. Joe ran to me and began grabbing and crushing hornets, getting his hands severely stung, I'm sure. They were the kind that goes into the hair. They were stinging me all over the head and face. I managed to keep them off the children and only Gary got a sting on the ear. Finally, we were able to escape them by getting off the boat.

We started out to trek around the rapid and get below it so that the men could portage our things around and then let the boat down through the white water. We found out, of course, that we were on the wrong side of the river as Joe had thought. There was no trail, so they had to cut a trail through as we went. Biting ants falling down our necks and vines and thorns grabbing us just added to the misery. Finally we got around the rapid and the boat was let down through to calmer water below.

We loaded up and were once more on our way again. All the way downriver, Calijoco and Shani had a good time laughing at my reaction to the hornets. One sat in the front of the canoe to guide and the other sat behind me in the back of the canoe.

"How did she scream?" one would call out. The other one would scream and paw wildly at his head. Then they would both laugh uproariously. Believe me, with my head still aching violently, it was not funny to me!

109

Another near tragedy on the same trip was when we pulled the canoe onto the bank above another stretch of bad water. Shani, who sat in front, was supposed to jump off, grab the prow of the boat, and pull the boat up on shore so we could get off. We were to unload the boat there and portage around the rapids and then let the empty canoe down through with a rope as before.

However, when Shani jumped out of the canoe, the momentum of the jump pushed the canoe back out into the swift water. We went broadside right down through the rapids. We were all scared stiff. I looked back at Calijoco. His eyes were bugging out in fear; he looked about ready to just leap from the boat and try to make it to shore. Then Joe's voice rose above the roar of the water. He shouted in Yanomamö, "Don't be afraid! Don't be afraid! God will protect us!"

The prow hung out over nothing and then suddenly a huge wave rolled in underneath it, lifted it up, and carried it down through the rapids. Suddenly it was all over. We were all still in one piece and still sitting safely in the canoe. We bowed our heads and praised the Lord! After other hair-raising experiences, we finally arrived safely.

15

FURLOUGHS HAVE THEIR DANGERS ALSO

After almost six years of living in the Venezuelan rain forest, we were going home on furlough. That furlough proved to be as challenging as the jungle.

We now had seven children. Sandra Page was born September 15, 1958 in Puerto Ayacucho. When we left for furlough in 1959, Sandy was the baby. We were living in Huntington, West Virginia, in a little cabin that a Christian group had fixed up for us. While there, we used a small wood-burning stove for heat in the winter.

One evening we came back from shopping. Thirteen-month-old Sandy was on one of my arms and a bag of groceries was on the other. After I put Sandy down, she immediately toddled off across the floor.

Joe had left some kerosene in a little tin can by the stove, intending to start the fire again as soon as we got home. Sandy, thinking of course that it was something good to drink, picked up the can and drank some of the kerosene. It took away her breath. She came staggering up to me with glazed eyes. As she dropped the can, we realized what had happened.

We grabbed her up and rushed out the door, pushing the other kids ahead of us. Herding them into the car, we started for town at breakneck speed. Sandy's face was blue, her stomach distended. I kept breathing into her mouth. Finally she breathed a little and then vomited a bit.

We lived out from town a pretty good way, but we were pushing the old car to its limits. When we hit the town, Joe kept his hand to the horn, ran a red light, and frantically prayed a police officer would see us and get us to the hospital quicker. Wouldn't you know it? Not an officer in sight!

We got her into the hospital, where I spent the night with her. She was strapped to a board with intravenous solutions dripping into her. She kept vomiting, and I had to keep ringing for the nurse so we could keep her from strangling. There was only one nurse on the packed ward. She was run off her feet. Several days later, when Sandy was out of danger, she told me that on the floor that night there were two patients who had not been expected to live through the night. Sandy was one of them.

When the time came to get Sandy out of the hospital, the people who had furnished the cabin for us to live in were very concerned about how we would pay the hospital bill. They wondered if we should try and get help from the county.

Joe said, "No, the Lord will provide."

The day he was to come in to the hospital to take us home, he opened the mailbox and found a letter from a church in Williamsport, Pennsylvania. He had spoken there a couple of months before at a missionary conference. They had enclosed a check apologizing for not getting it to him sooner. The amount was exactly what he needed to pay Sandy's bill. It was a real testimony to the folks who had been worried about what we would do.

Everything was new and exciting to children who had never even tasted an ice cream cone. I overheard Faith and Velma, who were ages six and five respectively at that time, talking as they sat by the wooden radio that we had been given. They had never seen or heard a radio before. It was a cause for amazement to all the children.

"Faithie, do you think those people really live in that little house?" Velma asked, as she stood on tiptoe and tried to look inside the glass over the dial.

"Of course they do. Don't you see that they have the light on in their house?" Faithie replied. I chuckled to myself then tried to explain the wonders of radio to them.

Then there was the Christmas program in the small school that they were attending. Faith and Velma were both enrolled in first grade. One day as the teacher stood in front of the class teaching the song "He'll be Coming Down the Chimney When He Comes," she made wiggling motions as though forcing herself down the chimney and instructed the class to do the same. All the children immediately began gyrating in imitation of the teacher, except for two little missionary kids who stood straight and very noticeable in their refusal to wiggle down the chimney with the class.

"Come on. Can't you wiggle down the chimney with the rest of the class?" the teacher asked.

"No ma'am. Our daddy doesn't allow us to wiggle like that!" Faithie solemnly replied, as Velma nodded her head in agreement.

The teacher laughingly told me about it at a PTA meeting later and said that it had greatly impressed her to see two children who were so young stand up for what they believed, in front of their whole class.

We returned to Venezuela after spending only seven months in the United States.

16

HEADING BACK TO VENEZUELA

We left Huntington, West Virginia, where we had spent our seven-month furlough and headed by train for New Orleans, Louisiana, where we planned to leave by Dutch freighter for La Guaira, Venezuela.

In those days, these Dutch freighters carried twelve passengers. By taking our storage barrels and boxes with us on the ship, we went cheaper than we could traveling by plane and sending our cargo by ship separately.

When we arrived in Cincinnati, Ohio, we found ourselves stranded. It was January 1960. The trains were full of service men returning to their bases from their Christmas leaves. They had priority, and the trains were filled to overflowing. Dejectedly, we watched as our train chugged off, leaving us behind. After sitting and walking around for many long hours, tired and hungry, we realized that it was about time for the next train headed for New Orleans to arrive. Joe left us to talk to the ticket agent at the counter. He asked what our chances would be of getting on the next train.

"Well, I would say they're mighty slim unless of course you find yourself a redcap and tip him about ten dollars and have him put you on the train before it pulls up for loading," the man replied.

Joe turned away dejectedly. We did not have ten extra dollars. We did not even have money for food for the long wait that we had there in the station. We had not realized we would be sitting there all day, waiting to board our train.

In the meantime, as the children and I sat waiting on the bench in the station, a lady came up to us and began a conversation. She wondered where we were going. There I sat with seven children, the oldest one nine years old, the youngest sixteen months, all lined up in a row on the bench.

"I've been sitting over there watching your family," she said. "I'm amazed that even though they're so young they just sit here obediently waiting. What is your secret?" she asked. "Where are you going with this lovely family?"

I told her we were missionaries and most of the children had been born in the Federal Amazonas Territory of Venezuela and all had spent most of their lives there.

"We spent six years there working with a tribal group of people who call themselves the Yanomamö," I explained. "We have been home for about seven months and are now returning to our work there in the Venezuelan rain forest," I said.

She was quite impressed. She wanted to hear of some of our adventures. I shared some of the stories from our work with her. As our conversation came to a close, she told me she was with the Salvation Army. When she left, she pressed a bill into my hand and whispered, "Maybe this will help out a little on your trip!"

I thanked her as she turned away, just as I saw Joe approaching from the other direction. I opened my clenched hand and looked down. There lay a ten-dollar bill. Joe came up looking a little discouraged.

"Well, I'm afraid the news isn't good," he said. "The ticket agent said that if we tip a redcap ten dollars, he might get us on the train before it pulls into the gate for loading, but we don't have ten dollars."

I opened my hand again with a smile. "Yes, we do," I said and told him the story of the Salvation Army lady and her generous gift of ten dollars to help us on our way.

"Praise the Lord!" Joe said and took the ten dollars from me. He found a cheerful redcap standing nearby and told him of our dilemma.

"Boss, yo' troubles am over," he said with a huge grin as he pocketed the ten-dollar bill and motioned for all of us to follow him.

He took us outside and led us to where the train was standing. He ushered us aboard and seated us in the empty train. When it chugged up to be loaded with the passengers, the train filled up quickly. We realized that but for the Lord's mercy in sending the Salvation Army lady to talk to us and give us the ten dollars we would never have gotten on that train either.

"Thank you, Lord, for your watch care over us and for the way you are taking such good care of us. We know you will see us to our destination. Our trust is in Thee," Joe prayed once we were settled in our seats. Our hearts were full of thanksgiving as we were once more on our way back to Venezuela and the Yanomamö tribe of people.

Somewhere on the long trip, all the passengers were startled to see paper and junk flying past the windows. Suddenly the train came to a screeching halt. After some of the passengers got off to investigate why we were stopped, they returned saying that the train had hit a garbage truck that had been crossing the tracks. The garbage truck had been demolished. An ambulance and a tow truck had arrived. The engine of our train had also been damaged and removed.

We had to wait hours for another engine. We were told later that the first train that we would have traveled on if our original plans had worked out had derailed. There were many casualties. Once again, we thanked the Lord for His watch care over us. We were all still safe and sound.

Since we pulled into New Orleans many hours later than expected, there was no one there to meet us. We had planned to stay at a home that put up missionaries traveling to and from the field, and we had expected the man to meet us at the station.

However, since we were so much later than planned, he had given up on us and had gone home long ago. The kids were all stretched out asleep on the wooden seats in the train station. I wearily tried to get comfortable, wondering just what the night held for us. Joe found a phone and called the home where we were to stay. The missionary who ran the home came to the train station. However, his words were discouraging.

"Our home is still full," he said. "The missionaries who were to leave yesterday are still with us. They have been having bad rains in Texas, so they have not been able to unload their ship's cargo there. So our guests are still waiting for their ship to come in from Texas to New Orleans before they can leave," he told us.

He finally drove us to a hotel. I worried as I saw our money that we needed to get through Caracas and on down to Puerto Ayacucho dwindling away. However, there was nothing else to do. We checked in at the hotel and soon had the kids bathed, in their nightclothes, and in bed.

When Joe and I finally had time to relax, I expressed my fears to him. I remember him saying, "Well, look what a nice birthday present the Lord has given you. He's letting you spend the night here in this comfortable hotel."

Sure enough, I realized it was January 4th and my twenty-ninth birthday! How good is our God! He remembered me, and I slept soundly knowing He would see us to the end of our journey, taking care of us all each step of the way.

The next morning Joe called our ship's company and found out that they would be unable to sail for a week. We told the man at the company our situation and explained that it was impossible for us to spend a week in the hotel, but we got no satisfaction from him. Then the manager from the homes where we had originally planned to stay called us and told us that he had gotten us a place to stay in a Salvation Army women's home. He came shortly and drove us there.

The lady who was in charge of the homes was very pleasant and friendly. She showed us to a couple of rooms upstairs for sleeping.

"You and your family can eat with us in the main dining hall," she told us. "Your wife will be required to help us by doing some kitchen work and helping serve in the dining hall, but we will not charge you for your stay here," she explained. I considered this a very small price to pay for being able to stay there for a week until we could board our ship.

"Since this is a woman's home, you'll not be allowed to use the front entrance. You'll have to come and go by the side entrance," she told Joe.

"That's no problem at all," Joe replied. He was happy to oblige.

"Oh yes, and another thing. . . " she continued, "my husband works nights and sleeps days. His bedroom is just under the room that you will be in upstairs. Will you please keep the children as quiet as possible?"

Well, it was a big order, but we did it, determined to be a good testimony and to cause no problems for these good people who were helping us out in a difficult time.

One of the things I remember about that time was crowding all the kids onto our bed and reading to them. We had little with us in the way of entertainment for kids, nothing like you see the kids of today have. I read the Book of Revelation to them. Why I picked that book, I have no idea, but it did the trick. The kids asked all kinds of questions and listened quietly as I read. Of course, there were times in the day when I could take them down to the indoor gym and let them get rid of some energy, and they were still young enough to be put down for naps. Those things helped keep the room above the sleeping man quiet during the day.

By the time we were leaving, I had gotten to be friends with the lady who had shown us the rooms. She told me we were the quietest people who had ever stayed there and marveled how we had kept the kids so quiet.

She said her husband kept saying, "I don't believe they're up there. They must have gone out."

She had replied, "No, they're up there. They haven't gone out."

Then she said, "Some families who've stayed here before have let their children jump from the top bunks of the bunk beds onto the wooden floor beneath. You cannot believe what a racket that makes below. Thanks for being so quiet and thoughtful. I know it wasn't easy with so many small children!"

How thankful I was that I had made a special effort to keep the kids quiet and happy, so as to be a testimony for the Lord!

17

HOME AGAIN! HOME AGAIN!

J anuary of 1960 found us fresh back from furlough. Shortly after we arrived back in Tamatama, Joe, along with another missionary as his companion, made a trip back up into the Cuntinamo area to visit Calijoco's village where we had put in a lot of work during our first term. Joe was interested in finding out if they wanted us to move there and establish a base there.

On their way back downriver, they passed the village of Coshilowa-teli, at the mouth of the Metaconi River where it emptied into the Padamo River. We had had contact with this village for a number of years when they still lived inland and only visited us at Tamatama to work for machetes and axes.

Once one of the men, whom we later named Octavio, said, "If we build you a mud house will you all come and live with us?"

To this we replied "Yes," meaning that some missionaries would be willing to do that, not necessarily us. We ourselves were still involved in the ministry in Calijoco's village. We were thinking of another young couple who was also in the Yanomamö work and wanted to get active in a village. They were a man and his wife with small twin boys.

We took this young family to the village of Coshilowa-teli and left them there to get acquainted with the people and to practice the language. The chief men in the village had been expecting us to move there and did not know or want these other foreigners. They were angry.

Joe explained to them that we had other commitments to another village but that this couple were their friends and wanted to live with them and learn their language and their customs. The village leaders finally agreed to give them a chance.

We left the missionary family behind and continued on our way up the Padamo River and then around the large falls that emptied the Cuntinamo River into the Padamo. After pulling our large canoe up around these falls on land, we then continued up the Cuntinamo River.

However, since we had returned from furlough, we had discovered that things had not gone well with them in that village. During their time there in Cosh the village raided an upriver group and stole some women. Dimiyoma (Dee-mee-yo-ma) was one of them. After a couple of days, two of these women escaped and went back to their own village. Dimiyoma preferred to stay in Cosh as the man she liked was living there. The Coshilowa village war chief was furious that these other women had escaped, and a warring party left to go after them again. They planned to raid the other village and take these women back as well as get more for their troubles.

The missionary did not understand the culture of the people. He did not realize that he would appear to them to be taking sides and thus become their enemy. He traveled in his boat to a spot below the other village and fired his shotgun in an attempt to warn the other village to be on the alert so they would not be taken by surprise and possibly wiped out. The surprise attack was foiled.

The war party from Coshilowa village looked on it as an enemy act and thereafter shunned the missionary and his family. They were so hostile to him that he was afraid to leave his family behind to hunt or fish or try to provide food for them. Learning language and culture from them was, of course, out of the question, so we found them very discouraged on our return. The family came down to Tamatama as it was now getting close to the time for their first furlough.

Now, as Joe and Paul passed by there, they met Octavio sitting on the bank of the river in front of his small house. He immediately began telling Joe how much they wanted us to come and live with them and teach them God's Word.

"Well, I don't believe that my leaders will allow me to come here to live," Joe replied. "Your people were so unfriendly to Waldo. You all hated him and his family and were very mean to them," he told Octavio.

"Yes, we became angry with him because he warned our enemies. So, we treated him badly. But now we realize that he was ignorant of our ways. We are not angry anymore. We greatly desire to hear God's Word," Octavio replied.

"I can make no promises," Joe replied. "I must talk to my leaders."

"You have a large family of small children," his single missionary friend, Paul, said. "Why don't you put a base there on the Padamo, and I will continue your ministry with the villages up the Cuntinamo," he said.

The mission leaders were thinking of abandoning that work, as the people had been so unfriendly. We felt that they had gotten off on the wrong foot and that we would like to try to reach this group for Christ. The leaders agreed for us to move there.

This was truly of the Lord, for this was the very group of people where Bautista and his father lived, the man who was trying to find out how to escape the "Big Fire"!

Thus, we found ourselves moving to the village of Coshilowa-teli or Honey Village. A couple of the women that had been stolen in the previous raid had escaped again and made their way home, leaving Dimiyoma behind so the village was sweating out a return raid. It was not really the healthiest of times to move there.

We had left our four oldest children behind in Tamatama in the mission school and dorm to continue their education. This was by far the hardest thing we had done to date. No one who has not experienced it can know what it feels like to leave your small children behind in the care of someone else. You think about all the things you will miss out on, that first tooth lost, that next birthday, the cute and catchy things that kids say growing up.

Someone else would be there when they ran home from school, excited to tell what they had learned. Would someone else take time to listen like Mom would? Someone else would take care of skinned knees, cuts, and scratches. Would they do it with love and care as Mom would?

We had to believe that God would see them through this time, just as we had to believe Him for our own hearts' needs. The pain in our hearts was great, but we assured the Lord that we would absolutely do this for none else but Him. He comforted our hearts and gave us peace!

18

RAIDERS!

We barely got moved in the little mud house with the palm thatch roof and got our meager possessions in place when, to our surprise, the door opened and a group of Yanomamö, dressed only in loincloths, surrounded us. They had smeared black on the upper portions of their bodies and faces. As their eyes gleamed out of their black faces, they were fearful to behold.

We realized in despair that these were raiders from the village called Forgetful Village. They came seeking revenge for their woman who had been stolen and mistreated. The Cosh people were all gone. They had risen early and gone to the forest to look for fruit that was in season. We breathed a sigh of relief that the village was empty except for some old women and small children.

We invited them to sit down, and we fixed them some yucuta, a drink made by mixing water with a dry cereal made from the manioc root. This drink is a great favorite of these people. Soon they were all happily gulping down huge gourds of the sour-smelling liquid.

Joe made conversation with them while they took turns drinking from the huge pot of yucuta. He explained that we had just moved in and that we wanted to be friends with all the Yanomamö.

"There is one true God who created the heavens and the earth and everything you see," he told them. "We have come here to tell all of you Yanomamö about the one true God. He loves all you people and wants all you people to come to know Him personally," he continued. "We want to be friends with your village too. We hope you will allow us to visit with you people in your village. We'd like for you to come here often to visit us and be taught this good message we have come to tell you," he said.

"Put away your anger," Joe kept saying to them. "Don't fight. You can all settle this quarrel peaceably. Fighting will only bring more troubles. Fighting is not good. It causes more bad feelings."

Joe went from one to another, trying to get them calmed down. They became friendly, and we were soon doctoring the sick. We treated sore eyes, stomach pains, bad colds, stopped-up noses, and even a sprained ankle. We also took advantage of the situation to give out malaria preventative medicine to everyone.

Then I remembered the little Gospel Recordings record player that we had brought with us. We had helped make some gospel tapes in our first term that had been used by Gospel Recordings to make these records. Now we had some of these records with us in the Yanomamö language. Each side contained a short sermon and a Yanomamö song or two with Joe playing the guitar and the two of us singing Yanomamö songs that had been translated.

We soon had the player cranked up and playing. To say they were fascinated with their words coming out of that contraption would be an understatement. They absolutely could not get enough and begged us to play them over and over again. On one record, there was a rooster that had crowed in the background when the tape had been made. This rooster crowing was a great attraction. They asked for that particular record over and over again. We praised the Lord anyway that they were hearing God's Word for the first time in their language and understanding what was being said.

They now seemed to be relaxed and enjoying themselves. We were also feeling more comfortable about the whole situation. Just then some of the villagers returned and a shout went up as the man who had stolen one of the women stepped out of the forest with Dimiyoma. The Cosh villagers had been taken unaware, but they rallied their forces.

Pandemonium broke out. People ran everywhere, screaming and yelling. Heads were bleeding freely from big open gashes. Arms and legs were gashed open.

I hastily tore up a white sheet for bandages. Joe began leading in the wounded from both sides. We were kept busy sponging out wounds and bandaging them.

We heard the screaming, shouting, and sounds of war increase in volume. We ran outside to see what else was happening. Now they were in a tug of war over Dimiyoma.

One village was on one of her arms, and the other village was pulling just as hard on the other arm. I was sure that she would be pulled in two. One of the men raiders kept slapping her on the back and thighs with the broadside of his machete. Finally the man who had come to get her back, seeing that they were not getting anywhere, walked up with his machete and chopped her right across the kneecaps. She fell to the ground screaming with blood gushing from her wounds. Now that she was mutilated and undesirable, they let her fall to the ground in a heap.

Two of the Honey Village (Cosh) women helped her into our house. By that time, her legs were a bloody mess. Grabbing

127

a pan of water, I began cleaning off the blood. Blood was gushing out of the wide gashes in her kneecaps. One knee especially was cut badly. I could not get the blood stopped.

In those days, we had no sutures, no anesthetics, no antibiotics, and not even any real bandages. We did have some sulfadiazine pills. After I had sponged out the wounds, I filled them with ground up sulfadiazine pills. I hastily tore up one of my white sheets and bandaged her knees with my torn sheet bandages. After I had gotten her bandaged up and elevated the leg to try to stop the bleeding, I gave her a sedative. Having done all for her that I knew, I left her and went outside to see what was happening.

(When they had started fighting, I had locked our three smallest children who were with us in the village in the bedroom with instructions to swing in the hammock and be quiet so that no one would try to get in where they were. They were doing this and seemed to be taking the whole thing calmly.)

I heard horrible groans coming from the battle area. Soon I saw them staggering toward our house, supporting one of the young fellows from our village. He appeared to be mortally wounded. They laid him on the floor, left him in my charge, and hastily took off back to the battle.

His young wife had followed him in, weeping. I asked her where he was hurt. She showed me a puncture wound in his elbow. He had been stabbed with a spear. It had bled quite badly, and he had blood all over him. His back was covered with bruises where the enemy had slapped him with machetes.

I cleaned and bandaged his elbow and gave him a sedative. A few minutes later, he began to shake all over. He seemed to be getting worse. I ran out to find Joe to tell him that the boy was going into shock. We managed with the reluctant help of another warrior, who had dropped out of the battle, to get him up on our table, where we covered him with a blanket.

Joe took advantage of a lull in the fighting to run outside with our small suitcase of trade goods. Many of the men had already stopped fighting and had gathered around. I guess they figured they could fight any old time, but getting fishhooks might be a one-time thing. Everyone from the other villages received fishhooks and matches, which definitely helped to put them in a happier and friendlier frame of mind.

With the tension eased, they began a begging session with the folks from our village. It was hard to believe that this group standing around laughing and talking in a friendly manner was the same group that had been fighting, clubbing, and shouting insults not too long before. Finally, everyone left happy, except the two men who wanted Dimiyoma. The suitor and his older brother left fuming and fussing.

It took many months for Dimiyoma's knees to completely heal. We had the daily chore of doctoring her, but we were happy that she did not lose the use of her legs. Her knees finally healed, and a last she was able to walk normally again.

Dimiyoma still lives here in the village of Coshilowa-teli. She is not young anymore. She has led a hard life of physical and mental suffering, but she is now a fine Christian woman with a compassionate heart for those in need.

The boy who was stabbed in the elbow with the spear later became known as Freddie. His young wife who was sickly died. Later he married her older sister, and they moved upriver to live in the village called Forgetful, where the raiders had come from to get Dimiyoma. There he became a shaman and practiced his sorcery for years.

Finally his heart softened to the Word of God, and he professed faith in Christ. He was so changed. He always had a big smile on his face. But something happened to take away his joy, and he was never the same again, in spite of the teaching he received of God's willingness to forgive and cleanse.

His wife and most of his children died in the years that he walked away from the Lord. He tried to go back to his sorcery but admitted that he was never able to get in contact with the spirits again. He was finally killed in a village downriver where he had gone to take another wife. The news saddened us greatly when we received it.

19

FLOOD WATERS—OUR FIRST MOVE

We had pretty well adjusted to village life. We had gotten our little routine together. Everything—all teaching and meetings—went on in our little mud house. We arose very early, had our devotions, fixed breakfast, and roused the children to eat. Mike was not quite five at the time. Susan was not yet four and Sandy not quite two. They were a handful, yet we managed to live there in primitive conditions and maintain a reasonable state of health and happiness.

Once our morning chores were done, I would remove the colorful flowered oilcloth from our one and only table, which Joe had built. Then we arranged benches around the table. After that, we would beat on one of our pans. This was to attract the attention of anyone who wanted to look at funny marks on paper and try to decide what it was saying to them. Pretty soon, the table would be filled with those anxious to show us that they were willing to be friendly and keep us happy, and if this is what it took, they were willing to suffer through it.

In the beginning, we taught literacy mostly to the adults. We did not want them to think that this was something just for children and so scorn it as beneath them. Also we were careful to aim for the men first, especially influential men in the village, so they would know we placed importance on what we were teaching. We had worked up little primers to teach literacy by the syllable method. All of it was new to the Yanomamö. They had never seen paper or pencils before. They had never seen a match before the missionaries came. They had still used fire sticks to make their fires.

Everything was new. Everything was a curiosity. Their favorite expression (next to "Give it to me!") was "Let me see it." This meant they wanted to take the object in their hands and examine it, turning it over and over from one hand to the other. Finally, I wearied of the objects getting dirty or broken and said, "Look at it with your eyes, not your hands."

As we became more familiar to them, they knew we were their friends. They knew we were there for them in sickness, willing to do what it took to nurse someone back to health, and in death, crying with them at a loss. This made them willing to accept my request. Visitors from other villages were another story. We still had to allow them to satisfy their curiosities by inspecting objects—spoons, knives, plates, notebooks, pencils, and more—with their hands as well as their eyes.

One day as some of the women and I were talking in my house, one of the women looked around and said, "Well, when the rains come, this will all flood out where your house is."

"What?" I asked. "You're just fooling, right? The water will not really come this far up, will it? Look how high the bank is."

"No, I'm not fooling," she said. "The water always comes up here in the rainy season."

They all looked around nodding their heads, agreeing with her.

Her assertion left me a little apprehensive to say the least. That evening when Joe and I were talking, I shared with him what the ladies had said. He looked around him at the mud walls of the house.

"No. I don't think the water has ever come up in here," he said. "Look at the walls. There is no watermark there. They're just teasing you."

The next day, as the women and I visited again, I remarked that Joe had said there were no water lines on the walls, so he did not believe the water had ever risen up on them. The women laughed.

"Oh no, the water never came up on these mud walls," they laughed, appreciating the joke. "There was no mud in these walls last rainy season, just poles and roof. So of course there are no marks." They shook with helpless laughter.

To me it was no laughing matter. I was expecting my eighth baby in July, and the high water came always in June. That did not make me too happy.

By the end of May, the water was rising higher and higher. I was getting very uneasy, but Joe felt that it still had a long way to go to come over the bank and up to our house. However, in June it did just that. It came over the bank and close to the outside wall of our house. The Yanomamö saw my fear.

"No, no," said one man, "it surely won't come into the house. It'll probably stop right here," he said, indicating a place well beyond our wall. Joe had some of the men heap sand up around the endangered wall.

That night, about 12:30 a.m., Joe woke me up. "The water's in the house and rising fast. We're going to have to leave the house and go up to higher ground. The long communal house at the end of the village is on higher ground, and we can go there," he explained, comforting me as he saw my fear.

I looked around. Water covered the floor. Everything that we had not moved into our little wooden loft the night before was getting wet. I hurriedly dressed myself, woke the children, and dressed them.

"We'll have to go in a paddling canoe," Joe said. "The water's already too high for you to walk through it to the other end of the village."

I held Sandy on one hip; my other arm held a pile of clean diapers. My movements were clumsy to say the least. As I awkwardly tried to get myself into the canoe, it tilted and threw me into the water. To make matters worse, the water covered a pineapple patch, and I landed on a prickly pineapple plant. It was the middle of the night. The water was cold. Sandy was crying. The diapers were now a soggy mess. I was eight months pregnant. Right about then, in the vernacular of today's youth, "I was not a happy camper."

A Yanomamö helped me up and into the canoe. Mike and Susan were already sitting there, looking forward to the big adventure of a paddling canoe trip by moonlight. I wished that I could be so enthusiastic. One of the men paddled us over to the long communal house made of leaves, which was sitting on a higher spot, but even there water was seeping into the lower end.

I huddled close to the fire, trying to get warm, shivering in my wet clothes. Joe paddled back to the house and got dry clothes for Sandy and me and a sheet to hold up for me to change behind. He also brought another stack of dry diapers.

To say this was a long night in the room filled with smoke and smelly bodies and no place to lie down is putting it mildly. Somehow we made it through the night.

The next day Joe went to our house and moved a table, some benches, and Sandy's high chair up into the loft. The Yanomamö had helped him put our bedding up the night before. Joe waded around down below and fixed our food, which he handed up to us. Mike and Susan thought Daddy was surely having a lot of fun down there tromping around in the water and begged to get down there with him. Yanomamö paddled in and out of the house in little paddling canoes.

After three days, the water went back down and we were able to go back downstairs, although the mud floor was a muddy mess. We had no sooner gotten set up again when the river made its second rise.

This time Joe had had enough. He had some of the men go downriver a short ways and build us a small leaf house on a high spot of land. The village headman had cleared this small spot off for a garden. We bought the land from him for many yards of red loincloth material, a machete, and a large cooking pot. There the men built a one-room house with a thatch roof and leaf wall. We moved down there all alone, in the middle of the rain forest, as the villagers were still living upriver.

20

ARMY ANTS

We had only been in our new house a couple of nights when we heard a peculiar sound advancing towards our house. Joe went out to investigate and found a column of large army ants in about a three-foot-wide swath, the line stretching off back into the jungle, making a beeline for our little leaf house. We panicked, to say the least. We had visions of being eaten alive with our flesh picked from our bones by these biting monsters. That they bite was soon proven out as Joe got too close to the edge of the horde.

In desperation, Joe thought maybe he could turn their course away from the house with his blowtorch. He fired it up and began unmercifully to burn the ants leading the column. As the leading ants died, the rest swarmed right on over them and just kept coming. Finally, Joe dashed back into the house shouting, "I can't get them turned away. Let's just get up on the beds and stay off the floor. Maybe they won't eat us up."

In our situation, there was really no place to run. The children were asleep in their beds. Joe and I climbed up on our bed, making sure nothing was touching the mud floor. Then we heard them hit the leaf walls and begin to pour into the room. It sounded as though it was raining hard.

Soon, the floor was black with ants scurrying everywhere. Roaches, crickets, spiders, and every kind of little bug imaginable began to scamper out of the walls and from every nook and cranny of that little leaf house. On a clean-up mission, those ants killed them every one and began piling up their bodies in a corner of the house. None had a chance for escape. They were doomed from the start.

"Oh," I moaned, "they'll eat up all our food before they go."

We could only watch from our bed, praying they would not finish cleaning up on the insects and then start on us.

We watched them for hours and then fell wearily asleep. A couple of times during the night, I awoke and shined the flashlight on the floor. The army ants were still scurrying around on the floor. The rain-like sound of their bodies thudding against the leaves as they ran up and down continued on.

Finally I slept. When I awoke in the morning, the ants were gone. It was as though they had never been there. Nothing remained. Not one roach. Not a spider or bug. Nothing! The only remaining ants were those that Joe had burned as they came in. The house was clean with not a single pest in it.

We were thankful for these house cleaners that the Lord had sent to us. We had learned that these were friends, not foe. From then on, when army ants came to visit, we just got out of their way and let them do their job. They never touched food or clothing. They only killed the insects. These they would stack in a pile and take with them when they left.

In a few weeks, it was time for us to go down to Tamatama and await the birth of our baby. Sharon Rose was born there on July 29, 1960. When she was ten days old, we left and went back to the village of Coshilowa-teli—or I should say—to our little leaf shack downriver from the village. The villagers had not as yet moved down with us.

21

THE STORY OF JOB

The people paid us visits every day. Every morning we closed up our foldaway beds and pushed them into a corner. After a quick breakfast of hot oatmeal and milk, we would begin getting organized to teach literacy.

The oilcloth would come off the table and onto the two beds to protect them from dirty hands. Then we arranged the benches around the table and got out our notebooks, pencils, and little primer books. Soon the students began to come in and sit down at the table. Many learned to read and write their language in those classes.

As time went by, we learned more about the Yanomamö, their language, their customs, and their needs. I remember once they were all sitting around the table doing literacy. By this time we had built a mud house with several rooms, so we could have a little privacy. Most of the villagers were already moved down to our area and had built houses here also.

Joe had built another small table from hand-hewn boards. He taught the beginners class at one table while I taught those who had learned the syllables and were trying to put them together to read fluently.

On this particular day, my class was reading. I had chosen the story of Job. Each reader was reading a small paragraph for practice. As they read, I realized that some of them were getting a little excited about something. I began to listen more closely to what they were saying.

"Yes, that certainly sounds like Clämö," one said.

As they read a little more, they became more excited. "Yes, it really does sound like Clämö with all those boils," they said.

By now, I was all ears. Who on earth were they talking about? When they came to the part of the story where Job sat in the ashes and scratched himself with a pottery shard, they could contain themselves no longer and began talking together excitedly. By now, Joe was wondering what was going on with my class.

"Come here and listen to them," I said. "They seem to know this story of Job."

Joe began to question them.

"We have a story like this," one said. "Only his name was not Job. Our ancestors called him Clämö. But he was like Job. He suffered greatly; he had many boils, and he sat in the ashes and scratched himself with a piece of pot. It must be the same man you are talking about."

Well, we really got excited.

"In the beginning your ancestors had the knowledge of the one true God," Joe said. "But because they refused to worship him as God and turned to their spirits, they lost the knowledge that they had. They began to walk in darkness instead of the light of God's truth," he told them.

"Some of the stories of truth that your ancestors had known you still have," I exclaimed

"But your stories are all mixed up with just portions of truth still mixed in, enough for all of you to recognize the story of Job," said Joe excitedly.

"You know how it is," I said. "When something happens here in your village, someone tells the story to someone else in another village. They tell it to someone else and so it is passed along from village to village until finally the story comes back to your ears. By now, many people have told the story, and in the telling they have changed the story. So you set the person straight.

"'No,' you say, 'that's not the way it happened. I was right there and saw it happen and I know the truth about that story,' and you tell them just exactly the way it happened. Well, that's the way it was with the story your ancestors had of Job. They did not have it written down, so as they told the story, it was changed in the telling. But we have the true story because God had it written down for us so it could not get mixed up. This is God's story of Job—or Clämö as you call him."

Years later, they told us it was then that they really began to believe what we were telling them about God was true.

"How can those people from way across the big waters know our story unless what they are saying is true?" they asked one another.

22

A BABY'S CRY

Joseph Alan was born on January 30, 1962. We had left
Tamatama on our supply boat and gone to Puerto Ayacucho
with our younger children, leaving the older ones in boarding
school in Tamatama.

Joe had just come back from a long, hard trip upriver. He
had been trying to keep up with a teaching ministry to the "babes
in Christ" that we had left there in the village. He had sat in a
dugout for hours with just a plastic held around him to shield
him from the cold driving rain. The right side of his face had
borne the brunt of the slashing rain as he sat back at the motor,
peering out of the plastic at the murky waters, keeping the dugout in the right channel to avoid rocks and sand bars.

As we prepared that morning to leave on the supply boat,
he complained about one side of his tongue and lips feeling numb,
but we did not have time to think on it too much.

However, on his way downriver on the supply boat, the right
side of his face became partially paralyzed. His right eye would

not shut. When he tried to eat, food ran out of the right side of his mouth, as that side of his face just did not respond. By the time we reached Puerto Ayacucho, we knew he needed a doctor's help for his problem. We found out that he had Bell's Palsy. That side of his face never completely recovered. We stayed in Puerto Ayacucho until Joey was born. When he was a couple of weeks old, Joe returned back upriver to the work. I stayed in Puerto Ayacucho with Sandy, Sharon, and Baby Joey.

In 1964 another baby was born. However, she was not born into our growing family. Her parents had come from the village of Jalulusi-teli to visit their relatives here in Cosh. When they arrived, we could see that the woman was soon due to deliver her baby.

One morning some of the women were talking to me as we sat around fellowshipping.

"That Jalulusi-teli woman is going to just kill her baby when it is born," said one.

"What?" I cried. "She can't do that. That is murder. God forbids us to kill!" I said.

They all nodded in agreement. "Yes, but it is true," said another. "She says her husband wants to be rid of it if it's a girl. They don't want any more girls," she said.

Later when the visitor woman came to my house to visit, I had a long talk with her. She denied the charges, declaring that the other women had just been lying about her. I accepted her word and was much relieved.

Imagine my surprise and horror a few weeks later when some of the Yanomamö came to tell me that the woman had given birth out in the forest just before daybreak but that she had killed the baby and thrown it away out there. She had returned to the village empty-handed.

We were heartsick, feeling that we had been warned what to expect but had carelessly taken this woman's word that she did not intend to harm her child. At about 1:30 p.m., one of the men came running to the house.

"Come quickly," he called. "The baby's still alive out in the forest. I just heard it crying when I was walking out there. Come get it before it dies!"

I could not believe what I was hearing. The baby had been born before daybreak. It had been misting a cold drizzly rain all day. Could a newborn baby have survived about eight hours of lying out there in the rain and cold? Impossible, I thought.

By that time, having heard the man's shouts, many of the women had gathered around.

"Be quick!" I cried. "Go get the baby! It's cold and wet. Go quickly!" I implored as they all just stood there looking at me. No one made a move. All of them had young babies on their carrying straps. None of them wanted another one.

"Please, go get the baby," I said. "I'll give you a bottle and the milk for it if you will go get it," I promised. Still no one moved.

Finally, in disgust at their insensitivity to the plight of this newborn baby, I said, "Well, go with me and show me where it is so that I can go and get it myself. I won't leave a baby out there to die like an animal." I found out later that the person who picks it up is responsible for it. No one wanted that responsibility.

They quickly ran ahead of me and showed me the trail to take out into the forest. Faithie, who was then about twelve years old, was with me also. We went on into the forest until we came to a place where an old tree had blown over, its roots grotesquely sticking up in the air, leaving a deep crater in the earth. The baby had been pitched down into that black yawning hole.

We could see it lying there on the wet, soggy leaves and the mulch and black dirt from many leaves that had rotted before.

Once again I tried to get the women to climb down into the hole and pick the baby up. Once again I was met with silent refusal. Faithie climbed down into the hole, picked the baby up, and handed her up to me.

"She's all full of ants, Mom," she said.

I saw that this was true. There were biting ants all over the little body. The raw area of her dangling navel cord was eaten badly and bleeding. One of her ears was badly eaten also.

"Oh God, please not her eyes," I prayed.

I had seen chickens, which had fallen off the roost at night and slept on the floor, blinded by these vicious little ants.

The baby's eyes were tightly closed, so I could not tell. The important thing now, I realized, was to get her home out of the cold and wet and to take care of her.

"Run home quickly," I told Faithie, "and tell Dad to heat some water so we can take care of her as soon as I get home." Faith ran down the trail the way we had come.

The women and I had not gone far down the trail when we came to a fallen log that I had to clamber across. To climb over, I had to lay the baby face down across one arm to allow freedom of my other hand and arm. As I glanced down at the baby's little back and head, I was alarmed to see the knot of a vine sticking up out of the folds of skin in her little fat neck. I called a halt to investigate. All the women gathered around me. Together we found the vine that had been knotted around the little neck and removed it.

With her breath restored, the baby gave a weak protesting gasp and started to cry. We realized then that the mother had tried to strangle the little thing and then had thrown it in the hole for dead. Only the cruel ants eating on her defenseless body had roused her from her stupor and given her the strength to cry out in spite of the vine choking her. This had given her enough air to survive.

When we got her to the house, I immediately went to work, giving her a warm bath and treating the open bleeding wounds where the ants had eaten. One ear lobe was eaten off. Her stomach, back, and face were badly bitten. I gently pried open her eyes and was relieved to find that they looked fine. We had to give the poor little thing a penicillin shot to ward off infection and some baby aspirin for the pain. A bottle of warm milk quieted her down and put her to sleep.

Joe then went up to the house where the parents of the baby were staying. The mother lay there in her hammock by the open fire just as though she had not just given birth to a beautiful little baby girl and then tried to destroy it.

Joe walked up to her hammock. "Your baby is alive," he said. "She is in my house. We have cleaned her up, and she is sleeping. If you want your baby, come to my house and get her."

She angrily turned her back to the wall and did not answer. The father lay there in silence. It was obvious that as far as they were concerned, their baby was dead and if we had a living baby now, that was our problem.

We got very little sleep for the next couple of weeks. The ants had crawled into her ears and nose. She sneezed out pus and ants for days. Her throat was so sore from being strangled by the vine that she became unable to cry. Her distress was shown in a tightly screwed up face and open mouth from which emitted tiny mews like a kitten. We were afraid to put her down and leave her—afraid that she would just quit breathing. We took turns walking the floor with her and whispering or singing softly in her ear. Finally the worst was over, and we felt that she would make it.

When the word got out via radio concerning the little discarded baby, a missionary couple in Tamatama who were unable to have children of their own called in and begged us to let them adopt her. We had been praying about her future. Despite of the fact that we had already fallen in love with her, we wondered if it would be wise to raise her in the village with her own people. Would we be able to teach her, train her, and discipline her in a society that would eventually feel that she was theirs? Also, we had nine children of our own. Tom and Lila had none. Could we be selfish with this lovely little girl who would be the apple of their eyes? No, we felt that we could not. So we turned her over into their loving care, and she became their lovely daughter, Jenny.

Years later we were living and working in another village, where a baby boy was unwanted by his unwed mother. She planned to abort him or kill him at birth, but the Ye'cuana medic there asked her to go ahead and have the child. He told her that he and his wife would take the child as their own. When the woman went into labor, the medic took her to the dispensary to keep a check on her. Just before the baby was born, she went outdoors, squatted down beside a small gully, gave birth to the baby and the placenta, and then took her foot and pushed the baby down into the gully.

The medic and his wife seeing what was happening, ran outside, retrieved the baby, and scolded the mother.

"I felt sorry for you," he said. "I had planned that if later you repented of your decision to give your baby away to me, I was going to give him back to you. But now I will never give him back. You don't deserve this little baby," he said.

A few days later they went off to attend their Ye'cuana Bible Conference being held in the village of Aacanana, taking along the newborn child.

When they arrived, they walked up the path lined on both sides by all those people attending the conference, who stood in a long line to greet and give an abraso (hug) to all visitors coming in. When the Ye'cuana medic, Juan Gonzales, came to Tom and Lila, he placed the baby in Lila's willing arms.

"Take him and raise him as your own," he said.

After they caught their breath, Tom and Lila thanked Juan for this wonderful surprise of receiving the little "Tommy" they could not otherwise have known.

Jerald Wayne, our tenth and last child, was born on January 28, 1966. He also was born in Puerto Ayacucho. Joe had stayed in the village, keeping the rest of the children. I went to Puerto Ayacucho on the supply boat by myself.

I flew back to Las Esmeraldas by MAF (Missionary Aviation Fellowship) plane with baby Jerald. The plane was a new addition to our field. I admit I got into that little plane with my new baby with my heart in my throat. But we had an uneventful flight to the grassland at Las Esmeraldas. There were no other interior airstrips at the time.

Joe met me there in a boat with the other children. Darkness came upon us before we had gone very far upriver. Joe had come prepared. We pulled onto a sand bar and soon had a cozy fire going. We cooked our supper, ate, and just rejoiced in the Lord and in the fact that we were all together again. We were soon sleepily bedded down on the warm sand. We pulled our blankets tightly around ourselves and went to sleep. Myriads of stars twinkled brightly in the sky overhead. God was in His heaven and all was right with my world.

23

RAISING TEN KIDS

As you can imagine, with ten children growing up in our house and a tribe of Yanomamö at our doorstep, we didn't suffer from boredom. With all those children to raise at the "back of nowhere," far from a doctor or emergency room, we spent some anxious moments. We found the Lord sufficient for all of them.

I remember when Sharon was about three years old and tried to follow her bigger sister, Susan, who was walking across a large log that had fallen a couple of feet off the ground. About half-way across, Sharon lost her balance and fell down into a prickly pineapple patch, which we had planted there. Worst of all, she fell into a large nest of biting ants. Hearing her screams and Susan's cries, we dashed out to rescue and soothe her.

I remember when a large poisonous spider ran out and bit Mike on his big toe. He ran screaming into the house and put me in a panic. Joe was not there at the time. I cleaned Mike's toe off with alcohol. By this time, all the kids were crying in sympathy and fear. We knew poisonous spider bites could be very bad.

I gathered them around me and told them, "Look at me. Dad's not here, and I don't really have anything for a spider bite. But the Lord's right here with us. He can take care of a spider bite without any medicine. Let's ask him to do it."

With that we bowed our heads and prayed. In a little while, Mike's toe quit hurting and never gave him another minute of trouble.

When Joey was just a little fellow of about three years, he saw the other kids picking flowers for me for Mother's Day. He also wanted to present Mom with a beautiful flower. Looking up on a bush beside him, he saw what he thought was a beautiful white flower. He reached up his little hand, grabbed it, and pulled it off the bush. His screams of pain filled the air. We ran to find him still holding the "flower" in his tightly clenched hand. He had pulled off a caterpillar that had long white hair. The long white hair that he had mistaken for a flower was in reality the caterpillar's protection. The hair gives a terrible sting that pains for many hours. We finally got him to sleep with his hand on a hot water bottle. How our hearts went out in pity to the little fellow who only wanted to give Mom a Mother's Day present. We were reminded again of the verse in Psalm 103:13: "Like as a father pitieth his children, so the Lord pities them that fear Him."

Once during a rainy season, when water stood in every hole around, the pit where the men had been making mud blocks for some houses was full to the top with water. An old cut-off half-barrel floated on top. Velma and Faithie, thinking this would make a fine boat, had crawled in. They were paddling with glee in the large hole of water. Seeing their dad coming out of the house, they remembered he had told them to stay away from the hole because one of the smaller kids might fall in. They paddled hastily to the edge of the hole and hopped out. In the rush to get on land, Velma gave herself a nasty cut on her foot on the jagged side of the rusty old barrel. Joe had to give her a tetanus shot.

Then there was the time when Jerald was about twelve and we were in Tamatama for one of our field conferences. He and one of his friends were out on the river in a boat with an outboard motor. He was thrown into the water and received a nasty deep cut on his arm which laid it wide open. With that bad, bleeding arm he swam to shore. One of the missionaries stitched up his arm, and it finally healed. Truly the Lord takes good care of us!

On another occasion, we had taken our old, leaky, palm roof off and had replaced it with new palm. Some of the old palm was still lying on the ground. Sandy and a couple of her little Yanomamö friends hooked arms together and skipped merrily around, singing. Somehow, Sandy hit one of the old, brittle, palm fronds just right, and a large sliver drove into one side of her foot, just under the anklebone and almost out the other side. She hobbled and cried into the house. At the time, Joe was away at another village. The kids and I were alone. I panicked.

Steve, who was a teenager at the time, said, "Mom, we've got to get that sliver out before her foot swells too big to get it. Then she has to have a penicillin shot," he told me.

I had never given one of my own children a penicillin injection before. I didn't know if I could do it.

Then the Lord took over. There's no one else here to do it but me. I have to be strong for Sandy's sake, I kept telling myself.

Steve was braver than I was. With a sterile razor blade, he cut the skin where we could see the bulge of the sliver. Then with tweezers he managed to pull out a long piece of it. (We thought we had it all, but for months afterwards small pieces continued to work out of the skin where the sliver had come out.)

I braced myself and gave her a penicillin injection as though I had perfect confidence in myself and had been doing it for years. In reality, my insides were mush. Joe returned the following day and took over the injections, for which I was grateful.

Even on furlough in the United States the kids kept us on our toes. In addition to Sandy drinking kerosene, which I mentioned earlier, we had another scare. When Susan was about three years old, she ran her arm through the clothes wringer on an old washing machine we had. By the time I got to her, hit the mechanism to release the pressure on the rollers, turned the machine off, and retrieved her arm from the wringer, she had a large injury on her small forearm where the rollers had bounced up and down on it. I was all by myself, out in the country, without a vehicle or a phone. Joe was in Williamsport, Pennsylvania, speaking at a missionary conference. I didn't know how badly her arm was injured, but all I could do was to doctor it the best I knew how and call on the Lord to do what I was unable to do. By the time Joe came home, her arm seemed to be doing so well that she never did see a doctor. She still has a scar, but it never gave her trouble. The Lord is so good!

The children could get into trouble on their own too. When Faithie was about four years old, she set our palm roof on fire. At that time, we didn't have electricity. We didn't even have a Coleman lantern. We had kerosene flares, which we used at night for light. I cooked on a fire table that Joe had built against one of our walls. He had built a wooden box with legs and filled it full of red clay. On this I built my wood fires and cooked my meals, using a three-legged metal stand to set my pots on.

We had left the flare upstairs. Faithie, who was up there swinging in a hammock, saw the flare and lit it. Then, not knowing how to put it out again, she became frightened at what she had done and pushed it out of sight behind the mosquito netting that we had tacked against the palm ends of the little house. She was too young to realize that the flare could set the netting on fire. She was blithely swinging in the hammock when someone outside began yelling, "Fire! Fire!"

We dashed out to see what the commotion was all about. Seeing smoke coming out of the palm roof at the end of the house, Joe ran upstairs. He grabbed the flare and blew it out. Then he yanked the burning netting down and put out the smoldering flames in the palm. He was able to get back outside in time to stop the men who were just about to start hacking at our palm roof. We had a long talk with all the kids on the dangers of playing with burning flares or fires of any kind.

Then there were the things kids do when you're not around and you don't find out about until later when they're telling the story to someone—things they knew better than to tell at the times they happened. It's just as well. I would've been gray much sooner.

One such event occurred as Joey and Jerald were returning home for a break from the school in Tamatama. They stopped at an island on the way upriver. There they discovered a huge anaconda snake asleep at the base of a high rock.

Feeling extra adventurous, they decided to kill that snake and take it to the village, where the people would have a feast.

"You get a big rock and climb up there and drop it on the snake's head. When he wakes up and lifts up his head, I'll hit him in the head with this paddle," Joey told Jerald.

So, taking the largest rock that he was able to carry, Jerald clambered to the top of the rock.

"Let it go," Joey hissed with a wave of his hand. Jerald let go of the rock, which dropped with a thud on the sleeping snake. The snake didn't even move a muscle but slept right on.

Joey motioned for Jerald to descend. "You didn't drop it hard enough," he complained. "Here, you hit him with the paddle when he lifts his head. I'll drop the rock. I'll get a bigger one."

When the second rock hit with a big thud, the snake slowly started to uncoil and raise its head. When Jerald, who was standing by nervously with the paddle, saw the huge head and snake eyes looking at him, he forgot about using the paddle and ran off toward the boat as fast as his legs could carry him. After a breathless Joey caught up with him at the boat and they were safely out in the river again, they laughed together uproariously over how frightened they had been when the snake woke up.

Years later, when I finally heard the story, I said, "I'm amazed that I raised any of you. It's just the goodness of the Lord that any of you survived."

24

Gary's Fall

We returned from our second furlough on September 29, 1967. We had spent a good fifteen months living out in the country in Linden, Virginia. The only hard thing had been the cold winter in a board house that was not insulated against the cold blasts that blew against our house on a hill.

Some of the children had never even seen snow, so the feathery, white flakes sifting down fascinated them. They begged to play outside and were soon sliding down the hill on old plastic garbage can lids and making snowmen in the front yard. However, not being suitably clothed and not being used to cold weather, they continually ran back inside to warm up and to dry wet mittens before running out again.

Now back in Venezuela, our school-age children would spend nine months in the mission school in Tamatama. Joe planned to continue the village work from there. When the children had a ten-day break, we made a trip to Coshilowateli. While there we discovered that during our absence the village of Coshilowa-teli had split into two factions; one group was now living up the Metaconi River.

Bautista was very concerned for his people and grieved about the split and the toll it was taking on the young church. He asked if Gary could use the small three-horsepower motor that we owned and take him up the Metaconi. He wanted to talk with those who had moved and try to restore peace. Gary, sixteen years of age, had a real rapport with the people. Bautista felt that Gary would be able to talk with them from the Word of God and heal the breach.

On the way up the Metaconi River, they saw some monkeys in the trees, so they quickly tied up to the bank and started in pursuit, hoping to have a couple of monkeys to give the group and thus soften their feelings toward the whole situation.

"If we can take them some meat, they will at least listen to us," Bautista told Gary.

As the men chased them, the monkeys darted from tree to tree, moving farther and farther up the mountain. Finally, Gary was able to shoot one in the top of a large tree. In falling, the monkey lodged on one of the branches. Gary climbed the tree to shake the monkey off the branch and down to the ground. He did not realize that something had eaten into the limb on which he was standing. As he shook the tree, his weight and the swaying of the tree caused the defect to give way and the limb broke, dropping him from the top of the very tall tree.

As the darkness began to recede, Gary realized that Bautista was rubbing his hand over his face and weeping freely. When he fully regained consciousness, he was able to estimate the damage he had done to himself. He found that he had a compound fracture of the right ankle and had lost a lot of blood. He had broken his right arm near the wrist. Some ribs were broken and his back was hurting abominably. They knew it was impossible for Gary to get himself back to the river again on his own power.

Bautista is a very small man. Gary, even at sixteen, was bigger and taller than he was.

"Leave me here, and go for my Dad," Gary begged.

But Bautista was adamant. He knew that the blood and someone in a helpless condition would soon draw a jaguar or some other predator to the scene. Gary would be helpless, maybe even unconscious, at the time. He refused to leave Gary behind. He cut a trail as far away as he could still see Gary. Then he returned, hoisted Gary onto his back, and carried Gary to the end of the trail he had made. Then he began the process all over again. The pain of being repeatedly lifted and carried was excruciating for Gary because of his broken bones. Finally they reached the river where the boat was tied.

Then they had another problem. Bautista knew nothing of starting a motor. Gary could not start the motor for him. The canoe was so small that it would start to fill up and would eventually sink if both men were back by the motor.

Therefore, Bautista paddled all the way back to Coshilowateli. The accident occurred about 9:30 in the morning. They arrived at the port in Cosh at 2:30 in the afternoon. Hearing the news, we rushed to the river. We were horrified to see all the blood in the boat, to learn of Gary's condition, and to see his white face.

We gave such first aid as we could. We tried to call the MAF plane to tell them we had an emergency and to ask them to fly in and take Gary out to the hospital in Puerto Ayacucho. We found out to our dismay that the plane could not be contacted. It was in Ciudad Bolivar for an inspection. In those days there were no small commercial planes.

Immediately, Joe started downriver in his boat and outboard motor with Gary lying on a mattress on the floor.

They stopped in Tamatama where the mission nurse, Freda Toews, worked on his arm, putting splints and a sling on it. She did what she could for his fractured ankle and gave him medicine for pain.

With someone to drive the motor and a helper along, Joe was able to sit by Gary and minister to his needs. He thought more than once on the long trip downriver that Gary was gone. He cried and begged the Lord over and over to spare Gary's life. The Lord was gracious and heard his prayers.

Gary arrived very weak and in bad condition, but—praise the goodness of our Lord—he made it through the ordeal. He had a staph infection in his ankle and had to be taken to the States where it was nursed and operated on. Finally he healed. His arm, which had healed crooked, was corrected in surgery and reset. He spent many months in the States with his Uncle Wes and Aunt Sylvia as he recuperated from his operations.

Several years later we found that he had three crushed vertebrae in his spine and was developing a large lump on the side of his back where his muscle had enlarged, trying to compensate. He returned to the States for a back operation.

The Lord had preserved his life to use him in reaching Yanomamö for Himself.

25

He Has a Tail

M any interesting and unusual things have happened through the years. To tell them all would be impossible.

I remember one man whose name in Yanomamö was "He Has A Tail." People said that he was a little slow in his mind because he had almost died as a young man when someone hit the back of his head with a war club. They said that he had lain unconscious for days and that when he awoke he was not completely himself.

In those early days, meat and food were hard for us to get. Everything we bought had to survive the long supply boat trip from Puerto Ayacucho to Tamatama. Then, another trip was made up the Orinoco River and another up the Padamo River to get our supplies to us. We supplemented this with food from the gardens of the Yanomamö. We exchanged trade goods we had bought in Puerto Ayacucho for the Indians' food.

Since the only meat we could get was that from the Yanomamö people, we bought bush knives called machetes to exchange for meat. The Yanomamö greatly desired the machetes that they could obtain only from the outside world. They didn't give meat willingly. Since they're a warring people, they didn't like to hunt far from home, so meat was so hard to come by. They preferred to eat it themselves.

This one time in particular, Joe had purchased twelve machetes and told them that he was willing to exchange them for meat. At first the tribesmen tried to get the knives by working or by exchanging them for large stalks of plantains, but Joe refused to be swayed by this ploy.

"No," he insisted. "I'll only give them in exchange for meat for my family. My family needs meat to survive," he said.

The man named "He Has A Tail" tried his luck in talking Joe out of a machete.

"Bring me some meat, and I'll greatly delight to give you a machete!" Joe replied.

A couple of hours later, the man returned, shoving inside our front door and carrying two huge stalks of plantains on his back. He shook himself and shrugged his burden off onto our floor, where they lay dripping the sap from their newly cut stalks onto our tamped earth floor.

"Now, give me my machete," he said with a big grin, thinking to disarm Joe in this friendly fashion.

"No. I already told you. I want meat for a machete," Joe insisted. "I'll give you fish line and fishhooks or some red cloth for those plantains. But I won't give a machete without meat," he said.

At those words, He Has A Tail became so angry that he grabbed up the ugly little piece of metal with no handle that he used as a machete and ran out the door. He had tied a rag around the metal to protect his hand. In his rage he left the two stalks of plantains lying on the floor. Outside the house he ran back and forth in great anger, brandishing his makeshift machete and daring Joe to come out or to stick his head out the door so he could cut it off.

We weren't sure, but we were afraid that he meant every word he said. Joe didn't go out or stick his head out the door. Later, when his anger was spent, He Has A Tail came back and received pay for his plantains and was happy with it. Then he killed some wild game, brought Joe the long-awaited piece of meat, and happily received a shiny new machete.

This man eventually became a believer and remained faithful to his Lord until his death as an old man. His Christian name was Alejandro. The name He Has A Tail faded out of use and was heard no more.

At every meeting old Alejandro would rise to his feet to give a testimony of how the Lord had saved him and how happy he was. He always said that he was looking forward to getting to God's beautiful land where he would sit under the tree of life and eat of its fruit.

He was recuperating from malaria when the flood hit the village of Coshilowa-teli in June of '96. The Yanomamö fled to the higher ground across the river. The rigors of the move and the harsh dampness of the jungle was too much for his weakened condition, and Old Alejandro passed away to be with the Lord he had faithfully served.

I greatly miss this old man because he had become such a good friend to Joe and me. Whenever we were expected to return to the village after a trip away, even if our trip was just a very short time, Alejandro met us at the plane and hugged us.

"Are you back?" he would ask, and we knew he was truly glad we were.

Another event also stands out in my mind: the time a little girl was badly burned. One of the girls who was nine or ten years of age was boiling a stolen chicken egg in a tin can of water over a hastily built fire. She had on her sister-in-law's dress. It was, of course, too long for her and dragged on the ground. Suddenly the long skirt burst into flames. Fire quickly engulfed her whole body.

She screamed and began to run when suddenly the words of a story in her little school primer book came to her mind.

"Never run when your clothes are on fire. Lay on the ground and roll."

She flung herself to the ground and rolled in the dirt, screaming at the top of her lungs. This quick action saved her from being burned beyond help. By the time they had gotten the fire put out, she already had second- and third-degree burns on the left side of her body.

That happened in the days before we had planes or radios. The only medical help that little Cosilemi received came from us. Every day we cleaned her burns and applied gauze covered with petroleum jelly over all the burned areas. When the gauze was all used up, I tore my white sheets for bandages. When we had no more petroleum jelly, we had to use our cooking grease, which was actually hard grease made from coconut oil. This kept the bandages from sticking and opening up the wounds again.

Cosilemi's mother and father had both died years before. She lived with an older brother and his wife Dimiyoma. Early every morning they brought her to our house, where she lay on a bench that I had fixed up for her in our front room. We fed her and gave her water when she was thirsty and doctored her burns every day. She lay there all day long, patiently waiting for her brother and sister-in-law to return in the evening from the forest or garden or wherever they had gone for the day. I don't remember hearing her complain, even though it was surely not a pleasant time for her. The burned places gradually healed and the raw open places became smaller.

After many long wearisome months, her burns healed, and she had only the scars left to show the ordeal she had gone through. Now she's a fine Christian woman here in the village of Coshilowateli. She's the wife of Ramon Rivas. Her name is Linda.

Many funny things happened during the years also. I remember one occasion when our daughter Sandy taught a Sunday school class of Yanomamö children. They began to ask her about the Scriptures concerning the End Times, which they had heard discussed in church. So Sandy began to tell them that Jesus said there would be "wars and rumors of wars . . . and earthquakes in divers places" and then the end will come (Matt. 24:6–7).

One day not too long after that lesson, war broke out here in Cosh as another village arrived to raid our group. They were angry at Cosh because they had accepted the Word of God and turned to the God of the Bible, leaving the teaching of spirits and shamanism.

As the fighting escalated, Sandy tried to comfort some of the children who had run for safety into one of the houses. Timoteo, just a little fellow at that time, looked at Sandy with big frightened eyes and said, "Yes, Sandy, it's just like the Bible says: Today we're having wars and rumors of wars, and tomorrow we'll probably have an earthquake."

In spite of the gravity of the situation, we could not help but laugh at the little fellow's logic.

26

OUR YEAR AT BISAASA-TELI

In 1970, the mission leaders asked us to move to the village of Bisaasa-teli located at the mouth of the Mavaca River where the Mavaca flows into the Orinoco River. The missionaries there had left for furlough, and the mission would probably have to close the base unless we "held it down" during their absence. We moved there to spend a year.

These Yanomamö of Bisaasa-teli had heard the gospel presented for a number of years but had never really committed themselves to following Christ. Some professed faith, but whether they possessed Christ or not was questionable. They still clung to their old ways. They appeared more interested in possessions than in the Word of God.

We began literacy and Bible classes with them on our arrival in their village. Many of the villagers attended our classes and meetings. One problem we had in that area was the presence of anthropologists who talked against our message and us when we weren't around.

The Yanomamö told us that they were telling the people that there is no God, that the God we proclaim does not exist, and that it did not matter what we said. The people said the anthropologists told them to continue living as Yanomamö in the way their forefathers had always lived. They were in no way to change any of their Yanomamö culture, because the foreigners were just trying to frighten them with tales of hellfire, so that they, the foreigners, would be accepted with their message.

The anthropologists said, "No such place as hell exists, so you need not fear."

Some of the Yanomamö who traveled with these anthropologists said they were warned. If they attended our meetings, they would not be allowed to go along anymore and would find no friendship and no more possessions from the researchers. Since the anthropologists were very liberal with their trade goods to those they catered to, this was a dire threat as far as the Yanomamö were concerned.

To help with the evangelization of these people and villages close by, we had brought Bautista over from Coshilowa-teli. He lived with us for a time, and helped us greatly in presenting the Word of God. He was a living testimony of what the Word of God could do in a Yanomamö life.

At this time he still had no wife, so it was easy for him to travel around unhampered. He was still single due not to his youth but to an earlier adulterous affair with his uncle's wife. His uncle was a fierce warrior who often led the group on war parties. During his absence, Bautista would have his uncle's wife for himself. Because of this adulterous union, all of his garden produce and all of the meat he hunted went to that family. He was not good son-in-law material since he had nothing left to offer to in-laws. However, he seemed satisfied with this arrangement and was content to have his uncle's wife during the times of his absence.

Content that is until he heard the message of salvation through the blood of Jesus Christ. He put his trust in Christ to save him. Then his troubles with his conscience began. Before too long he had to confess and forsake this sin, realizing that to continue therein would be displeasing to the Lord who had saved him. By then there were no other girls available for him to marry in his village. He remained single, and the Lord used him mightily in proclaiming the Word to the Yanomamö people.

One day our girls came running excitedly into the house.

"Mom," said one, "they're making the visitor's call in the shabono. A visitor must have arrived. Can we run over and peep through the back wall to see who it is?" Permission granted, they ran off excitedly.

The shabono of the Yanomamö, who are a warring people, is encircled by pieces of standing wood layered thickly for protection from enemy arrows of warriors who might sneak up from behind and shoot them. This wood also serves for firewood, but it is constantly replenished lest it grow thin in spots and not afford proper protection.

The girls came running back to the house.

"Mom," one cried, "it's the anthropologist. He came prancing into the village like a visitor."

"He has on only a red bathing suit, and he is all decorated up like a Yanomamö," cried another.

"He has a monkey tail around his head and arm bands with feathers dangling down like the Yanomamö always wear," Sharon finished up breathlessly.

Why would he be doing that? I wondered. But many things they did made little sense to me, so I was not too concerned about it.

"But, Mom . . . that's not all," they squealed.

"He's going to take dope and do witchcraft," said one.

"He was getting all ready to do it when he saw us peeking through the wood piled up in the back," cried another.

"He glared at us and said in Yanomamö, 'Foreign girls go home! Foreign girls go home!'" Susan said.

"He looked so mean that we were scared and ran," said Sandy.

"Well, you did the right thing by running home," I said. "Stay away from the village. You don't want to be around where they're taking dope and doing witchcraft."

Glancing out the window, I saw the women villagers streaming out with their pack baskets on their backs. The baskets were piled high with their hammocks and some of their other possessions. I went outside to speak with them as they approached my house, grumbling to themselves and each other.

"Where are you all going?" I asked. "Are you moving out to the jungle for a while?"

"No," they replied. "We are just protecting our possessions from that foreigner who's taking dope and invoking the spirits. He'll surely be crazed with dope and demons and tear up our shabono," they said tearfully. "Can we leave our baskets here in your house until he's sane again?" they asked.

For answer I opened the door and watched them tromp into the house and set their pack baskets down. They gathered around me for a little chat.

Some of the villagers told us later that the anthropologist had told the captain of the village, a man by the name of Kaobawa, that there is no God to fear. He told him that it was not wrong to take dope and invoke the spirits. To prove it, he said that he himself was going to do it then and there, which he preceded to do.

Joe, Steve, Gary, and Bautista were working on an outboard motor at the river. So the girls along with our two youngest, Joey and Jerald, ran downhill to the river to tell them what was happening.

When Bautista heard what they were doing in the village, he and Gary walked back up the hill and entered at the village opening. The anthropologist, deep into the drug, pranced around shuffling back and forth as they entered and approached the dope takers. He didn't notice them observing him. After a few minutes Bautista said, "Come on, let's go. I'm unwilling to stand here and watch that foreigner make a fool of himself!"

So they went back down to the river, where they told Joe what they had seen.

Joe walked up the hill from the river to observe for himself just what was happening. He entered the shabono. The anthropologist was prancing and dancing and throwing himself into a stance with arms outstretched in front of him and yelling, "Wa-a-a!" Just as Joe walked up to him, the man turned.

Facing Joe and standing with arms outstretched, he yelled "Wa-a-a!" right at Joe. He hadn't expected to look into Joe's face. Joe jumped back at him, imitating his stance and yelling, "Wa-a-a!" right back at him. The man became so unnerved that he walked to and sat on a log.

Joe pulled his eye down at him in the manner of a Yanomamö insult. Then he turned and walked out of the shabono, leaving a shaken anthropologist yelling after him.

We lived in that village for a year but did not see many results for the Lord, even though many children came to our school classes and many adults came to hear the Word of God taught. It was as though they could not open their hearts to receive the Word of God, which would have set them free.

Years later, from time to time many of them came to Coshilowa-teli to visit or just pass by on their way upriver. They told us many sad tales of so many we had known who had gone into eternity.

"We know now that we should've listened when you told us about the Great Spirit," many of they admitted.

"If we had listened then, we might still be a big village instead of almost completely gone," lamented others.

It reminded us of Agrippa's words to the Apostle Paul, "Almost thou persuaded me to be a Christian." To be "almost persuaded" is not enough. Faith in the Supreme Being—Almighty God—and His Son Jesus is what it takes to save a soul.

27

LIVING ON A HOUSEBOAT

After our third furlough we returned to Coshilowa-teli in 1973. This time we lived in a houseboat that Joe, Steve, and Gary had built, which we named "La Mensajera" (The Messenger)

Another missionary—an Englishman, who knew what he was about—had built the fifty-five-foot hull. He built it for hauling supplies for the mission, but by the time it was finished, they had decided to go with a commercial merchant who had established a business hauling supplies upriver.

We bought the hull. We wanted a houseboat so we could travel and take the Word of God to many villages along the river. We were asked to accept an itinerant ministry working on the Orinoco, Mavaca, Manavichi and Padamo Rivers. We had hoped that this would take us into contact with more than twenty villages.

However, at that time in our lives, the Lord had other plans for us. We became involved in the Yanomamö translation of the New Testament and worked on that for the next ten years. The houseboat made a perfect place to work with Bautista, away from the noise and uproar of the village life. We spent seven years living on this houseboat and many are the tales that could be told.

One that our kids love to tell on me is not really a favorite of mine. It was the time I decided that the frame built on the back of the houseboat, where an outboard motor was mounted, would be the ideal place to hang onto while getting some much needed exercise in the water. After I had gotten into the water and kicked and splashed and had a great time, I finally decided I had had enough and would get back up on the wooden frame. To my chagrin I was unable to hoist myself far enough to get onto the frame. There I hung, kicking my legs out behind me and wondering how on earth I had gotten myself into such a position.

Finally I called out to the kids on the boat. "Go call your Dad," I said, "so he can help me get back in the boat."

"Just put your feet down, Mom," one of them called down over the side of the boat. "You can stand up there."

"My feet are down," I replied, "and no, I can't touch the bottom. Go get your Dad."

They just kept laughing and assuring me that if I would just put my feet down, I would be able to stand.

I became more agitated all the time as my arms ached and my hopes of getting Joe to rescue me grew dim. Finally in exasperation I yelled up at their grinning faces, "Just don't bother to call your father; I've already drown."

I guess my desperation finally got through. They ran off and brought Joe, who also spent time chuckling about my predicament, Finally he came down to the board frame and hauled me up. I crawled back into the houseboat, and that was the last of my exercises.

However, it has been a standing joke in our family ever since. Someone just has to say, "Don't bother to call your father; I've already drown," and everyone goes off into peals of laughter. They also have one they tell on Joe. It was April 1st. We had been busy on the houseboat that morning. Joe was up on the bank where he had just pushed off the boat and retied it. He was talking to some of the Yanomamö.

Velma suddenly had a brainstorm. "Mom, I'm going to April Fool Dad," she said. "I'm going to run out and tell him that you fell in the river and are floating down the river. Then, when he comes running, I'll yell, 'April Fool!'"

"He'll never believe you," I laughed. "He'll know that if I fell in the river, you all would jump in and help me," I said, but she ran to the front of the boat, shouting.

"Dad! Dad! Mom just fell overboard, and she's floating off downriver."

All the other kids were standing by to see what would happen. They were shocked to see their dad wheel around and tear down the bank to the houseboat. He was in such a hurry that he tripped over the rope he had just tied up and rolled down the bank.

"Dad! Dad!" Velma screamed again. "April Fool!"

"I'll forgive you this time," her dad said after he had untangled himself and gotten to his feet, grinning sheepishly," But don't ever do that to me again!"

And to this day April Fool pranks have never been played in our house again.

28

TRANSLATION WORK

I n 1975, the month of January found us at the mission base in Sierra Parima spending time with the Jank family who worked there. We were there for a get-together with other Yanomamö workers to discuss the translation that we had been checking and redoing.

We had our language consultant, Bautista (who had also become known as Mamicö Zapatowä or Shoefoot because he had taken to always wearing shoes) and his young wife, Marilu, with us. At first Marilu didn't like any of our food except bread. By the time we left from there she was eating margarine on her bread, oatmeal with milk, rice, and macaroni. We spent a profitable time with Bautista and another Yanomamö from the Parima village, who helped out in comparing the difference in the dialect.

Then, on February 3rd, our son Mike and Franny Cochran left for a trip up the Ocamo River. The boys, now graduated from high school, wanted to be a part of the Yanomamö work. They planned to spend almost a month there helping and encouraging the village of Wabutao-teli to make an airstrip. Word had come that the village had already started it on their own, so the boys wanted to check their progress and help where they could.

While we were in Parima, the Mensajera was tied up at Tamatama until our return. On our way back from Parima, we left Bautista and his wife at Coshilowa-teli. He was anxious to get his garden planted during the dry season. We found the river too low to risk taking the big boat back upriver, so we spent some time doing some needed repairs. We had one of the young men from Cosh, Joaquin, with us. He also served as a checker on the Scriptures we were working on at that time.

The Yanomamö who were living in Tamatama had moved downriver about thirty minutes away. While we were there working on repairs, our men started going down there to teach them from the Word of God. The head shaman made a profession of faith. Our hearts were thrilled as he prayed, "Lord, you know that I've thrown away my dope stick, my demons, and my anger. Now you help me keep them thrown away."

Mike and Franny came back from their trip up the Ocamo greatly encouraged. They had helped to complete the airstrip. The plane had landed, checked out the strip, and pronounced it good.

However, we were concerned. Mike had returned with his left arm swollen to about three times its normal size from the shoulder to the fingertips. We didn't know whether he had been bitten by something or if something else had caused his trouble.

The Yanomamö were anything but encouraging as they kept telling us tales of others who had developed this malady and had not recovered. Still, we prayed and did all we knew to do. Gradually the swelling went down and Mike was fine. We praised the Lord again for His goodness to us.

Now the village of Wabutao is no more. Most of them have died out from warring and from Falciparum malaria. We were never able to take advantage of this airstrip, so we never got in to them with the good news of salvation through Christ.

Individuals who came out and visited our village from time to time heard the gospel but received little teaching, so we don't know if any came to know Christ or not.

Our efforts to reopen this airstrip and get a work going there were thwarted, opposed by those seeking to keep the gospel from the tribal people, so these ones for whom Christ died are now gone out into the Christ-less eternity. Many of them had never heard the gospel. None had been really taught in His Word!

In November of 1976, we were at a Translator's Conference in Puerto Ayacucho. We had left Gary, his wife, Marie, and our girls to hold down the fort in Coshilowa-teli. While in Puerto Ayacucho we received this letter from Sandy. You can see the anguish of her heart as she doctored the people in our absence. She wrote:

> Bautista prayed this prayer as he knelt by the hammock of his little niece: "Father, you can make this little child that I call mine well. But, Father, you do what You want to do, because we don't know what could happen but You do. And Father, you do what You know is best. And give me the courage and strength to take it."

Dear Pop and Mom,

I stood by the hammock where little Jenny was lying in her mother's arms, her body racked with fever and pain, gasping for breath. As I listened to Bautista pray, let me tell you I found it hard to believe that just a week ago Jenny had been well, following her brother Timoteo all over the village. Or down by our houseboat calling to Sharon or me to give her some candy. Could it really be true?

Was it just Sunday afternoon that her mother had brought her down burning with fever and vomiting? I started her on the malaria medicine right away, but it hadn't seemed to touch the sickness. The second day they came running down and called me. Well, we went up and she was burning with fever. She had a temperature of 105.3 and after that she did not act right. She just lay in the hammock sort of semi-conscious, not really knowing anybody at all. Nothing we did altered her condition. Now it was the sixth day and she did not look good at all.

Night after night Sharon, Paula, and I had gotten up at midnight to check on her and give her medicine for pain and fever, but it just didn't seem to help.

After Bautista finished praying she seemed to quiet down a little bit, so Sharon and I went on around to the other houses to give medicine to the rest of the sick people. While we were busy washing an old Sejal-teli man down to relieve his fever Timoteo walked into the house. When he saw we were busy he didn't say anything, just went on back outside.

When Sharon and I got back home Marie told us that Timoteo had been looking for us, so we went running up to see Jenny again. I knew there was nothing I could do and man, I felt sick! After worrying day and night with the little kids it really breaks me up to see them lying there dying, knowing that there isn't a single thing I can do to help them. . . .

She was in convulsions and we started working with her to try and bring her out of the convulsion. We were there for about three hours. It was 12 o'clock when we got home, but at 1 o'clock they came down calling for me again, so we took off running for their house, but as we walked through the door, they started to wail! Boy, one of the saddest sounds I have ever heard is the Yanomamö death wail. And I don't think I can stand much more. It tears you all to pieces watching these people die. I feel so helpless knowing there isn't a thing I can do! It makes me wonder who's gonna be next. . . .

Three people have died since you all left. Maria's little girl, Bautista's sister's little boy from Jalulusi-teli and now Jenny. The Yanomamö here are really getting scared of the malaria, so pray for them.

Love, Sandy

29

JOAQUIN

Much heartache goes along with the work of living with a group of people, becoming their friends, and becoming involved in all the things that concern their lives. February of 1977 found us facing one of those hard times.

We first met Joaquin when he was a little boy of ten or eleven years old. He grew up with our boys and seemed almost like one of the family. Joaquin was one of our dear friends, so it is really hard to believe he won't be dropping by to sit and chat with a big smile on his face. He was sick only three days, but he could not stop vomiting. Nothing we did helped him. It was hard for us to believe he could go so quickly. Three days before he had been sitting on our steps, talking and laughing, and now his body was being placed on the fire to burn away to blackened bones.

Just before his death, he had called his father and mother to his hammock and said to them, "Father, Mother, I'm going on ahead to God's house. My Father God has already called to me, and I've answered for you to come on to God's house later. Teach my little brothers to serve God for I want to see them in heaven," he said.

"Older brother, I'm going home," he had told his cousin Ramon. "Don't get angry and upset and stop following Jesus. People will come from other villages when they hear of my death, and they will tell all of you many lies, but don't listen to them. Don't get upset by lying tales. Don't give my bones to them to carry off to other villages to drink," he said.

Joaquin's older brother Augusto was in Coyowa-teli with Gary. They had gone in to teach the people God's Word. It was so hard to call by radio and tell them of the death. The plane came bringing Augusto home. Everyone met the plane weeping, wailing, and carrying the basket containing his charred bones.

The next day as they all gathered around to grind the bones to powder, the unbelievers began telling the family to get something to put the bones in to keep them. They began talking wildly about how they would all go kill meat and hang plantains to ripen so that they could have a leajumou (a bone drinking feast). The Christians loudly protested this, saying that before Joaquin died he had said he didn't want this allowed.

The father's younger brother who had always been strong against the gospel sent his wife to get a can to put the bones in. The father started scooping up the bone powder and putting them into the can.

Finally Augusto walked over and took the can away from his father. Then he took the bones and went into his house. There he dug a hole under the spot where he had his nightly fire. After they had prayed, he poured the bones into the hole and covered them up. This was a terrific stand for him to take against his elders.

Just as Joaquin had said, there were those who came telling the family that they had found the tracks of people who had lain in wait and had blown on Joaquin to make him sick. They tried to get Augusto and Ramon and the others to go on a raid and kill someone in another village to avenge his death. The Lord wonderfully strengthened them, and they stood firm for the Lord. The father, Dino, and the mother accepted the Lord and began coming to all the meetings.

In this culture it is expected that when a son of this age dies, they will lay in their hammocks and be mad for months, hardly eating or drinking. However, they didn't do this. They went about their work as usual and even broke their taboo of not mentioning the dead, as they kept talking about what Joaquin had said before he died.

30

JAIL

One of the hardest things we have faced as a family in this work was Gary's arrest on false charges.

On April 11, 1982 on Easter Sunday, a day when we should be filled with joy and gladness, it was not to be so for us. Our family had just sat down to our Easter dinner when suddenly a plane buzzed the village. Right behind the first plane we heard the sound of another one buzzing the village. These sounds struck fear in my heart. A group of National Guards had been here several days before to investigate charges brought against Gary. It was being said that he was responsible for the death of a Yanomamö child who had been injured and died several years before. Everything had been explained to the Guards in detail. We thought it was all taken care of.

Both planes landed and the governor from Puerto Ayacucho got off with his comisionado, who was a Yanomamö go-between for the governor. National guards poured off the other plane with their big guns in their hands. They immediately circled our house with all those guns aimed right at us. I got a taste of what Christians in other lands are going through for their faith.

They asked for Octavio Silva and Bautista Perez. They walked across the village, entered Octavio's house, and shut the door. They would not allow anyone else to hear what was going on.

The captain of the police and captain of the national guards were here. They asked to see all of our identification papers and our permits to work here.

The captain of the guards saw me crying and said, "No lloras [Don't cry]." Then, in broken English, he said, "Are you crazy?"

I don't know if that is all the English he knew or if I truly thought that I had nothing to cry about.

He called Gary aside and said, "Do you understand Spanish? Do you know what I am saying?" When Gary answered yes, he said, "The military is behind you, but the governor is against you."

We were well aware of this, as the new governor had fought us ever since taking office.

One of the planes had returned to Esmeraldas and picked up several more people and returned to Cosh. We were surprised to see Julio Jimenez (the Julio mentioned in the beginning of my story). He came up and hugged us. He greeted us and asked us what the trouble was. We told him what the situation was. Then he walked on over to where the guards were all standing together.

About that time, everyone came out of Octavio's house. The governor called the captain of the guards. After talking to the governor, the captain went out and called his men together and stationed them strategically around the village. You would have thought we were a gang of hardened desperados armed to the teeth.

The governor then called Gary out and told him that he was taking him to Puerto Ayacucho to clear up the accusations against him. He did not tell Gary that he was under arrest, nor did he cite any charges against him, but somehow I knew in my heart that he was arresting Gary.

I had told Marie to have him a small bag packed just to be ready. We were thankful she had done so, as they barely gave Gary time to come in the house, get his bag, and say goodbye to his family.

Gary turned to Bautista, who stood nearby, hardly able to grasp what was transpiring. He said, "They're taking me, Bautista."

At this news Bautista became so overwrought that he shook all over. He turned to Octavio and said, "Keep out of our way, or we will strangle you with our bare hands."

Octavio just puffed himself up spitefully and said, "Kill me! Kill me!"

Faith and Sharon and I were crying along with Gary's whole family. When the Cosh villagers realized what was happening to him, they all began to wail and cry. It was certainly obvious to the guards and everyone else that the people loved Gary and didn't want to see any harm come to him.

They were all wailing, crying, and chanting about what they would do to Octavio when the guards left. Joe became concerned. He approached the governor and told him that he would be wise to station a couple of guards in Cosh for a time.

"The people here are very angry with Octavio and may try to hurt him. I may not be able to stop them if they get started. They may very easily harm him," he said.

The governor just turned away, but he did have the captain of the guards tell the two guards from Tamatama to stay in Cosh until further orders.

Marie went to the governor and told him that Gary was subject to severe allergy reactions and could become asphyxiated, which could result in death if not treated promptly. The governor just ignored her.

However, the pilot of the plane came up to her and said, "Tell me about his problems. I'll listen." Then the pilot would not let anyone smoke on the plane that Gary was on.

During all this time, the new Venezuelan doctor from Esmeraldas was here making the rounds of all the sick people. Faithie, who worked in the dispensary at that time, was taking him on his rounds to show him where the sick people were. He began to ask her just what was going on with the governor, the police, and the national guards there. She tried to explain the situation to him.

After the governor had told Gary that he was taking him out and all the people began to cry loudly and wail for Gary, the doctor said, "Well, it's obvious that you people are doing a good work here and that the people love you and want you here."

He walked over to the governor's comisionado and rebuked him.

"You're a fool. Can't you see what you're doing here?" he asked. "I haven't known your Yanomamö people long, but I can see that they really love these people, and the people love them."

Julio Jimenez and the two guards from Tamatama called us into the house and sat down with us. They asked us if we understood what they were charging Gary with. Then they told us that the governor was charging Gary with murder, bribery, and the possession of military arms—all of which were ridiculous charges.

That was a terrible day and a long night. We notified Don Bodin on the radio that they had taken Gary and asked if he had seen him, but he said, no, he had not seen Gary, but that Julio Jimenez had gone by his house and had told him that Gary had been arrested on serious charges. He had suggested that they get him a lawyer and get to work on his release.

We all met together in the church and lifted our voices in fervent prayer for Gary's health and safety. The two national guards from Tamatama also joined us. We could only find comfort in laying this burden at the throne of grace.

The next day Marie went to Puerto Ayacucho by MAF plane. We kept the children with us. We knew she might have to go to Caracas if Gary were sent there.

We waited anxiously by the radio for news. Don said on the radio that they still had not been allowed to see or talk to Gary. Only the Word of God and prayer helped to keep us calm so that we did not completely panic in this situation.

I kept thinking about Gary's allergies and praying that he would be kept in good health in spite of his ordeal. We met for prayer again that night in the church with all the Yanomamö brethren. The two national guards came again.

April 13, 1982. Gary was still in jail in Puerto Ayacucho. No one had seen him or talked to him. Our mission leaders in Puerto Ayacucho assured us that they were doing all they could. They were in contact with Caracas and Dr. Pablo Anduze, an old man revered in the Venezuelan government and a real friend to us—especially to Gary. Gary had led him to the Lord several years before. He had gone right to the president himself.

"Don't worry," they told us. "We'll have good news tomorrow."

We all gathered again that night for prayer for Gary. The Yanomamö people were so wonderful in this time of testing that we were going through. They tried to comfort us, but they were grieving as much as we were. They were faithful to be there every night and morning to pray with us.

Ramon's old mother went up to the guard Pablo and said, "Where's my son {meaning Gary}? What have you people done with my son? I'm a sick old woman and I'm just going to go out like a light is extinguished, if you don't return my son to me."

Sandy interpreted what she had said.

"It wasn't me," protested Pablo. "It wasn't me. The police have him, not the guards. We are friends."

On April 14th the governor's plane flew in again. They took out Octavio and Bautista. Octavio's wife and mother began to cry and wail.

Octavio's brother Juancito turned to Octavio and the others and said, "Now you know how Millie felt when she saw her son taken away. She cried for her son too. Now why don't you quit your lying, Octavio? Go down there and tell them the truth."

But Octavio was still unrepentant and said, "That's all right. Just let the guards kill me if they want to. I'm ready."

I felt sorry for Octavio's mother as I saw her tears and how upset she was. I went up and put my arms around her and said, "Don't cry. They won't hurt him. They just want to question him to find out the truth. He'll be back."

When she heard those words of comfort she quieted down.

We had prayer meeting again that night and our prayers were fervent. It was so hard to sleep not knowing just how Gary was doing in his ordeal. They told us on the radio that night that they had seen Gary from afar. He was making his declaration. They would not allow any of our people to be with him.

We received word by radio on the night of April 15th that Gary had been released and was at the mission. We all cheered!

Their superiors had recalled the two national guards to their base in Tamatama that morning. Pablo called in from Tamatama on their radio to tell us how happy he was upon hearing of Gary's release.

We had a praise service that night thanking and praising God for His infinite mercy. The spirit of sadness that had hung over the village like a pall lifted and everyone was happy again. No one had come to work since Gary had been taken. The boys wouldn't even play soccer.

An investigating committee of congress came down from Caracas to investigate the whole situation. It seemed that the governor was behind the whole thing. He was against us politically and wanted to see all missions and us particularly out of the territory. Octavio was just a little pawn in his game and didn't realize that he was just being used to further the governor's ends. He had been told that if he cooperated and said what he was told that Gary would have to give him a large sum of money. The thought of getting the money had put him on their side, even though he knew that what he was saying was false.

We were expecting the plane in with our field chairman, some of the congressmen, and Gary. We heard a plane. Of course we thought they were arriving and ran outside only to find it was an ambulance plane.

The doctor from Esmeraldas had sent the plane to get little Freddie who had been bitten months before by a poisonous snake. His leg was finally healing but was all drawn from the tendons being destroyed. The doctor said that Freddie would never walk again unless he had several operations on his leg and foot to replace the tendons. We scurried around trying to get everything ready. In the bustle, I misplaced Faith's Venezuelan identification card. We felt that it was very important that she go out with the boy as she had treated him ever since the snakebite in January. I was becoming very uptight when Sandy found the identification card where I had set it up on the shelf.

By the time we got them all off, I felt like a nervous wreck. Faithie also took little Donny, Gary's youngest, to turn him over to his mother in Puerto Ayacucho.

I was trying to cook dinner for the planeful of people who were coming—our field chairman, two congressmen, the pilot, and Gary. To make a bad situation worse, we had run out of propane gas that morning. I was cooking a big pot of beans when the propane gas ran out on my stove, so I was trying to cook them on a wood fire outside. I knew they would never get done in time, so Joe finally rounded up a kerosene primus stove and got that going. Soon the beans were bubbling merrily in the pot, and I was able to relax and get on with preparations for the rest of the meal.

The plane arrived. Everyone ran up to give Gary a big hug. One of the fellows from Caracas stood back and snapped pictures of it all. Everyone was so happy to see Gary that they almost cried again.

We finally got the meal over with. Gary took his two little girls, Vicki and Jeanne, back to Puerto Ayacucho with him. They were so afraid that they weren't going to go that they stayed out by the plane the whole time so as not to get left behind. We felt they needed the assurance of being with their parents at this time as who knows just what they were going through.

Jim Bou, our field chairman at that time, told us that a television crew would arrive the next day. We weren't happy to hear that as we had hoped for some peace and quiet and a chance to rest our nerves.

Nick Bauman from Caracas and a crew from VeneVision television station came in the next day. They interviewed us and found out all that had happened. Then they talked to Octavio's father, wife, and brother.

They wanted someone who could translate from Yanomamö into Spanish besides us so that it could not be said that we were changing what was said. Bautista's brother, David, had spent several years with the Maiquirtari people and had attended one of their schools at one time and was able to converse in Spanish. We asked him if he would do the translating, and he agreed to do it.

With the television cameras lined up on the group, Octavio's father told how the accident had taken place, for he was the only one who had really seen it happen.

"I was paddling up the river in my canoe, coming home from my garden," he told them. "My little grandson was leaning over the backboard of a dugout canoe that was tied up at the bank of the river. He was happy and excited, calling to me, his grandfather. Then a tall pole that had been standing up against a tree on the bank fell. It struck the front of the canoe that the child was standing in. He was tossed up into the air and came down hard striking his head on the backboard of the dugout. No one was near the pole," said Octavio's father. "The pole just fell."

The child's mother testified that she had not even been in the village at the time of the accident. She and her husband, Octavio, had been at another village and arrived back just after the accident happened.

When asked who they felt was to blame for the death of the little boy, Octavio's brother, Juan, said, "No one was to blame. It was an accident. The pole just fell. No one pushed it. It just fell. We are not saying that anyone was to blame."

The truth of the whole thing was that the child had not died from that blow on the head, which had fractured his skull. Gary had flown out with him and took him to a hospital in Caracas. There, they operated on him and the operation was a success. The boy was doing fine when he was released from the hospital. His speech had been affected, and the doctors felt that as young as he was he would recover his speech quicker by returning home. However, shortly after arriving home, he was accidentally injured again while in a hammock with his sister. Gary rushed him back to Caracas to the hospital again. But that time he did not make it. The doctor's "cause of death" statement had read, "Bad care of the parents." There was no blame accredited to Gary in this thing at all.

With the Yanomamö standing all around us, Joe gave just a brief account. This was on national television in Venezuela. We prayed that it would help undo some of the bad publicity that Satan had inspired against the work and us.

We talked to Gary that night on the radio. He told us that they had still not been able to find Bautista. We were all very concerned about him, wondering just where they had taken him and for what purpose. We turned once more for comfort to a long siege of prayer that night for Bautista.

Octavio's parents and relatives were very worried and concerned about him also. I had to really ask the Lord for grace in order to be able to pray in sincerity for him that night.

Now there was sadness over the whole village again. Everyone was worried about Bautista. Where could he be? Since Gary was no longer in jail, why were they still keeping Bautista hidden away?

The next day we heard the drone of an approaching plane, and we ran outside. Yes, it was the mission plane. It landed and the crowd surged forward, trying to see who was on the plane. Everyone clapped as they recognized Gary and looked anxiously to see who was sitting in the back. Yes, it was Bautista. Happiness flooded through the whole crowd assembled there.

They told how Bautista had been kept hidden and how they had moved him from place to place. Each time Gary heard that he was in a certain place, Bautista was moved to another place by the time Gary arrived. But, praise God, they had found him. He was home again. They had tried to get Bautista to change his story and lie about Gary, but he had refused to do so. How we thanked and praised the Lord for faithful men like Bautista.

Gary said that he had seen Octavio and told him that he would take him back to the village, but he wouldn't even answer him. He just turned his back and walked away. I felt sorry for Octavio's mother as she cried at the plane when she saw her son wasn't on it.

Eventually Octavio came back home, but he has never really had a close walk with the Lord since then. Even though we talked to him and assured him that we had forgiven him for his part in the whole affair, he has still never been the same again. Bautista has thrived and grown spiritually since his stand and has become a real strong man of God.

31

EXCERPTS FROM GARY'S NOTES

Here I would like to add excerpts from "Notes That I Kept in Jail." These are notes that Gary kept during his time in jail away from all he knew and loved.

Sunday, 5:30 p.m.

On order of the governor I was put in jail in Puerto Ayacucho. I haven't even been told what the charges against me are. I was not allowed to call or talk to anyone since I arrived in Ayacucho. This was also by order of the governor. He told the police that I was to be put in solitary confinement, and I was not allowed to make any phone calls or talk to anyone. The guards were ordered to keep quiet about the Yanomamö people crying for me when I was arrested.

Monday

I still don't know what my charges are. I had a pretty bad day until Fran sent me a New Testament and Psalms. What a blessing! Thanks a lot, Fran. May the Lord bless you for this! Just praising the Lord for what has happened makes it easier. Everyone here (the police) have been very nice. I'm glad that I'm in solitary confinement when I hear the noises from the other cells.

Tuesday

Got a note from Marie—I find out my charges. I can't believe that the governor is really trying to pin murder and bribery on me. I'm thankful that it is not true and that my God knows I'm innocent. I saw Marie from afar today. It was good just to be able to see her. It was also good to be able to wave to Larry (Fyock) and Jim (Bou). I can't believe that I was arrested on such serious charges and never told by the authorities what my charges were.

I have almost finished the book of Psalms. It is such a precious book for encouragement in hard times. Example: Psalms 139:17—"How precious also are thy thoughts unto me O God."

6:00 p.m.

They just gave me Jim Bou's note. It encouraged my heart.

God has been able to use this suffering in my life to show me that I had become too busy. So busy that I had neglected the Word and my family. The Bible says that God is a jealous God. I know that lately I have given Him cause to be jealous of my time.

Thank you, Lord, for what has happened to me. Use this to bring us all closer to yourself. I have been very worried about being interrogated, but I just read in Matthew 10:18–20 that God will give me the words to say. Thank you, Lord!

The captain of the guards just came to visit me. He was very nice but didn't say much. I finished reading Psalms and am halfway through Matthew.

Wednesday Morning

I had a bad night last night—my allergies really acted up. Someone was smoking a cigar or something. My chest is still hurting, but I feel better. My insides hurt all night. I'm sure that when I get out of here that I'll be a changed person in just appreciation. I'll appreciate my family more. I'll appreciate all my fellow missionaries more and all the dear Indian brothers who are pouring out their tears and prayers on my behalf. Thanks again, Father, for your work in our lives. Just knowing that God's people back in the United States are praying for me is an encouragement.

I keep worrying about Jody [his small son in boarding school in Tamatama]. I hope he won't worry too much. I hope he'll be able to keep his grades up. Thanks Chuck and Darlene [Jody's dorm parents] for your love towards him. I know it will help!

It is sort of exciting being here and being so defenseless, just to see God work on my behalf. My brother Mike's letter said to me that it is a privilege to suffer for the Lord. I can hardly believe the quiet peace He has put in my heart. It certainly isn't me! The book of Hebrews says He gives us grace in time of need. PRAISE THE LORD!

I was interrogated today by the Captain. I just can't believe the lies that Octavio told on me. I didn't think that the guards noticed much, but they saw how all the people were standing behind me. That said more to them than all of Octavio's lies. They were suspicious of the comisionado's translation from Yanomamö into Spanish, so maybe God will move him from his position.

Well, I wasn't given much choice on whether to sign or not; however, I understood and was satisfied with all that was written.

I had a bad time all day with my allergies. I just don't know what will happen to me if I get worse tonight. A note of praise: I finished the book of Matthew today. I hope to finish Acts tonight.

Psalm 21:11—"For they intended evil against thee: they imagined a mischievous device, which they are not able to perform." What a blessing!

It must be around 3:00 a.m. I am having a bad night and can't sleep. I just asked God to quiet my heart again and to cause me to rest in the fact that He is in control. They had told me at the interrogation that my seventy-two hours would be up that evening. [The length of time you can legally be held without formal charges against you.] But I guess the governor must have ordered me kept longer. The Bible says: "The eyes of the Lord run to and fro throughout the whole earth, to show himself strong in the behalf of them whose heart is perfect toward him" [2 Chron. 16:9]. PRAISE BE TO THE LORD for His everlasting kindness to us, His people. Today has been hard, but He tells us in EVERYTHING to give thanks. Thank you, Lord, for this difficult day. Use it to draw me closer to you. Amen.

Thursday

During my interrogation I was asked fifty-one questions and had to make my declaration on all the accusations against me. I have no complaints except that they would not let Jim Bou in with me.

But God allowed me to understand all that was said. I pray that God will richly bless Jim for the way he has handled this thing in my behalf. He has done all he could. I saw Marie yesterday and I am very concerned for her. I realize just what she has been going through as I saw how bad she looks. I pray that all those who are praying for me will send up a special prayer for her, asking the Lord to sustain her during this trying time.

I just found a very disgusting newsletter on my floor. It is so full of lies that it is hard to believe that someone is that evil. Scrawled on it are the words, "If you're given your freedom, remember Chet Bitterman—the same thing will happen to you!"

As the psalmist says: "Let burning coals fall upon them; Let them be into the fire; into deep pits, that they rise not up again" (Psalm 140:10). Sitting here in prison all I can say is, "God rebuke them!"

Psalm 118:6—"The Lord is on my side; I will not fear: what can man do unto me?" What an encouragement!

I didn't get a note from Marie with my breakfast, so I figure that things must be worse. I believe that Satan realizes that his time is short, and he is doing everything he can to stop the gospel of Christ from going forth; Jesus said that He is going to build His church and the gates of hell will not prevail against it. PRAISE THE LORD HE IS ON THE THRONE!

The Captain just gave me Marie's note. She tells me that they are bringing Bautista out from the village. I don't know if bringing him out will help me or not. I'm sure that Manuel Valero will not truthfully translate what he says in my behalf. The will of the Lord is done, and may He bring glory to Himself! Amen.

I finished the book of Acts today. One thing is sure. The Christians back then really suffered for the Lord. Also they surely accomplished things for the Lord.

The Captain called me to his office again this morning just to see how I am feeling. I hope he is a friend. He treated me very decent in my interrogation yesterday. He spoke very slowly and clearly for which I praise the Lord.

Thursday 1:00 p.m.

Praise the Lord I have been released. God answered prayer on my behalf. They gave no explanation—just told me that I was completely free.

Friday

I spent most of today preparing and talking to the Investigation Congressional Committee. They were very cordial and heard me out on everything.

I feel sorry for Octavio because they are the ones who could be charged with lying and perjury to the government. I told the attorney general when he met with me that I did not want to present charges against Octavio because his family stood with me, and I don't want to hurt them.

Praise the Lord that the charges are all considered false and God has once again proved that He is on the throne.

I was sick today and had a bad attack right in the middle of my questioning. I have finally decided that I need a furlough.

Nick, an American friend from Caracas, told me today that God works in mysterious ways. Truly God has shown himself strong on my behalf. Nick has been a true friend to me. I'm grateful to him.

Now that I have gotten out of jail, everyone has been telling me just how much all our very precious Venezuelan friends did for me. I have been left amazed and speechless, and in the closing of these notes from all my heart I pray to the all wise and only living God that He will forever remember the kindness of each of these dear people. I ask Him to richly repay them for all they did in my behalf. Thanks especially to you my dear friend, Dr. Pablo Anduze, for your great concern and all your many efforts to get me released. God who sees all knows of your great labor of love for me.

Note: The congressional committee that came had Juan, a Ye'cuana who speaks Yanomamö, present to listen to the comisionado's translation of what Bautista and Octavio were saying. It was proven that he was adding and downright lying in the way he was translating.

After Gary and Marie's ordeal, they decided to go on furlough, which they did as soon as all these things were cleared up.

Still there was much to be thankful for in 1982. We finished up the translation of the Yanomamö New Testament. Jean Johnson from the NTM Language School in Missouri came to do a translation check. Finally it was finished and turned in for printing.

32

A BIG DAY — A DAY OF BLESSING

June 10, 1984. This was a big day for our Yanomamö brethren. They had waited a long time to have the whole New Testament in their own language. They had watched us through the years as we wrote down words in their language. In the beginning they were amazed that we could later look at these marks on the paper and speak their words back to them. Later as some learned to read, they realized that the written word was for them too if they would apply themselves to the work of learning what all the syllables meant.

At last the day had come. The goal of the tribal missionary was to place the Word of God into the hands of the people whom he has come to reach for Christ. This was the highlight of our thirty-one years with the Yanomamö people, presenting God's wonderful message to the people in their own language.

The setting was the jungle village of Coshilowa-teli on the Padamo River. Throngs of visiting Yanomamö from outlying villages milled around in happy excitement. Most of our ten children were on hand to join in the celebration, for none of them had been excluded from the many years of hard work. The service took place in the newly painted chapel. The New Testaments were stacked on the communion table in front of the pulpit. On the wall hung the sign that proclaimed "Diez de Junio—Día de Bendicion" or June 10—Day of Blessing.

The director of New Tribes Mission spoke as Gary Dawson interpreted for the Indian brethren. Captain Gilberto Perrera, representing the National Guard of Venezuela spoke in behalf of his countrymen. He said, "In the words of a famous man: Never has so much been done by so few with so little."

Macon Hare from the NTM Executive Committee in Sanford, Florida was there to make the presentation. Bautista Perez, the faithful translation helper for so many years, brought a stirring message in which he told how the entrance of God's Word into their lives had brought them light for their darkness and hope for a better future. He declared that even though many were saying, "Just leave the tribes alone; they are happy as they are," this is not true. They too have the right to choose what they desire for themselves.

The children's choir, composed of thirty-three Yanomamö children and led by the four Dawson girls, sang a repertoire of Yanomamö and Spanish songs, ending with the Venezuelan National Anthem.

Copies of the New Testament were presented to those who in some way shared the burden of seeing the Word of God translated into the Yanomamö language.

As Mike Dawson closed the service in prayer, we all realized that God had done a great and mighty work. All praise and glory belongs to him.

Marg Yank, another Yanomamö worker, wrote the following in the NTM Headwaters magazine.

An earlier presentation had already taken place in the jungle village of Coshilowa-teli; however because so many who wanted to attend were unable to get permits to travel into Indian Territory, a second program was planned.

The setting had lost a bit of its charm by being moved to Puerto Ayacucho, the capital of the Amazon territory. But the emotion felt by the Venezuelan believers and national Christian leaders was unequaled. Eduardo Ruan, nationally known evangelical leader, had pronounced the opening words and directed the program. Jim Bou, chairman of New Tribes Mission in Venezuela, had shared some background of the missionary endeavor among the Indians. A choir of Yanomamö children all dressed in red and white uniforms startled the audience with their songs, a repertoire of hymns in Spanish and Yanomamö, under the direction of the four Dawson girls who were participating.

Joe and Millie Dawson, the missionaries who had completed the final translation, spoke a few words to the assembly. Their translation helper, Bautista, who had worked at their side through the years, addressed the crowd through an interpreter.

The four Dawson girls stepped forward and sang two patriotic songs which they had written. Then the dedication of the New Testament took place as hands were laid on and God's blessing asked upon the Word to the reaching out to many unreached people. The audience rose to their feet as the Venezuelan flag was raised by one of the Yanomamö children, and the children's choir closed the program with the national anthem.

From the days when Jim Barker finished the first draft, until the past ten years when Joe and Millie have been working on the final translation, the Yanomamö New Testament has taxed the energy of many people. But as Millie said, "All the praise and glory belongs to God."

33

FAITH TESTED AND FAITH REWARDED

In January of 1986, following another hard trial for us, I wrote: Yesterday the portals of Heaven opened and a little Yano-mamo boy slipped in. All of heaven rejoiced as another of the redeemed ones came home. Little Unabewa had lost his battle with the cancerous tumors that were invading his frail body.

They had discovered the tumors some months ago and brought him down from upriver to us here at Cosh for treatment. We were not able to help him, and Marie took him out to Puerto Ayacucho to the doctor.

They said he would have to go to Caracas, so with only an hour's warning, Marie had to pack and was soon on her way on an army plane with him to a hospital in Caracas. There too they were unable to help him as the tumors had invaded his whole body. They did a biopsy, found the tumors were malignant, and said they could do nothing to help him as he was not strong enough to stand the treatment.

As soon as he arrived back here on the plane, his people met him and took him home to their village upriver, as they knew there was nothing we could do.

Yesterday they came to tell us that he was gone and to call relatives from this village to come up to mourn at his cremation.

David Perez, Bautista's brother from here in Cosh, returned today. He told us how the boy's stepfather said that just before Unabewa died he called him, the stepfather, to his hammock and said, "The Lord is calling me home. I'm going to the eternal land. Don't be sad when I go, because I am going to be happy there. When I'm gone, go ahead and burn me, but don't drink my bones. Just bury them. I'm a Christian [one who wants Jesus], and the Lord is calling me to his land."

When we heard that, it was hard to be sad about our little friend. Even though we would miss him, we knew he was in a much happier place, and we could not honestly wish him back. Little Unabewa had been one of our kindergarten students last year, so we had come to know and love him, but how we can rejoice that this little one has gone to a better land where there is no sickness, no pain, and no more sorrow.

In March of 1989, I wrote:

Once again we were made to realize just what the Lord has done here in this village and the strides that have been made with the gospel.

Rick Johnson, a friend of ours from California, came down with a friend of his. They came to help us out by putting in some badly needed wells in some villages where getting water was a problem.

He took some of the Christian Yanomamö from here with him. They were to help drill the wells and to have a ministry with the unsaved Yanomamö. So Pablo Mejias and Augusto Rivas from here went along. These are testimonies they gave when they returned.

Pablo said, "I was so very sad when I saw my people, the Yanomamö, in this far off village. [They had to fly in by plane.] Now I hear that people are saying, 'Just leave them alone. They are living so happy there in the jungle. Why are you bothering them?'

"Well, my people, I'm telling you that the Yanomamö are not happy when they are living alone. They are very miserable. The old people here in our village are very clean." [This was said by way of comparison because to us they surely didn't seem very clean. But in comparison they themselves seemed to him to be very clean.]

"Friends," he continued, "I saw one very old woman there, but if you would have seen her, you would have said, 'What is that strange creature they have taken for a pet?' She did not look like a human being. Her hair was so dirty that it had all become brittle and broken off. It stood out grotesquely around her head like a huge termite nest. The dirt was so thick and crusted on her face that you could not see her features. You wondered if she had a nose or mouth. Her hands were so dirty that she looked as though she had no fingers. Her hands looked like a black blob.

"My friends, when I saw her, my heart wept for her. I said, 'Mother, why don't you bathe? That dirt carries many germs. It will kill you,' but she didn't heed.

"I killed a wild turkey. I took it into the village. I saw a man. He too was filthy. 'Uncle,' I said, 'why don't you go bathe? That dirt will make you sick. Dirt carries diseases. Dirt makes us sick.'

"'Later,' he said, 'Later I'll go take a bath.'

"'No, go right now,' I said.

"'The water is a long ways away,' he said and didn't go.

"So finally I gave up. 'Well, Uncle,' I said, 'Here's a turkey. Cook it and eat it.' He gladly took the turkey. He was hungry. Even though there was no water nearby to clean the turkey, he began to pull off the feathers and pull out the entrails. His hands became full of blood, but he just pulled off some leaves and rubbed his hands. Then he wiped them in his hair and down his bare arms and across his bare chest. I felt like throwing up. I talked to him from God's Word and told him the gospel. He listened quietly. Then I left him to eat his turkey.

"The next day when I went back to see him, he still had the dirty dried blood from cleaning the turkey between his fingers and down the backs of his hands. Again I shared God's Word with him. 'Yes, yes,' he said, 'but who will teach me about God?'

"Another time a man called me and Augusto to eat with him. We did not want to appear rude, but later I thought, 'Why didn't I tell him I was full?' When we got there, he was preparing a banana drink. He was squishing the bananas up with his dirty hands. I thought, 'Lord, can I eat this?' He handed me a dirty pot. I saw it had black greasy dirt around it where he had cooked an animal in its skin earlier. There were some long black tapir hairs in the dirt. I looked at the banana drink that he had squished up into a pulp and had then added some water. The dirt from his hands and the dirty pot was swimming around on top. I looked at that and thought, 'I can't drink this.' Then I thought, 'If I don't drink it, he'll think I'm despising his food and be angry.' So even though I wanted to vomit, I forced some of it down my throat.

"Then I held the pot out to Augusto. He peered into the pot and said, 'No, I don't want any. I won't drink that!' He handed the man back his pot and walked away.

"Friends, here we eat from clean pots. Here we wash our hands before we prepare food. Here we bathe and wash our clothes. Why do we do this?" He held God's Word high. "It's because we are new people. We have heard the truth and the truth has freed us from our old ways that were out to destroy us. "Friends, give God the glory! He is the reason we are living so much better! He is the only hope for these others who still live in the old ways in spiritual darkness. They are not happy. We cannot leave them in their darkness. We must take them the light. It is not just for us. It is for all Yanomamö."

Augusto's testimony was much the same. This trip had shown them how blessed they were that they knew the Lord. They were experiencing His many blessings. This knowledge hushed the voices that were calling to them from other groups telling them that they should go back to their old ways as Yanomamö. These voices had been assuring them they would be happy if they returned to their old ways. But now they had seen first hand this so-called happiness. They didn't want any part of it.

They were both saddened and repelled by what they had seen. Now they had the burden to go and share what they had with those who were still living in darkness.

34

JOSEPH AND BABY BOO

G randma, Jesus died on the cross." Little Joseph, almost four years old, looked up at me with his big brown eyes wide. We were in the kitchen and I was preparing a meal. The kitchen was deserted except for Grandpa, who sat quietly at the dining room table off to the side, trying to snatch a few minutes of quiet time with his old Bible.

"That's right," I said.

"Jesus died for our sins," he said, "But he didn't stay dead. He rose from the dead and went back up to heaven."

"That's right," I said.

"He's coming back to get us again," he persisted, "And take us up to heaven to live with Him."

"Yes, that's right," I replied. "That's what He is going to do," I said.

For a long moment he looked at me—his brown eyes glowing. Then, he asked, "Well, what about Baby Boo?"

Baby Boo was a pet spider monkey we had. He was so named because his black wiry hair stood all out around his head like a hairy halo. The girls said that he looked as though someone had jumped at him and yelled "Boo!" and made his hair stand on end. He was semi-wild, spending most of his time up a tree or on the roof, coming down when coaxed down with a banana or other fruit.

Joseph loved him and enjoyed handing him his banana. Now I could see as I looked into his puzzled brown eyes that he was concerned for his little hairy friend, but I knew no way to break the news gently.

"Well," I said, "Baby Boo won't be going with us. He'll be staying behind."

"Why?" he wanted to know.

"Well," I said gently, "Baby Boo is a monkey and monkey's aren't going."

His eyes got rounder. He put his hands on his hips and looked at me reprovingly.

"Then he'll just cry and cry and cry," he stated. "Who'll be here to give him his banana every day?"

I really was lost for words. I hardly knew what to say and then, before I could think of a suitable reply, his eyes lighted up again and he said, "Well, probably all the Yanomamö won't be going, and one of them will give him a banana."

"Yes, that's right. Only the Christians will go, and probably some of the Yanomamö will be left behind. One of them will give Baby Boo his bananas," I said, relieved at his solution to a sticky problem I was having difficulty with answering.

"Probably Dino will stay and give Baby Boo his bananas," said Joseph.

"No, I think not," I replied, "Dino's a Christian and he'll go with us."

"No," he stated emphatically, "I think Dino should stay here and give Baby Boo his bananas." He turned and walked away.

Grandpa, who had been listening to the whole conversation, was really getting a chuckle out of the wisdom of this little fellow.

A couple of months later, Baby Boo was killed by one of the old dogs here. Joseph, by this time, had gone back to his home in Ciudad Bolivar with his Mom, our daughter Susan, and the rest of his family. When he heard the news, he was not crushed by it as we had feared. He seemed to be comforted that now Baby Boo would not be in danger of going hungry when the rapture takes place and we all go to be with the Lord, leaving Baby Boo behind.

35

SHICOIMA

"Milimi, give me some of that bitter medicine," she said. I turned and looked into the black eyes of Shicoima, a young woman from Shitali village. She was married to a man from Jalulusi village and had been here in Cosh for a couple of weeks.

"Is your baby sick?" I asked, feeling its forehead.

"No, I don't want it for my baby. I want it for myself."

"Do you have malaria?" I asked, transferring my hand to her forehead.

"No, I'm not sick," she said. "I want the medicine that kills babies inside of you."

I looked into her troubled eyes. "I can't give you medicine to kill babies," I said. "That would be murder, and God tells me not to kill."

She looked pathetic. "I'm afraid my husband is going to really hurt me, maybe kill me. They've already hurt me once. Now he will hurt me again. He's waiting to see if I'm pregnant, and if I am, he says he will really hurt me. I'm so afraid."

"Are you sure you're pregnant?" I asked.

"I'm pretty sure," she said mournfully, "and I'm so scared. My husband will know it's not his, and he will hurt me badly," she said again.

"If you're so afraid of your husband, why did you allow this to happen?" I asked.

"Even though I refused myself, I had no choice," she replied.

Elias, a young man from Jalulusi village, and Shicoima had arrived at Coshilowa-teli at night. The woman was badly injured and in much pain. Her husband's brother had chopped her with many gashes in the head with his machete and her ear lobes were dangling where he had grasped her ear ornament sticks and ripped them from her ears, tearing out the flesh. One ear was torn away from her head. This had happened several days before. She and Elias had run away and walked the trail to this village for medical help. She was in a pitiful state.

As Gary, Marie, Faith, and Sharon worked over her, we learned her sad story. About five months earlier, her husband had taken a young girl in another village to be another wife to him. He had gone to this girl's village to live with her and to meet the demands of his new in-laws, leaving Shicoima and her children behind to make it as best they could alone. Finally, her brother-in-law, her husband's brother, who also had a wife of his own, began making advances to which she did not respond. Then Elias, a young man without a wife of his own, began taking her meat. For this reason, Gabriel, the brother-in-law, had beaten her in a jealous rage. We shuddered when we saw her condition.

Gary was able to sew up her ear lobes and stitch the one back to her head. Since the wounds were several days old and had already begun to heal in their mutilated condition, it was necessary for him to reopen them and then sew them up. Thank the Lord we had anesthetics and sutures. We treated the wounds in her head, which were already infected, and gave her penicillin.

Now, her husband had left his second wife in her village with her parents and had come to get his first wife. As I looked at her, I marveled at how the Lord had so graciously worked. One had to look close to see where her ear lobes had been repaired.

"I'm sorry you're afraid," I said, "But I can't give you something to kill a baby. God warns me against that. Anyway, malaria medicine would probably not kill your baby, even if I gave you some. Many of the women here have taken chloroquine when they were very sick with malaria, and they did not miscarry. You don't need medicine to kill your baby. You need someone to protect you."

Then I shared the gospel with her. I told her that by taking Christ as her Savior, God would be her Father, and He would be open to her cries for protection. I explained how Jesus had died to cause all her evil doings to disappear and make her clean.

"Yes, that's what I need. I want my sin to disappear, and I want to go away from here empty," she said. Her mind was still on getting rid of her problem. She went sadly away.

"Leave them alone! They're happy like they are."

That's what people say, but I haven't found it so, and this sad woman was one more example.

Months later Shicoima did have her baby—a beautiful little girl. Her husband had not mistreated her as she had feared and had accepted the child—a happy ending to a sad story!

36

VANESSA

In one of my letters home I wrote:
Vanessa accepted Christ as her Savior this morning at the close of Ladies Bible Class. Vanessa is a petite lady, wife of Pedro. She's Ramon's sister.

Ramon serves the coffee to the Men's Prayer Meeting and Bible Class that takes place from 6:00 to 7:00 a.m. every morning, Monday through Friday. He then stays and serves the coffee to the Ladies Bible Class from 7:00 to 8:00 a.m. every morning.

Vanessa has been coming to Bible Study and meetings for years, but she had never openly professed Christ as Savior. I didn't know just what her position was. She was not openly antagonistic to the message of the gospel, but she never spoke up for it either or declared her faith in Christ.

I had taught once again through the Gospel of John, stressing throughout the deity of Christ and also the fact that He was man, stressing His love and His desire to save each one. This morning as I summarized it all up once again, I gave the invitation for those who wanted to publicly accept Christ as their Savior. Finally, after a struggle with herself, Vanessa rose to her feet and with utter sincerity spoke:

"I have never said that I was a Christian," she said. "I have never claimed to be a Christian. But I have sat here for a very long time listening to God's Word being taught. Now I want to say that the Word of God is a very good message. I am happy with the message that I have been hearing, and I want to say publicly before all of you that today I am accepting Jesus Christ as my Savior. I ask God to save me and make me His Child. I know that Jesus died and gave his blood for me so that I can go to His land and live with Him."

I was so thrilled that tears came to my eyes. It was so wonderful to hear her testimony. Every lady in the room was touched. There were several visiting ladies that had been here for a couple of months. They came to all the meetings and paid close attention as I spoke. I was praying for them also, that they would open their hearts to receive what Christ was freely offering them.

"For the preaching of the cross is to them that perish foolishness; but unto us which are saved it is the power of God" (I Corinthians 1:18).

37

Baby Killer

Bump ... Bump ... Thump ... Someone was bumping and thumping on the door, but I wondered why they did not just push open the door and come on in. The door was not locked. The Yanomamö usually didn't knock unless the door was locked. I went to the door and opened it. There on the ground in front of my door sat an old lady leaning back on both hands with legs raised and foot extended to give the door another thump.

"Why are you sitting there on the ground, thumping on the door with your foot instead of coming on in?" I asked.

"I'm sick," she whined.

"Well, you know that while the doctor from Sanidad is here, you have to go to her for medicine," I said. "I can't treat you when the doctor is here. She'll give you medicine."

"Well, I'm hungry," she continued to whine. "I'm too weak to walk to the doctor because I'm so hungry," she complained. Taking her arm, I helped her to her feet and into the house.

"I already went to the doctor," she said. "She gave me some of that bitter medicine, but I'm so weak, my legs are just trembling."

Seating her on a bench, I went to the stove, where I usually kept a pot of cooked rice. "For your welfare people," my kids laughingly said. I dipped her up a plateful and sent her away happy.

She was a visitor lady, and I had not recognized her, she looked so old and sick.

"That is Cojoima's mother from Jalulusi-teli," one of the ladies who had come in told me. Then I remembered. That was the old lady that they called "Baby Killer" because she was known to kill unwanted babies.

When her unmarried daughter Cojoima became pregnant, she decided that the pregnancy was the result of incest, so she told Cojoima when the baby was born that she intended to kill it. "Don't even think about keeping it," she had said, "because even if you go somewhere else and give birth to it and don't come right home, later when I see it I will snatch it from your carrying strap and kill it."

When Faithie heard this from her sister Susan, who, along with her family, lived and worked in Jalulusi-teli, she sent word in to Cojoima that she wanted the baby to raise as her own child and that she would take it as soon as it was born. She begged her not to let her mother kill the baby but to save its life by allowing Faithie to take it to raise as hers.

Cojoima was very happy to do so, as she did not want her baby killed, but she knew her mother well enough to know that she meant what she said. At first the old woman refused, but Faith and Gary went in by small plane to her village to talk to her. Finally, she seemingly relented. But Cojoima was taking no chances. She came to Cosh and stayed until it was time for the baby to be born. Faithie was with her when the baby came—a beautiful little boy.

"There lies your baby. Pick him up. He's yours," Cojoima said, and Faithie gladly did so. That's how she came to have little David Michael, who is now a lively, precious six-year-old.

I thought about this in the days when I was giving old Baby Killer her morning and evening bowls of rice. Now she was an old sick woman. Her unsavory past must rise up to haunt her. She needs a Savior. I pray before it is too late for her that she will open her heart and let Him in. He is able to save to the uttermost, even a baby killer.

Just five months after Faithie took little David to raise as her own, a family came to visit from the village of Jalulusi-teli. The wife was very ill with Falciparum malaria, which had greatly affected her spleen. It hung down huge and swollen. The problem was that she was also very pregnant. It was obvious that she would deliver within the next week or so.

She went into labor early in the day, and the baby boy was soon there. They sent for Sharon and Faithie to help her, as it was obvious to them that there was also another on the way. Faithie came running home with a very tiny baby boy that weighed only about 2 pounds in her arms. We quickly rigged up a cardboard box lined with hastily warmed blankets and wrapped the baby up snugly and placed him in the box. She ran back to help Sharon in the delivery of the other one. The other was a very tiny girl. They rushed back to the house with this one also because the mother was so sick that she was not able to even look at the babies.

We put a heating pad in the box to keep the babies as warm as we possibly could. We held out little hopes for them surviving. We knew that by all means they should be in an incubator. Even then, their chances of making it would be slim. They were so tiny and had no body heat at all. The little boy seemed to be having some trouble breathing. To make matters worse, they were almost completely covered with black hair—especially heavy on the face and back. Because of their size and their grotesque looks and the fact that they were twins, the people thought they were not humans but animals or spirits. They were afraid of them. Finally we were able to persuade the father and the sister to hold them and see that they were just little newborn babies.

As the mother became stronger, the father said, "We want the boy. The girl we don't want. We already have enough girls."

The babies were so very fragile that Faith and Sharon stayed up all night with them. They were so tiny that you could not hear them cry unless you were bending over the box. The girls were so afraid that the babies would just quit breathing that they just wouldn't leave them alone but stayed right by them.

The tiny boy, who had never seemed to breathe right, succumbed at a week old. We felt sure that now they would want the baby girl as the boy was gone, but they were adamant. No, they would not take the girl.

We begged, pleaded, and cajoled them. "If you want me to, I will keep her until she is the size of a newborn baby," Faith said. "The mother must come here to the house everyday and hold her and nurse her. Then she will not be a stranger to her when the time comes to take her to your village. I will take care of her now until she is out of danger," Faithie said.

But they refused to be persuaded. "If you make us take her, we will kill her on the trail as we go home," they said. "We don't want her and we won't keep her. Just keep her and raise her for yourself."

Tiny Nicole Renee, better known as Nikki, was six months old before she looked the size of a newborn baby. But with all the love and care she received, she has grown into a beautiful little girl. She is now very healthy and bigger for her age now than other children who were born here in the village at the same time she was.

She is a constant source of delight to all who know her sharp wit, her beauty, and her winning ways. She and David Michael, who are just five months apart, seem like twins. While they are quite a handful for Faithie, who has adopted them, she would not change a thing. Along with Samantha Joann (Sami), the little abandoned girl from Coyowa village that she adopted in 1990, Faithie has a little family of her own. Sharon helps out with their support and care also.

38

HE MUST HAVE BEEN AN ANGEL

We separated officially from NTM on May 31 of 1990. Joe and I retired and, along with the rest of the family, established Mission Padamo. Several months later it became necessary for us to take a new computer back to the United States for repairs.

Our youngest son, Jerald, who lives in Chicago with his family, had sent us a new computer. It had been damaged in shipping to Venezuela. Since he had bought it on his credit card, he wanted us to get it back to the United States as soon as possible in hopes of a refund or a replacement.

We decided to take the computer back to Chicago ourselves so that when it was replaced, we could hand carry it back to Venezuela. We left the village of Coshilowa-teli the day before. The next morning we went down to CANTV (the telephone company) to talk to Jerald by phone. When he suggested we come as soon as possible, so we went right to the Avensa Ticket Agency and were able to get tickets on the plane for that afternoon.

227

As we hastily packed for the trip, I remarked to Joe, "Now that we are no longer with the mission, we won't have anyone to meet us in Maiquetia at the airport, nor anyone to get us hotel reservations, nor plane tickets and reservations for the United States. We're going to be as helpless as babes, for this has always been done for us!"

"That's true," Joe said, "But we still have the Lord, and He'll work it all out, so don't worry about it."

We flew into the national airport in Maiquetia and went immediately to the international airport to get our tickets and reservations for Chicago. Imagine our surprise to find the American Airlines office already sold out and closed. While we were standing there wondering what to do, a porter approached—a short fellow with a big grin.

"Can I be of service?" he asked. Joe explained that we wanted to purchase tickets to get to Chicago as soon as possible but that the American Airlines Ticket Agency was closed up.

"Well, I can take you down to the Viasa Ticket Agency," he said as he put our suitcases on his cart. On our way to the Viasa ticket office, he probed us for information and found out we were missionaries working in Estado Amazonas and had been working there with the Yanomamö since 1953 when Amazonas was still a territory—The Federal Territory Amazonas.

He was a very friendly, bubbly fellow. He told us that he was an evangelical believer also, and he did a lot of street work. When we arrived at Viasa, Joe explained what we needed. The girl checked out the computer and told us that it was possible for us to get two round-trip tickets, but they would cost us over one thousand dollars apiece.

"That's a lot more than I wanted to pay," Joe sighed.

"Well," she said, "American Airlines has a special on tomorrow to Chicago for seven hundred dollars per ticket, if you can get on that."

"Well, American Airlines' ticket counter is closed now," Joe replied.

"Say," piped up the little porter, who had told us his name was Victor, "I know the people in the upstairs office of AA. I could take you up there, and we could try them."

So he took us to the elevator and pushed his cart aboard with our two suitcases. He took us to an upstairs office and talked at length with a man there.

"No, no, it is impossible. The office is closed and the cash box is locked," the man protested.

Victor would not give up, and finally the official turned to us and said, "Just wait right here. I have to go downstairs and make some phone calls and see what I can do."

He was gone fifteen or twenty minutes. Victor sat on the floor at our feet, talking about the Lord and the Lord's work. When the man returned, he handed Joe a piece of paper on which was written a name and a number.

"Look," he said, "I have fixed it up for you. But in order to get these tickets and these reservations, you must be at the ticket office at exactly 5:30 a.m. You must be the very first one in line. When you approach the ticket box, you must give this paper to the girl and then ask for this man," he indicated the name on the paper. "When you speak to this man, tell him you are from the man he talked to on the phone last night."

We thanked him profusely and left with this admonition ringing in our ears.

"Remember 5:30 a.m.!"

"Well, what next?" our self-appointed helper asked now.

"Well, now we need to get a hotel room—somewhere nearby," we replied. This little porter had been with us so long by this time that I figured he was really going to expect a big tip.

"Let's check with the tourist agencies," he said and led us over to another window. I saw him turn to a woman standing to the side nearby and heard him say, "Don't take off. We may need you."

Well, it seemed that all the hotels nearby were full—full—full! What were we to do now?

"You could go into Caracas," they told us.

But we knew that would mean a long taxi ride in to Caracas and back out in the morning. We might not even make it back for the 5:30 a.m. appointment that was so crucial.

"No, I don't want to go into Caracas," I said. "If we have to, we'll just stay here at the terminal until morning."

It was already 10:00 p.m. It had been a long exhausting day.

"Well, I know a hotel," Victor said, giving us a name. "It's not a very fancy hotel, and it's in a bad part of town, but they always have rooms open."

"OK, try that hotel," Joe said, and they made the call.

Sure enough, they were able to reserve a room for us. Victor turned to the woman still standing close by and said, "Take these people to their hotel and make sure you get them and their bags right into their rooms. Tell the man at the desk that they must be at the airport in the morning at 5:30 a.m. on the dot! That he is to get them a cab in the morning so they'll be sure to get there on time!"

He rolled our suitcases out to the cab and loaded them into the back of the car. Joe pulled some money out of his pocket and started to hand the bills to Victor, but he drew back and put up his hands in a gesture of refusal.

"No, no," he said, "I don't want anything. I did this for the Lord!"

We thanked him again and got into the cab, not sure if we could believe all that had happened. As the cab pulled away from the curb, we turned to each other and both of us burst out at the same time, "He must have been an angel!"

We were still marveling to ourselves as we sped along the busy road winding in and out of the streets we had never been on before. When our cab stopped, we got out and entered a hotel. Just as Victor had told her, the cab driver went up to the desk and helped us sign in and then carried our luggage to the room. She had also told the clerk that he was to get a cab in the morning and see that he got it in time to get us to the airport at 5:30 a.m. on the dot.

After the door closed behind her, I turned to Joe and said, "I'm starved. Do you reckon we could get something to eat here?" We had not eaten a bite since early morning. Even then, I had eaten only a piece of toast.

"I doubt very much we can get anything to eat at this time of night in this hotel. I doubt they even have a restaurant," Joe said. "And this looks like a really slummy part of town. I don't know if it would be safe to go out."

I sighed. "Well, I'm so hungry, I don't know if I'll be able to sleep." After the hubbub had died down I began realizing just how hungry I was.

"I don't think it will do much good, but I'll go ask if there is a restaurant here in the building," Joe said and went out. After about five minutes, he hadn't returned, and I was getting nervous. After ten minutes, I was beginning to feel panicky. I didn't dare to leave the room to go look for him, because Victor had cautioned us against leaving our bags unguarded in the room. By this time I was walking up and down the grungy little room, praying fervently. All kinds of horrible things crossed my mind.

What if he's gone looking for a restaurant in this sleazy part of town and been mugged? What if he got lost and can't remember the name of the hotel to ask directions? What if . . . ? What if . . . ?

It went on and on as I wept and prayed and asked the Lord to take care of him and bring him back safely. I promised I would not say another word about hunger. In fact, my worries had caused my hunger to leave me.

After an hour or so, Joe walked in—all smiles—with two boxes of take-out food and a woman carrying two Pepsis with straws sticking out of the bottles.

"It was incredible!" Joe said after the woman had set down the bottles and left. "The man at the desk took me down the street a few blocks and took me to a place that is open all night. He told them to fix me some food to take out. Then he told me that he had to go back to the hotel desk but that he would come back in a half-hour to check on me and see that I got back to the hotel OK. All the way from the hotel to the restaurant he had been telling people standing along the streets, 'This man is a friend of mine.' Well, they had to cook the food. The desk clerk came back in a half-hour. I was still waiting. When he found out that the food wasn't quite ready, he told them when it was finished to send someone back to the hotel with me. They were to help me carry the food and to make sure that I got back to the hotel. So they sent a woman along to help me. I couldn't believe how friendly and helpful everyone was," he said.

I was happy he was back safe and sound, and we thanked the Lord together for the way He was watching out for us!

We slept very little that night, anxious lest we oversleep. But when we presented ourselves at the hotel desk the next morning before dawn, paid our bill, and asked about a cab to the airport, the man ran outside, stood on the curb, and had soon hailed a passing car. He helped us inside and told the driver not to waste any time but to get us to the airport right away.

So, before 5:30 a.m. we were standing at the head of the line at the American Airlines ticket office when it opened. When the lady motioned to us, we stepped forward and presented the slip of paper and asked to speak to the man whose name was there. She motioned to a man standing near. He came over, took the paper, and looked at it. Then he said, "Where did you get this?"

"From the American Airlines upstairs office last night," Joe said. "He told me to tell you that he talked to you on the phone last night."

He looked at us again, then laid the paper on the counter. "Fix them up with tickets," he said as he walked away.

We walked away from that counter with the tickets to Chicago in our hands. Later, people who had tried to get on the flight told us that they were informed it was absolutely sold out and there wasn't a chance of their getting on!

"How in the world did you get on at the last minute?" they asked.

We knew that all the credit belonged to the Lord. He had taken care of everything for us!

39

RENEE

I'm sure the very hardest thing of all that we faced as a family and as missionaries to the Yanomamö people happened in June of 1992.

Our son Mike had been called to be guest speaker at a mission's conference in Puerto Rico. His wife, Renee, and their three little boys, Joshua (seven years old), Ryan (five), and Stephen (three), stayed behind here in Cosh. Just a few days after Mike left, Stephen became sick with Falciparum malaria. We were all very concerned. I had gone over that morning to check on him and to ask how he had spent the night. Renee mentioned that she was not feeling well either, but she felt that she was just getting some sort of flu.

Everything happened so quickly that it is hard to remember just exactly the sequence of events. I had finally coaxed Renee to take some malaria medicine, as I was sure she was having a malaria attack. She had come over to our house and was in a hammock there.

235

We all thought that she had taken the medicine. When she got worse and drifted into unconsciousness, we berated ourselves, thinking that she was having an allergic reaction to the medicine. She had been afraid of the medicine since she had had a bad experience the year before after taking it. That is one reason why she had gotten so badly ill so fast as she had refused to take the medicine.

However, when we moved her out of the hammock and unto a cot, which we had prepared for her, we found the malaria pills down in the bottom of the hammock and realized that she had not taken the pills. She was unconscious from the deadly Falciparum malaria. It was on a Sunday, and we were unable to get anyone at all on the radio. We called and called, trying to get in touch with the MAF plane which served our area, but we were unable to reach them. They were not on the air.

We sat up by her bedside all night, trying to bring down her fever and trying to do what we could for her, which was little at best. That morning we were able to get the plane by radio. They flew in and took Renee out to the clinic in Puerto Ayacucho. Marie flew out with her to take care of her on the plane and to be with her in the clinic. Little Stephen, who was still very sick, was taken out also.

Mike was notified in Puerto Rico about the illness of his wife and son. It was discovered that he too was very illustrate. They had thought he had a kidney infection, but it was then discovered that he too had a very bad case of Falciparum malaria. He was so illustrate that he could hardly make the plane back to Venezuela and on down to Puerto Ayacucho, where his sick wife and child lay in the clinic. Soon he too was in a bed there.

However, despite all our prayers, Renee continued to get worse. They flew her and Mike in an ambulance plane to Caracas. When the news came to us on the night of June 22, 1992 that Renee had gone to be with the Lord, we were unable to take it in. We were devastated as we thought of poor sick Mike, who was even then battling for his own life. We thought of the three little boys who were now without a mother.

The rest is like a nightmare. I remember sitting on my bed weeping. All the family was weeping. All the Yanomamö were in the house weeping loudly. Bautista came into the bedroom. He put his hand on my shoulder and tried to comfort me. "Milimi," he said, "I know how you feel because I have gone through this many times. But, Milimi, we have a hope. We will see her again. She is safe with Jesus. Someday we'll see her again. She has not gone away forever."

I thanked this dear man who had comforted me, and in spite of my sorrow I rejoiced as I told the Lord that this is what it is all about, this hope that we have that can keep us going in the midst of sorrow and tragedy.

They brought the casket home. Poor Mike was as thin as a rail and looking so haggard and ill, hardly able to comprehend all that had happened to his life. Little Stephen was now well enough to come home also, but oh, what sorrow, what upheaval these little ones faced.

Renee's mother and sister Debbie came too, and our two youngest, Joe and Jerald, came from the States, joining our sorrowing group. Our four sons stood at the plane that had just brought the two youngest boys in, huddled in a circle with heads bowed and arms around each other, and wept. Our oldest son, Steve, had been financially unable to make the trip. It was a hard time for all. But, by the grace of God, He took us through it, although I can't say that I have ever gotten over it. It is still very painful for me to remember.

Renee's body rests up in the little white-picketed cemetery that Mike had built for her. Her lovely spirit is with the Lord. We will always remember the beautiful black-haired girl with the lovely white smile who was part of our family for a short twelve years. We look forward to that day when we will all be together again.

40

THE UNPRECEDENTED FLOOD OF '96

I n the dark morning hours of June 7, 1996, I paced the floor when I was not putting hems in ten bright red skirts that I was making for the Yanomamö women. I had sewn them up during spare time in the previous two days and was using this time when I could not sleep to get them hemmed. They were washed away the next day in the flood, so it was wasted time.

Then, early in the morning, the water came into the houses in Cosh. By evening it was window high. Since our houses were made of rammed earth, we weren't sure just how quickly they would collapse, so we were afraid to stay in them. However, we kept moving things to higher places in the house and into other houses where the water had not come in.

By the end of the day, the water had entered all the houses, and we knew we were in for a long, hard night. The church was the first to go. It was heartbreaking to see the large sections of walls falling into the raging waters and benches floating off downriver.

We wearily bedded down on the upstairs floor of Faith's new (unused and unfinished) cement blockhouse. Some of us were on mattresses and others in hammocks.

All night long we listened to the waters splashing under us and the sounds of the houses falling into the floodwaters. Large sections of wall were still falling out of the church. Then we heard a loud crash closer by. Everyone dashed to the open door to see which house was going next, and we saw Bautista's house going down.

Each time we heard another crash we jumped up and rushed to the door to see whose house had gone. We never closed our eyes all night. The whole back wall of Steve's house had fallen out. They had just left for the States for furlough.

Our new school building was falling also. I had been so proud and happy to think it would be ready for a new term in October. Now it would never be used to see Yanomamö boys and girls being educated.

Animals were having a very hard time, as there was not a dry place to put their feet. The goats were drowning and some of the Yanomamö brethren came in the dark of night, dragging them into their canoes and taking them to higher land up on the cattle field.

Chickens and turkeys were given to the people to eat, as there was no way to save them from drowning. Dogs and cats were crying and yowling. We managed to get them up on my sofas that we had moved into Faith's house, thinking the water would not get there, as it never had in all our years here. Now it was two meters up the walls and still rising. The sofas were wet, but Sharon coaxed the dogs up on them, where they whined and cried all night.

In all the houses, furniture and articles that we had kept putting up higher and higher finally succumbed to the raging current. Refrigerators, freezers, cupboards—to name just a few things—floated around. Things that had been put up on them for safekeeping were plunged into the water. The walls that fell floated downriver too.

The Yanomamö had fled across the river when the water first came into their houses, so they actually did not lose their possessions, although their mud and pole houses were gone.

They took the kids and us women out to Tamatama by speed-boat on Saturday. As I climbed down the wobbly aluminum ladder into the speedboat below, I could see that the water was up to the top of my front door. Chain link fences were completely submerged. We flew from Tamatama to Puerto Ayacucho on Sunday.

It was so hard to leave Joe and the others behind in Cosh amidst the floodwaters. Joe had set up a kitchen in the upstairs of Faith's house (the only place out of the water). He was cooking and keeping the other men's spirits up.

They continued their early Morning Prayer meetings, though the Bible classes were suspended for a time. Every morning found the canoes tied to the upstairs porch poles and the Yanomamö men squatting on the floor alongside our men, all with bowed heads, lifting their hearts and voices to the One who was able to hear and answer their prayers for help and protection.

On June 12, I wrote to our faithful prayer warriors in churches at home in the United States.

Velma, her three children, Sharon, and Mike's oldest boy, Joshua, went up to Tamatama today by plane. We got word this morning that the water has gone down a good ways. They have just a short time to get in there and check to see if there are things that are still salvageable so they can clean them up before they ruin completely. Then, the water will come up again for a second rising. It always rises again after it has gone down.

They are going to Cosh by speedboat. Faith, her children, and Mike's other two boys will go to TT [Tamatama] tomorrow by boat, and she is going to stay in TT and keep all the small children there. The older boys will go up to help with the cleaning up work.

Now we will have to find a better, higher place and start over again. We were so close to being through with the building. All of us had good, comfortable homes, and we thought that now we could forget about all that for awhile.

This is a bitter blow, but we know that we are in a warfare. We may be "knocked down." but we are not "knocked out." We are counting on your prayers in these days!

41

TOTAL DEVASTATION

After the waters went down, I returned to the village to find a very dismal and discouraging sight of the devastation left by the floodwaters. Our normal work was at a standstill. We were now involved with survival, not only for our work and ourselves but also for the indigenous people.

Falciparum malaria was hitting hard. Bad living conditions out in the wet and chill of the jungle were making many ill. There were many new babies and pregnant women who would now suffer without a decent roof over their heads. With the help of a flood relief fund set up by some of God's faithful servants in the States, we began to hand out food, hammocks, blankets, and mosquito nets.

Yanomamö flocked to Cosh from villages far and near. Many visitors moved here and set up shacks across the river as the Cosh people moved back to their village and tried to get set up again.

This made the number very great of those needing to be fed, supplied with blankets, hammocks and nets, and given medical attention. A couple of Venezuelan army helicopters flew in some supplies that helped out.

We were kept busy as we continued with the hard and dirty work of trying to clean up things left lying in the mud and water. We managed to get some items operating again. Other items, for all our work of cleaning and polishing, had to be returned to the junk heap as unfixable.

Those of our number who had been there while I was still in Puerto Ayacucho had the hard and unpleasant job of cleaning all the mud, silt, and grime off the floors, walls, and everything we owned. I could appreciate what they had gone through to get it looking as well as it did.

Thank the Lord I still had my computer. I had had it moved first to Gary's house. Then, as it became obvious that the house was filling up with water, I had had it moved to the upstairs of Faith's house. My translation materials were still on the computer.

Everything that I had on paper and in notebooks was gone, but I thanked the Lord I still had my computer materials. I had stayed in Puerto Ayacucho and worked on translation, keeping the outside world informed of conditions upriver as I heard them via shortwave radio and praying for those still up there in the hard place.

"Brethren we need your prayers as we have never needed them before!" I wrote to our churches at home. "Satan is determined to put an end to this work," I wrote. "But 'Greater is He that is in you, than he that is in the world' [1 John 4:4]. We know that Jesus is the Victor. We stand with Him! Bear us up before the throne! Thank you!"

42

JUST TRYING TO SURVIVE

For two months we did not get out any word of our situation due to our being completely taken up with the work we were involved in and being too exhausted at night to do anything but fall into bed at night and sleep. In September 1996, I wrote again.

These last few months have been a time of just trying to survive and get on our feet again after all the devastation. At this present time, we are all living together in the house mentioned and are trying as best we can under these trying circumstances to live. We continue to serve the people with medicine, which is handled by Sharon, and with food, which is handled by Timoteo and Lanzo (two of the Yanomamö brethren), but it is distributed from our house.

We still have daily Bible classes with the men and also the women. We are slowly getting this house in a more livable condition. This included getting in a functioning toilet and shower and fixing the bathroom floor, which was still all dug up for the plumbing.

A door was also made into the bathroom from the hallway, giving privacy to our bedroom, and doors are hung at the two bedrooms upstairs. Upstairs the families have to make do with rooms made of sheets.

There are usually from fifteen to twenty or so people living here in the house. With so many people living here and visitors coming and going who must live right in with us, it makes for very close fellowship. We ask for you to continue to hold us up in prayer that we will keep close accounts with each other and to the people with all their demands on our time and strength. There have been and still are many, many Yanomamö visitors who come for food, medicine, and help in their despair and disorientation. It has been hard as there are so many sick to deal with, so many hungry to satisfy, and so many people around all the time.

Many of these people have sent word from their flooded villages that they need help and so our men have had to make long trips in the boats to go and get these needy ones and bring them here. Then when they are well and feel able, they have to be returned to their homes. All of these things take time and use strength and energy. Many of our own family have been battling malaria, diarrhea, vomiting, and aching bodies, so we are all in this together.

However, it has been a blessing in the fact that it has given a great opportunity for presenting the gospel to those from far off who were still unreached.

Jaime went on a three-day journey and brought back some people from the village of Auwei-teli. They were here for help and medicine. Jaime called them together each evening to his house. There, he proceeded to spend time giving them the gospel.

Gary was coming back from turning off the electrical plant one night and heard him as he passed by Jaime's house. Jaime was singing the hymns to them and then he would go over each song verse by verse, explaining exactly what it meant. He was doing a tremendous job sharing his faith with these ones who had never been taught God's Message! This was done spontaneously and all on his own! Praise the Lord!

He did this the whole time the people were here. They left having been presented with the claims of Christ. This has been being done not only by Jaime but also by many of the Christian brethren. Both men and women are witnessing and sharing their faith with those visitors who are living in their houses at this time.

In the midst of just trying to survive during these trying days, we had to also begin to prepare for moving the whole community to another location. During this time I also wrote in my letters:

Work is being done in getting the new location ready for rebuilding. It has been hard because there has still been so much rain, and the land already saturated from the flood does not absorb the water, so there is so much mud and puddles are still standing. We have been trying to get materials up to start our building program.

The first boat load we sent up filled with cement, flood relief food, gasoline, and diesel fuel sank to the bottom of the river. Everything was lost, and the owner of the boat almost lost his life. He is a good friend and Christian brother.

However, in this disaster also, Satan overplayed his hand. This man has been a Christian for years but has not had a strong testimony. He is now witnessing and says he can't keep quiet. He is a joyful and radiant Christian and is making the fact known everywhere that he was as good as drowned, but the Lord delivered him and gave him another chance to serve Him. This is what he wants to do. He just recently arrived in Cosh with 320 bags of cement and some reinforcement rods. One of his crew accepted the Lord while they were here in Cosh, so praise the Lord! Satan meant it for evil to us, but God brought good from it. He uses the wrath of men and devils to praise Him!

Another merchant who was bringing up cement and other supplies for us was hit by a big windstorm while tied up in one of the ports. Waves swamped the back end of his boat, and he lost our 200 bags of cement that were on board. So it is obvious that Satan does not want Cosh rebuilt. However, we have now managed to get over 500 bags of cement here and are pushing forward with the program.

Right now we are working on getting in the foundation for the metal building that Mike had brought down before. This will be used to store our supplies for building.

We have a Christian Colombian fellow working with us, Oscar Tovar, who is heading up the work on this. He seems very adept and knowledgeable of what he is doing. He hopes to bring his wife and four children up from Puerto Ayacucho so that he can continue to stay and help us in this big project of getting a new village set back up again. He is a tremendous witness to Spanish-speaking people who come through. Pray for him and his family.

43

NEW YANOMAMÖ TESTAMENTS ARRIVE

T HE WORK CONTINUES IN COSH!" I wrote in November of 1996.

Most of the land has been cleared. Three footers for missionary houses have been laid and the fourth has been started. The metal storage building that Mike brought down a couple of years ago for the Savannah project (which has never gotten off the ground) has been erected at the new site and will be used for storing building supplies.

Mike spent a month in Caracas when our container containing our new Woodmizer sawmill and our pipe for our sewer system came in, as the customs gave him a hard time. We had finished filling up the container with used clothing and blankets donated by friends and church groups. We also had a number of boxes of medicine that we had received for helping in the flood relief. The clothes and medicine were what held us up at customs even though Mike told them of the disaster of the flood and that this was given to help those suffering from the devastation of the flood.

It was finally passed through customs after we paid a large customs fee, and we are happy to have the things. The sawmill is already in Cosh, and lumber is being cut to use in rebuilding our homes and buildings as well as homes for the natives. I want to hasten to assure those of you I wrote who are concerned about the rain forest that we are allowed to cut into lumber only those logs felled by the Yanomamö in making their gardens. There is no devastation going on.

Everything was not bleak and dismal during this time. In spite of the chaos around us we were able to write in our October-November News Report:

PRAISE THE LORD! The new Yanomamö New Testaments have now arrived in Caracas from Korea, where they were printed up. Being completely out of New Testaments for about three years, we had had a reprint done of 5,000 New Testaments. Our first printing of the New Testament was done and presented in 1984. We have been waiting so long for them, and since most of the peoples' old Bibles were lost during the flood, they have been begging us for new ones. Since our supply had run out even before the flood, we had to keep sadly turning them away.

We received a call from our Aduana (customs) agent last night, as he knew we were supposed to be here in Puerto Ayacucho at this time taking care of correspondence. As soon as we get the necessary papers and the custom fees up to him, he will be getting them out of the customs and shipped on down here to us. We are so thrilled, and we know the Yanomamö will be too. A greenhouse owner in Virginia so graciously paid for having the New Testaments printed up and shipped.

44

TIMOTEO

M ilimi, do you have some extra song books that we can take with us?"

I looked up into Timoteo's sparkling brown eyes. He and Lanzo stood there, grinning at me. These are two of the young men who are being greatly used of the Lord in getting out the Word of God to other villages.

"Why do you need extra songbooks?" I asked. This was a Thursday morning, and they usually wait until the weekend to go out.

"Some of the Ocamo people just talked to us by radio, and they asked us to come and preach to them and teach them," Timmy replied. "So a group of us are going there and preach and teach today and tomorrow. We will return home tomorrow night."

I found some extra songbooks and, putting them in a plastic bag to protect them in case of rain, I handed them to him.

"Pray for us," he said. "Every time we come to your mind, pray for us. We will need much prayer to get through to these people because they think they are already good enough."

I promised him that we would indeed pray.

Saturday night Timoteo again walked into the house. "I haven't heard yet how your trip went, Timoteo," I said.

He obligingly sat down and with a happy grin and shiny eyes he told me the whole story of his time at the Ocamo-teli village.

"We arrived there about 4:00 p.m.," he said. "As soon as we arrived, some of the young men left to go to nearby villages and call people from those villages—Lechosa-teli, Cashalaowa-teli, and others. When they arrived back, we immediately started preparations for our meeting. I pulled the cord and started up our little generator and hung up the cord with our light bulb.

"People began filing in, and soon the building we were meeting in was crowded. We began to sing hymns of praise, and we sang and sang and sang. Then, some of the younger men came in, and they acted a little bit upset. 'Hurry up and finish singing,' said one. 'We are prepared to have a party, and we want to get started dancing.'

"'I don't know anything about your dance,' I replied. 'I don't do that. I came here to hold a meeting to preach and teach, because you people called me. That's what I am going to do. If you all want to dance, go ahead, but that's not what we are here for,' I replied.

"'Well, all those that are supposed to be at the dance are here listening to you,' he said angrily.

"But even though he called them, no one got up to go. They sat there and listened to the preaching and teaching. We closed at 10:00 p.m., and then everyone left for the dance. [They have learned the western style of dancing from their trips into Puerto

Ayacucho.] They turned their tape player on full volume and started dancing and making a lot of racket.

"The next day we started in to preaching and teaching again. Several from our group of nine spoke and gave the message to them. Finally one of the young men from Ocamo stood up and said that he wanted to speak.

"'I am a Christian,' he said. 'Just like you all are. I'm a Christian and just like you all have been baptized, I have been baptized. We are all the same. Even though you have different foreigners living with you, we have foreigners living with us too [Catholic Mission]. There is only one God, and so we are all the same. I like this word that you are teaching and preaching. I like to hear it. But there is something that you Christians say that I'm unwilling to hear. So, if you come to teach us, don't say that anymore. I don't want to hear it. We're just as good Christians as you are, but we won't listen to that one thing that you say,' he declared and sat down.

"I stood up," said Timoteo. "'What is it that you are unwilling to hear?' I asked him.

"'You Coshilowa-teli Christians say that it is wrong for us to go on in our old ways once we become Christians. You say we should not have our bone-drinking festivals and do all the things our ancestors have always done. I greatly delight to drink bones and have our festivals. You tell us not to take dope and do witchcraft anymore. These things are just our culture. They don't have anything to do with whether we are Christians or not. So I don't want to hear anymore about it. You all are just imitating the foreigners. We intend to keep our cultural ways,' he said.

"I started to speak and answer him, but just then Tito [one of the older men who had gone along] stood up and said that he would like to speak. Tito really spoke well.

"This is what he said: 'I'm an old man. I'm not just a youngster. I'm a Christian, and I've been a Christian for many years. I used to do all the things that you all are doing. I took dope. I delighted to do it. I was always right there for our bone-drinking festivals, and I delighted to take part in all of it. I walked around with my lower lip heavy from a large cud of tobacco. I painted myself all up and decked myself out with feathers and flirted with all the women, just like you all love to do. I loved it too. I flirted and sinned with the women. My older brother [Bautista] was a shaman. He took dope and called the spirits, just like you all like to do. Why are we different now? Because many years ago we found the true God, and we now worship Him. We have changed because we are His children, and He is our Father. He has made us new. Don't just keep saying that we are imitating the foreigners. We are following the teaching of God's Word. We have the Word of God in our language. We read it for ourselves. Whether there are foreigners living with us or not, we will continue to follow God's Word because now we have the truth,' Tito said and sat down."

"There was complete stillness in the room," continued Timoteo, "except for some of the older men murmuring amongst themselves that what Tito had said was true, because they had known him and his older brother since childhood. Tito and Bautista had indeed participated in all the things he mentioned and more too, but now they were different as everyone knew," Timoteo said.

"Then, I stood up, and I held up God's Word. 'You all say that we are imitating the foreigners and that it is not wrong for Christians to continue in their cultural ways. But I want to show you from God's Word that if your cultural ways go against the Word of God, you must put them away from you and walk in the light of God's Word. It's not me that you are arguing with, it is God Himself,' I said.

"I read Romans 12:2 to them. 'This tells us not to let our Yanomamö culture be what controls us but that our ways are to be pure and acceptable to God,' I said.

"'Most of our old ways and beliefs did not come from God. They cause us to think impure thoughts and do sinful things. Therefore, since as Christians we have new hearts, we are to live new and different lives,' I said.

"Then, I read to them many verses from God's Word where He tells us to cease from sinning and do good—strong verses where he tells us how to live in order to be pleasing to Him. The place was very quiet. After I closed in prayer, many men began to come up to me and tell me that God's Word was beautiful and that they saw now that it really was God Himself who was telling them how to live. We had not just been making it up.

"'Do you have other Bibles with you?' they asked. Everyone began clamoring for a Bible. I had eight Bibles with me and gave those away. Many more begged me to send them a Bible when someone else came back to preach again, which I promised to do.

"'Let's don't wait around. Let's call these Christians back again and again so that they can teach us this good word,' they said to each other.

"Milimi, I left there so happy. The Lord did a marvelous work there, and He will continue to work in their hearts. We had a wonderful time giving them God's Word," he finished up.

He shared all of this again at the Sunday morning service as he filled the congregation in on how the Lord had worked on the missionary trip they had made. We all left there with overflowing hearts at what the Lord is doing in Yanomamö hearts.

All of this happened in 1998 amongst the Yanomamö people in spite of the fact that rebuilding our village again was going awfully slow, due to lack of finances and building materials at the site. Still, we knew that God's time is not our time, and He does all things well. We were able to rejoice that Yanomamö are coming into the kingdom of God. That is what is all-important.

One of the most blessed things concerning our work here has been that all of our ten children and their spouses are born again Christians, and eight out of the ten are back in Venezuela in the Yanomamö work with us. Our two youngest boys, while not in Venezuela, are involved in the work by helping out with their finances and computer knowledge, even coming down to the field for months at a time to help us out in a project. Jerald was a big part in getting the manuscript ready for the reprinting of the New Testament. He and his family spent nine months with us in Cosh and much time after returning to the States working on this.

Joe's brother, Wes, and his wife, Sylvia, who took us to the training camp in Pennsylvania when we first started on this long journey of being missionaries to the Yanomamö, have continued with us through the years. They've supplied a home away from home to our children as they returned to the United States for Bible school or college. They've always been there for our kids when they needed them. Now they are doing the same for the grandchildren who, praise the Lord, are also entering back into the work. Wes and Sylvia also take care of business things in the States that we are not there to do and make purchases for us of things we can't get in Venezuela. We praise the Lord for them as they are valuable to our work.

45

WHAT GOES AROUND COMES AROUND

It's an old saying I've heard all my life, and I guess there is a lot of truth in it. What goes around comes around.

I remember that after "He has a mouth," "Shoefoot," or Bautista, whichever name you prefer to call him by, had become a born-again Christian and a real man of God, I said once to Joe, "Wouldn't it be something if the Lord would someday use some of the Yanomamö people to take His Word back to the United States from which we brought it to them?"

As we read our mail from home and heard many of the things that were happening back there, our hearts were saddened. We realized that, as the small group of believers here in Cosh was expanding, back home in our own country people were turning from the true Word and worshipped idols, things made by the hand of man. Spiritism and demon worship had become prevalent in a once great Christian country. "Professing themselves to be wise, they became fools" (Rom. 1:22).

Well, in essence, "What goes around comes around."

That is just what has happened. The Lord has used this little Yanomamö man in a marvelous way. In these last few years since Mark Ritchie, the author of *Spirit of the Rainforest*, portrayed Shoefoot's (Bautista's) life as an apprentice shaman along with Jungle-man, his mentor Bautista has made a number of trips to the United States.

There, he has spoken in well-known universities before well-educated people. This little Yanomamö man from the Amazon rain forest, probably not much more than five feet tall and probably weighing less than eighty pounds soaking wet, has astounded some of the more learned men in the wisdom which God has given him.

He stands fearless before these people. With Gary as his interpreter, he answers their questions. He's not ashamed of the gospel of Christ. He's always ready to point out the truth to these ones who are "trying to get back to Mother Earth and find the true beginnings." He tells them that what they're searching for they have already rejected in rejecting the Word that is nigh them, right there in their own country, for the taking and the believing.

In one of the big colleges, a young woman stood and asked a question. She wanted to know why he thought it was necessary to bring God into their picture in order to have all these changes in their lives of which he was speaking. She told him that she was not a believer. She said she had moved to the States with her parents. They had fled for refuge to the States to escape war in their country. She said that she now enjoyed all the benefits of which he spoke even though she herself was not a believer in Jesus Christ.

"It's not necessary for you Yanomamö to bring God into the picture. Your people can change without Him and be just as well off," she insisted.

Without batting an eyelash, Bautista answered her with wisdom from the Holy Spirit of God.

"You say that even though you don't believe in God or His Son, you are doing fine. You say that you don't need Him to live well and experience the good things of life and have peace and happiness," he said. "Well, take this as an example. Just suppose that I'm in my country, and I'm out in the forest. I realize that a storm is going to come up, so I quickly chop some small poles and cut some leaves and soon have myself a small hut to keep off the rain that's beginning to fall. Suddenly, there you are seeking to get under my shelter and get out of the rain. I move over and let you under the roof with me. So there you are keeping dry under my roof. You didn't do anything to help make the shelter, but you're enjoying it. I've been told that the people who first came to this country from across the great waters came seeking a safe place to serve the God of Heaven. I'm told that this country was founded on the teaching of God's Word. So now everything that you have and enjoy is a result of the message of Christ that made this country what it is. You're sheltering under the blessings of God's people here in this country. Someday when the shelter is removed, your blessings will be gone also, and then it'll be too late for you," he told her.

She sat back down and didn't say another word.

A few years ago a millionaire from California came down to visit the rain forest and us here at Cosh. He had been raised as a missionary kid but was seeking for himself to know Truth, not being satisfied that the faith of his parents was his faith as well. Before coming to Cosh he had even gotten into channeling spirits in his search for truth.

He went on a trip with Gary, Mike, and some of the Yanomamö Christians to another village. Through Mike as an interpreter, he began asking Bautista about shamanism. He was very interested in this side of Yanomamö life, hoping, I think, to find something he hadn't found before. Bautista had been told of his beliefs and his problems with accepting the faith that he had learned as a child of missionary parents.

Bautista looked him in the eye and told him, "You already have the truth. If you reject the truth that you have, then there is nothing else for you. Christ is the only way. You're seeking truth in the things that I've given up and thrown away because I found out it was all emptiness and lies. Now you won't find truth there. If you don't accept Christ as the truth, there's no where else to search!"

This man was so impressed with the testimony of this Yanomamö man and what he saw in his life that he returned at a later date, stood up in one of our church meetings, and testified that at that time he had put his faith in Christ to save him. He's been a changed man ever since.

Later he asked Bautista what he could do for him.

"Is there something that you need?" he asked Bautista. "I'd like to get it for you," he said.

Bautista thought for a few minutes. He knew that this man had a lot of money and if he so desired, he could buy Bautista just about anything that he might ask for.

"Well, I really don't need anything," he said. This little man who had a large family of small children and practically nothing material to his name felt that he had all he needed.

"I have the Lord," he said. "I have God's Word to read in my own language. I have a wife and family. I have a good garden. God has blessed me. I don't need anything," he said.

What a testimony to the power of God in a yielded life! To God be the glory! He has done a wonderful work in the hearts of many Yanomamö people who will be singing praises around His throne.

That's why as we have looked back over the years at all that God has done here in this place, Joe and I can say with joyful hearts, "This is my story, this is my song. Praising my Savior all the day long!"

Overqualified

Overqualifieder.

Joey Comeau

ECW Press

For Adrian.

Dear Reader,

Thank you for taking the time to read this, my second collection of cover letters. But before you start, I wanted to make something clear. This is a different book from the first. This volume is a collection of more funny letters, and not an experimental novel in the way the first sometimes was. There is no hidden narrative in these pages. No story of a doomed romance, no struggles with the death of a loved one. Though every letter is signed with my name, you'll find a different sort of crazy person at the heart of each.

Also worth noting: every one of these letters was actually sent to a company, and not one of them ever replied. It breaks my heart.

I hope you like the book.

Joey Comeau

Dear Disney,

I am writing to apply for a position as anything with your company. I don't care if you have me parking cars. Yesterday was my three-month anniversary of looking for work, and my dad says that I can't find a job because I'm not a gay, crippled immigrant, so you can understand why it'd be nice to move out.

Joey Comeau

Dear Radiotech,

Thank you for taking the time to consider me for the position of Radiographer with your company. The first time I ever saw an X-ray machine, I was coming through airport security, with my dad. I must have been eight years old at the time, and the customs official put my teddy bear through the machine just like my mom said he would.

He took my whole family into this little room, and I was terrified. But my dad wasn't. My dad kept smiling the whole time, and his voice was real quiet. He stood between the security guard and us, and he said, "We can do this the easy way or the hard way," and the official laughed nervously and patted the gun on his hip.

"Oh yeah?" he said, and my dad just nodded, real slow.

"The easy way," my dad said, "is I knife you."

Later on, when I was in my first year of university, I lived with a friend named Alex. When I found myself once again covering Alex's rent money, my mom told me, "Never lend money to a friend, because you lose both the money and the friend." My father told her to mind her own business. He said, "Let him make his own mistakes, Karen."

After three months of covering his rent, I was out of money and desperate. Week after week, Alex kept telling me that he'd pay me when he had "the money to spare," and I didn't know what to do. So I called my father, and he told me exactly what had to be done. Step by step. His voice was quiet and calm.

I woke up early the next morning and went into Alex's room, where he was sleeping. I carefully set a phonebook, open halfway, on his stomach and then I took a hammer to him.

Waiting for the taxi to take us to the hospital, I told him, "We can do this the easy way or the hard way," and Alex just stared at me, clutching his stomach, tears on his face. "The easy way," I told him, "is I knife you. The hard way is you start giving me straight answers about my money, and we can work on rebuilding the trust that is essential to our friendship."

At the hospital, I watched as the technicians X-rayed him, looking for internal damage. I thought, "This is a cushy job. All you have to do is push a button and keep your goddamned mouth shut."

I decided that I wanted to be a Radiographer.

Joey Comeau

Dear NSCC,

I am sending you my resume in the hopes that you will hire me for the position of Research Assistant with the Nova Scotia Community College. I have extensive experience working with GIS software, and I would like to take a minute to better outline my qualifications.

Last night, I was in bed with a boy (whose name escapes me just now), and afterward he said, "When did you know you were gay? Thirteen? Fourteen?"

I smiled as wide as I could, and I told him, "Oh, I wasn't gay when I was a kid."

"Oh no?" he said, with that knowing grin. He ran his fingers over the tattoo that runs across my torso, "GEOGRAPHIC INFORMATION SYSTEMS 4 LIFE."

"Nope," I said. "I turned gay when I was twenty-one years old, on February 15th." I gave him a playful kiss on the cheek. "It was cold and grey, and I was on my way home from the movies. I had just gone to see a showing of *Fight Club*, and I remember thinking that there had been too many shirtless men. A car came out of nowhere, and I didn't have time to jump out of the way. Later, the doctors said that it was unlikely the accident had caused my homosexuality. But I knew better."

"What?" he said.

"I was hit by a car," I told him. "And now I'm gay."

Sorry for the trip down memory lane, NSCC, I know it's not standard for a cover letter, but I think it is important to explain myself. You see, it's like that with GIS, too. A second, similar accident happened to me about two years ago: a bus stopped too quickly, causing me to lose my balance and hit my head, leaving me with the desire to devote my life to geographic information programming.

I've done nothing but study GIS and sleep with men since the accidents. I've never been one to question the hand I'm dealt.

I look forward to hearing from you about this position.

Joey Comeau

Dear Northwood Care,

I am writing to apply for the position of Marketing Director at Northwood Care. You want someone who can meet your subscriber and revenue growth needs. I believe I could help you surpass them. I'm including my resume, which details the extensive experience I have working in marketing, as well as my experience with the elderly and the physically challenged.

But allow me to propose something. Your company cares for the elderly and the infirm. In order to understand how you can increase the number of your subscribers, I think it is valuable to examine the reasons that people choose to place themselves or their loved ones in your care.

When people are no longer able to take care of themselves, or when their loved ones are no longer able to take care of them, it is sometimes best for them to seek professional care. But what if there were other pressures that led people to seek your services? What if you yourself were to introduce new market pressures, creating need where before there had been none?

Imagine, if you will, an elderly woman with an adequate retirement fund. This woman has no family, but she takes good care of herself and is in good health; she has no need for your services. Your old marketing strategists would have looked on her as being outside of your potential subscriber base, and that is a mistake.

What if that woman were to fall out of the back of a speeding car and break her hip irrevocably? If this woman lived in your small town, she would have several options for care. She may choose you, she may not. It's a free country. But what if someone had whispered a suggestion to her before she accidentally fell from that car? What if she felt she would be somehow safer at your home for the infirm and the physically challenged? Somehow less likely to find herself physically challenged again?

I hope that you will contact me about this position. I feel that we could make great things happen together, and we could help a large number of people find the care and, more importantly, the security they need.

Yours,
Joey Comeau

Dear Frito-Lay potato chip company,

I don't know if an email cover letter can properly express the admiration I feel for men and women who have become rich off potato chips. Thank you. Seriously, THANK YOU, for taking the time to review my resume. I realize that the last time I applied for a job with your company, I accidentally included an instant messenger transcript that reflected poorly on my character, but I have fixed the copy-and-paste bug that led to that particular CHRIS SAYS: also, i thought that a great new trend to start would be to yell something insane every time i orgasm with a girl.....like, "HERE COMES THE CRAZY JUICE." Wait. I told you that one, didn't I?

JOEY SAYS: You did. I mentioned it in bed this evening, actually.

CHRIS SAYS: What about the one where I yell "I HATE MY DAD" when I come.

JOEY SAYS: I love you, man.

Which is exactly the sort of experience and underlying motivation that makes for a valuable employee, I think you'll agree. CHRIS SAYS: or you could just yell "GIVE IT BACK. GIVE IT BACK."

JOEY SAYS: haha. Or "CAN YOU HEAR THAT MUSIC? IS THAT YOUR BEEF PEACH SINGING TO ME?" copy-and-paste problems are JOEY SAYS: or "MY

COLONISTS! MY COLONISTS ARE COLONIZING YOUR BEEF PEACH!" Technical know-how and potato chip enthusiasm. And that said, I look forward to hearing from you regarding this position.

Yours,
JOEY SAYS: "BEEEEEEEF PEACH" Comeau

Dear Alpin,

I am writing to apply for a position as Inside Account Executive, though perhaps I should wait until I'm less upset to send this email. I'm not a "racist." I respect people of all races equally, or I'm trying to. It takes time to check and make sure.

You can't just say "every race is equal" without doing any research. That's not SCIENTIFIC. What if the Chinese really were all monsters? Just because something isn't polite to say, that doesn't make it automatically false. Don't get me wrong, I had a Chinese girlfriend last year, so this is obviously just an example. I'm certain now that they're perfectly nice people.

The Arabs, too. After I went out on a few dates with the TA from my Semitic Languages seminar while at university, I no longer doubted that Arabs were indeed an equal people. In fact, if I had to compare, I would say that she was a little more equal than some of the white girls I've dated. She had a sense of adventure, anyway.

You can see why I'm so upset over this. I am many things — efficient, energetic, charismatic — all of which would make me an asset to your company. I would excel as an Inside Account Executive with your firm, and it tears me apart that she thinks I'm a racist.

So now I'm a racist. Why? Because she found my checklist?

I'm a scientist, is all that is. Should I just go around saying, "all races are equal" without having checked for myself? So, I keep a checklist of the different races of women I've been with. Every scientist keeps notes.

And I can't just trust the books other people have written, can I? You can't believe everything you read. People can just make up any old thing and write it down. Hands-on experience is the only knowledge that you can really trust these days.

She asked me why I hadn't put a check mark in the box next to Indian Women. (She's Indian, is why she asked.)

"Well, I haven't had enough time to decide," I told her. THAT's why she called me a racist.

In any case, I have included my resume for your review, and I think you'll find that I have a lot to offer your company. And, judging by the list of surnames I found for some of your lady executives, your company has a lot to offer me as well.

Yours,
Joey Comeau

Dear Spherion Recruiting,

I am writing to apply for the position of Warehouse Assistant because "Warehouse Assistant" sounds so innocuous, so unassuming. I am writing to apply for the position of Warehouse Assistant because this morning was the first time I ever thought seriously about killing myself, and if I'm going to do it, I want to do it right. I'm not going to do this half-assed. I have a plan.

I want the newspaper listing of my death to start off with "Joey Comeau, a hard-working family man, who, in addition to his office job, worked weekends as a Warehouse Assistant in the suburbs to make ends meet, killed himself today." I'll leave a note for the police, with a list of names, some of them underlined in red. At the top of the list it will say, "I couldn't keep quiet any longer. The public is in danger." When they investigate, they'll find that these are people from my past, but they won't remember me.

After time, the police will realize that these men and women all work for companies that have at one time used the warehouse I'm working in. This second connection will be the clincher. When they can find nothing there, they'll look deeper; they'll start finding connections of their own, connections that are nothing more than coincidence. The human brain is a pattern-recognition machine.

If suicide is all I have left, it has to be something more than just spectacular or horrifying. This morning, staring at myself in the mirror, I almost decided to just write a normal, honest letter. But no, my suicide has to be everything my life should have been. My suicide has to be a mystery, a quest, a story worth reading.

It has to be my legacy.

When they talk to my wife, she'll say I've been distant for the past few years. She'll say that our money is gone, and she doesn't know what I did with it. And these will just be clues. These will just be infuriating pieces to a puzzle that will hang over everyone's head. My children will grow up in a world with a sense of the hidden, of the wondrous. In five years, when my son turns sixteen, a law firm halfway across the world will mail him a letter.

As each of my children reaches sixteen, they'll get a letter in the mail.

"I did what I did," it will say, "for you, for my God, and for my country. Please forgive me."

I took a picture of myself in a suit, and the letter will have a copy of that picture attached to it with a paperclip. I look very serious in that photograph.

Their father was more than just a screw-up. He was SOMETHING.

This is all I have left. Please help me. Please hire me to work in your warehouse. I have no trouble working machinery, lifting boxes, filling out forms. I am a dedicated worker.

Joey Comeau

Dear MoneyMart,

You posted seeking a Cash Applications Manager. Good. You can't lump cash under the umbrella term "money." Cash is a creature with its own needs, with its own inclinations and territories. Cash is a pervert, with desires that aren't easy to understand. You need someone with experience living outside the world of plastic. You need someone who can successfully guide your company under the radars of government taxation.

You're gonna get a lot of applications from people with business degrees. I should mention that I did not graduate high school. Three weeks before graduation, I was all set to head to business school. We had a party, and after everyone left, I was in the shower drunk and fell. I fell from the tub sideways, gashed the left side of my face, and lay there in silence. I could feel the hot water on the bottoms of my feet, which jutted into the tub. When I got up to face the mirror, I thought, "That's going to scar," and then I thought, "Good."

The cut ran down through my eye and gave me a dangerous look. Fuck this life tied to names and plastic money. I decided then and there, facing that mirror, to become a grifter, a shark, a con man. I would live under the radar, off the grid, outside of the movie euphemism for the interconnected computer systems that track and manage everyone in terms of credit, worth, and funds. The man in the mirror was a rogue agent now. He was a cowboy. I tried to squint like Clint Eastwood. It hurt.

I took my mother's purse and used her credit cards to get as much cash from a bank machine as I could. I left home, money strapped to my body in little hidden packets, and hopped a boxcar heading south. Nobody knows where I am or who I am. I can go into a delicatessen and buy a sandwich, eat in silence, and leave without a trace. Did I buy a drink with that sandwich? You'll never know.

I have a few questions before we meet regarding this position. Firstly, I assume that you can pay in cash? If not, would it be alright if I had you make the cheques payable to my mother? I can mail them to her, and she'll mail the cash back to me. It's inconvenient, but ultimately the cost is worth the freedom!

Yours,
Joey Comeau

Dear RIAA,

Thank you for taking the time to review my resume. It outlines the fifteen years of law enforcement experience at my disposal, and my many awards and honours accrued in that time. You do good work at the Recording Industry Association of America, but if you'll pardon my frankness, you are a joke to the very pirates you should be terrorizing.

I can teach you how to deal with those punks who thumb their noses at you. Just last month, a young man in an anti-WTO t-shirt was attacked in my neighbourhood. He was badly hurt, with a broken nose and something horribly wrong with his eye.

But when I offered to help him, the little bastard said, "Fuck off, pig. Shouldn't you be somewhere else, intimidating the men and women of this neighbourhood? Abusing your power so you can feel like a BIG MAN?" He sounded like the guys down at the station. They have the same problem you do, RIAA: they're not willing to go far enough. Only this kid wasn't trying to guide me toward the light like my pussy co-workers. He was just being disrespectful. "You're nothing but a government-subsidized playground bully," he said. "All police are."

So I laid it on thick. "Son, we're human beings, the same as you are. You can't paint a whole group of people with one big brush. I became a cop, because I wanted to help. I wanted to make my father proud. He died in the line, trying to save a woman from a gang of attackers, and I . . ." This is when I start to cry.

He had no idea what to do. He put his hand on my shoulder, and I cried harder. Eventually I managed to pull him into a hug. While he was nervously patting me on the back, I stuck my finger in my mouth and got it real wet with spit. Then I stuck it in his ear and gave him the nastiest wet willy anyone has ever given anyone.

He was like "WHAT" and I was laughing, man, because who would ever believe him?

"A police officer gave me a wet willy!" wouldn't last a minute in court. And people would think twice about pirating music if it called down the wrath of the RIAA in the form of crooked police officers grabbing them outside their schools or daycares and giving them painful and embarrassing wet willies.

Think about that.

Yours in blue,
Joey Comeau

Dear Apple,

Resumes and cover letters aren't my thing. But if that's
how you do it then that's how you do it. Here's my resume.
Here's my cover letter. The subcontracting situation that
I'm proposing, well, it already exists. I just want to let you
in on it. You and I are business partners already. You've been
putting shoes on my kids' feet for six months now.

When I was growing up, there were days when the milk ran
out. I didn't know what it meant that I ate my Cap'n Crunch
with cola at the end of the month. I didn't know what it
meant that we ate Kraft Dinner every day for lunch. Fuck,
man. I loved that stuff. It wasn't until my sister and I got a bit
older, and we didn't have a Nintendo, and we didn't have a
Super Nintendo. We didn't have a Genesis.

I wasn't like my sister, though. I didn't blame my mom for
that. I could see how hard she was working to get us what we
needed, without a dad around. Not a lot of kids would have
been able to see through their own shit, but how do you put
that on a resume? I guess that's why you need a cover letter.
Well, here's mine. I made friends, and when I didn't have a
Game Boy, I took someone else's.

Now I'm twenty-four, and I make my money the way I make
my money. A large part of that is you. A cellphone could
always catch you a few bucks, but it used to be luck of the
draw. Now it's all changed. Now you can't walk downtown
without passing twenty or thirty people, all sporting the

little white headphones, advertising that they're packing a thousand-dollar piece of equipment in those pockets. You got billboards all over the place, making that shit into fashion.

So, you and me, Apple, we're working together already.

Joey Comeau

Dear Microsoft,

Thank you for taking the time to review my resume. I am
excited for the opportunity to work for the company that
saved my marriage, and you can rest assured that I will
give my all. As my resume indicates, I've been a Computer
Programmer for sixteen years. Wanda and I were married
for eight of those.

My resume indicates my professional experience, which is a
good rundown of my skill set, but I'd like to talk about my
personal projects, which I believe show my ability to think
outside the box. You see, in the months before I lost Wanda
in a car accident, I started teaching her to program.

Those few programs that she left behind were simple, and
very often flawed, but they are all I have left of my Wanda,
besides her journal entries. She programmed on your
operating system, and with a little internet research I was
able to make a list of net-connected appliances I could
adapt to my needs.

It was short work to program each of those appliances
with the remains of my lost wife: fragments of her journal,
snippets of her programming. I was suddenly living in
a William Burroughs romance novel. Cups and plates
rattle when I pass and speak in their Microsoft-approved
synthesized voice, "July 31st. Joey is still spending more
time with the computer than with me. I am worried that the

romance is gone for good this time. My mother suggests that I pretend to share his interest, so that we can . . ."

The vacuum drives around in circles in the living room, saying, "We must have left the condom wrapper in the living room, but I can't find it for the life of me. If Joey finds it, how will I explain? Jack says not to worry. He'll be there to . . ."

Sometimes, my doorknobs won't let me inside at night. "September 16th. He's forgotten the anniversary again." But it's a success, Microsoft. Not a single day goes by where I don't get a glimpse of my wife. Not a day goes by where I don't hear her voice, simulated and authentic at once.

I would be an asset to your company. I look forward to hearing back from you about this position.

Yours,
Joey Comeau

Amazon,

Let me first thank you for taking the time to review my Resume. Enclosed, it should help illustrate just why i Am the right choice for a database programming position. Don't be dissuaded by my lack of professional experience in this field, as there are many similarities between my full-time hobby picking fights with fortune tellers and shamans, and developing best path and rudimentary artificial intelligence algorithms. i am certain that You will find me a valuable addition to your team.

I Have fits, sometimes. Unconscious, my body continues to act, Neither awake nor really asleep. Generally my unconscious body is only capable of watching reality television or reading books by doctor phil. Except, once, i woke to find that i'd written scraps of poetry and computer code with the red pen i use for practising my spelling and capitalization skills. Red ink stained my fingers.

For life is a grey slug lifting weights to impress a lady unicorn

Or, as Rimbauld said, "a fax machine that runs on broken hearts"

a Backend position with jungle books

will sate my

and when i typed in the source code, when i compiLed it and executed it, my screen flashed once, and i thought i caught a glimpse Of my father's face and just two words, all in capitals like some hidden message frOm the machine itself. the encyclopedia-assed gypsy i slapped said that my evil would come forth and "consume all of existence" or something. it's harD to tell what someone is saying when their head wobbles like that.

it almost seems now, as if every time i sit to program i have one of my fits, and when i wake there are pages and pages of code i don't understand. still, the programs all work just fine. my whole computer is new, and corrects me as i type.

i wish i could remember those two words. i feel like i'm not sleeping well at night.

yours,
joey comeau

Dear Walmart,

I am writing to apply for a position with your company, and I am including my resume for your review. It outlines my years of experience in retail and management, as well as my credentials and degrees in business. I hope that you will take the time to consider it, as well as this cover letter. Whenever I hear about Walmart in the newspapers, I think, "That's the company for me."

Everyone must be tired of women complaining 'bout the "glass ceiling," it can't just be you and me, Walmart. Glass ceiling, glass ceiling, glass ceiling. What is their PROBLEM? Have they ever even seen a glass ceiling? Greenhouses have glass ceilings. Glass ceilings are nice, man. They're classy. And anyway, they act like they're the only ones hard done by.

If they have a glass ceiling, what do we men have? That's right, a glass floor. Do you know how hard it is to concentrate on your job when you're constantly worried whether you've got gum or something on the bottom of your shoe? What if the breeding stock downstairs can see? Who will I fuck then?

It's not like they'd stop complaining if they were on the glass floor and we had the glass ceiling. They'd complain that we're constantly looking up their skirts! They'd organize some kind of media fiasco, demanding the right to wear panties so we can't see their unflushable pink toilets. Women will always demand more, Walmart. I'm glad you've drawn your line in the sand.

Hire me! I've got a dick.

Joey Comeau

Dear Random House,

I am writing because this morning I woke up with a phrase on my lips that I haven't been able to shake all day: "The girl's guide to being an asshole." Such a perfect title for a book.

One day soon, Random House, women are going to look around at the fat asshole men, at the sexist monsters in their workplace, at the sweaty throng of criminals and the quiet guile of thieves and assassins, and they're going to start wondering why they aren't having any of the fun. They're going to start asking, "What has the culture of victimization ever done for anyone?" and "Why can't we be degenerates and monsters and still be feminists?"

This is a genuine cultural movement, Random House, and you and me, we can profit. Big time. We can put together a guide, a guide to spitting and fighting dirty, a guide to coercion and date rape, a guide to vandalism and assault. It's idiotic to think that women are somehow incapable of these glorious pastimes. History has shown that on occasion they have revelled in these very acts. And, Random House, what woman has never felt debased hearing someone say, "I honestly don't believe a woman could be capable of such a crime," be it about child abuse or violent murder? Women are capable of anything.

Ours will be a guide to living outside of an outdated feminist culture that defines itself by vilifying the other. Our guide will help women embrace all of their potential, both good and bad, polite and vulgar, heroic and gloriously untoward. This is the next true step toward the destruction of sex-based barriers, toward equality, toward a better future.

A better future where our paycheques are very large, Random House. Can you honestly tell me that doesn't sound good? I look forward to hearing from you regarding this.

Yours,
Joey Comeau

Dear Toyota,

I am writing for a job in your marketing department, and I hope that you will take a moment to review my attached resume. I have been selling used cars for the past fifteen years, and over that time I have discovered a few tried-and-true selling techniques for reaching certain demographics.

I hope that I am not out of line by speaking my mind here, but let me be frank. Automotive technology has reached the point where — at the consumer level — it doesn't matter what's under the hood anymore. All that today's consumer cares about, functionality wise, is that it gets them from point a to point b. Aside from that, they want a car that's individual. Look at the new models of cars you've been shipping out recently. The Matrix and the Prius are idiotic looking, but people are buying them to have a car that they feel is distinct.

People want to believe that their car is special, individual. When I was working the lot at the used-car place, we used to keep a car out back and we would shove dead pigeons under the hood. Dead pigeons, man. That car was waiting for the perfect customer, a little old lady with a wicker purse. We convinced her the car ate pigeons. She was thrilled. We sold haunted cars, cursed cars. We sold cars that made you lucky in love. We sold cars that famous people had spat on.

A series of marketing campaigns, all aimed wildly into the demographic shooting-barrel. Campaigns running in the middle of the night, claiming that when the Garden Estate

Slasher was captured, he had a dead businessman in his trunk and we just rolled that shit back out on the lot without cleaning it. Somewhere, we'll say, is the Camry we emptied all of them hookers out of. Somewhere there's a Camry that mister big-shot movie star got blown in. Somewhere there's a Camry that is also a time machine. There is a Camry that can bring your children back to you. People want to feel like they're picking their car, Toyota, they don't want to feel like we're picking them.

People want something special. They want the house with the broken cellar stair and the wind tunnel that swings the doors open and closed like it's haunted. They want the neighbourhood where the race riots first started. They want to feel like they're a part of something bigger and stronger, and they want to be able to tell their children they are participating in history, not just standing off to the side. This is the house where Marie Curie died. I drink at the bar where Hoover used to go dancing. This is the Camry they found all those dead businessmen in. We're going to live forever, kids. We're a part of the story, now.

Joey Comeau

Dear RIAA,

You should note first that my experience has all been military, and that my position was cook. I should also mention that I do not believe the diagnosis indicated on my medical discharge was correct.

I have always been interested in copyright law. It has always been a hobby of mine. The doctors are correct in stating that I have been paying more attention.

You can violate copyright these days by taking a picture of your family standing next to your DVDs, by talking on the phone with the radio in the background, by emailing your friend about an interesting article in Oprah's magazine. The laws will get crazier and crazier, until I find myself surrounded by criminals.

But without laws the world makes no sense, RIAA. Maybe these laws are too strict, too geared toward the profits of corporations, but what is our alternative? Chaos? A world where terror is our only rule?

My neighbour has the same deadbolt on his door as everyone else in this apartment building. I can pick that lock in less than a minute without a sound. He talks in his sleep, RIAA, quoting lines from movies. I have been making notes of the date and the time of each. What he's doing isn't illegal yet. What if it is tomorrow?

The hairs on his head are arranged in a strange pattern. The spacing between each is irregular, but not completely. I'm certain that there's something here. I have been photographing his hair follicles, and I'm encoding them onto the computer, looking for a pattern. There's nothing yet, but I know I am close to finding the key. What if he has a leaked copy of the Avengers sequel in his hair? Tonight I will photograph the eyebrows.

His hair is so soft, RIAA. It used to be that criminals were all rough men. Now this? Now ten-year-old boys are committing crimes in my own apartment building? I only hope the juvenile correctional facilities here can redeem him in time. Because soon, RIAA, the day will come when we must protect this country with our knives and not our laws.

Joey Comeau

Dear Armdale Tea Room,

I am writing to apply for the position of Dishwasher (Casual), because, let's face it, dishwashing isn't a career. I'm not going to sit up all night and worry about the stats on my quarterly dishwashing report. I want to show up for my shift, wash gross half-eaten food off plates for a few hours, and then go home. It sounds like the sort of job that I don't even need to think about while I'm doing it. I can think about weird sex things or about what if zombies were racist, would they not eat you if they hated the colour of your skin? Would you be safe? Or would they eat you out of spite?

I need to make a few extra dollars to pay rent, to buy groceries. I don't want to have to care what your company stands for, or try to make myself sound like some kind of inhuman perfect employee.

It's like meeting girls. A relationship is just another kind of job, isn't it? In the beginning you pretend to be that perfect employee. You lie in the interview and then you do your best for a while. You never step out of line. You always wait until you go home to use the bathroom if it's number two. You shave and brush your teeth every day. When you're kissing, you never pull out the pen and ask her to write "whore" on your body. You behave. But how long can that go on before you start going crazy? You have to be yourself. That's why it's called being yourself.

And soon you start slipping up. You think, "Oh, I'll just use the bathroom a little bit. Just a bit of a number two, to hold me over until I get home." You start chewing gum just before you see her, because you forgot to brush today. You find yourself writing, "who" on your own stomach while she undoes your pants, and when you see her confused face, you scramble for a weak explanation. "Oh, I just didn't want to forget to look something up, later. Who, uh . . . Who played the girl in *The Apartment*? Was it Shirley MacLaine?"

In the end it never works out. You are who you are, no matter what you pretend at the beginning. So I'm not pretending. I drink to ignore my problems. I spend more time with my computer than with my friends. I am angry and lonely, but I can wash dishes just fine. I'm being honest. Please don't be an asshole about this.

Yours,
Joey Comeau.

Dear FCC,

I am writing to you because I am looking for a position with your agency. As my cover letter will indicate, my experience encompasses a variety of positions with a wide range of agencies.

Often, in interviews, I am asked why I have spent time with so many different agencies. There is a worry, I think, that I am unable to commit my skills to a single agency. This is based on the false premise that for a business relationship to be successful, it has to last forever. Every agency will surprise me with new positions, and I'll be forced to adapt, to enhance my skill set to allow me to satisfy the needs of this new agency. These skills have served me well, and I believe they will serve you well.

Allow me to present an example of one of these professional situations in which I was well served by the expanded skill set that I have developed through my experiences in various positions with agencies over the years. I accepted a contract with a small agency downtown. I contacted this agency via an internet site devoted to establishing such business relationships, a "headhunter" site.

I was unaware that there would be two companies involved, and when I arrived to work I was initially skeptical. I had never worked a position that required me to coordinate business relations between two agencies concurrently. However, I found that my skill set allowed me to successfully bring the contracts to their conclusion. Three times with one of the companies.

Sometimes, however, I share the concerns of potential agencies that my experience is too broad-ranging, that I may in fact be overqualified. There is a part of me that believes very strongly in old-fashioned careerism, that believes you should spend your entire life with one company, loyal and true. I'm too young, though. I have too much to do. Don't I?

I wish there was a clear answer, but in the interim I hope you will consider me. I've included some photographs of my resume for your review. It's 8.5 inches, uncut.

Yours,
Joey Comeau

Dear Security Services,

Thanks for taking the time to consider my application. I understand the need to review the criminal records of potential employees, and I support your position in this matter one hundred percent. When you are hiring someone to guard a property against burglary and vandalism, the last person you want is a vandal or a convicted thief. That makes all the sense in the world, I totally agree.

A repeat burglary offender is likely to steal from his own employers. He would make a horrible employee in a security capacity, being a security risk himself. But you need to ask yourself this: Does it really matter if he's been convicted of first-degree murder? Could there be anything less relevant? He isn't likely to encounter his backstabbing best friend on the job, or anything. That friend is already dead.

He's already dead and buried, and I have already served my time. I've paid my debt to society, and now I would like nothing more than to resume the career that I laid out in a guidance counsellor's office oh-so-many years ago. I would like to come to work for your company, and I think I would make a fine addition to your team. I am crazy tough-looking, with prison tattoos all over, and have a raspy voice cultivated by a combination of the harsh air conditions in my cellblock and an unreliable supply of good herbal tea.

I am a people person, and I love to work with the public. I have extensive experience working in a security capacity, having worked security on such high-profile accounts as Microsoft headquarters and McDonald's head office, and with Securitas Canada in a number of important capacities.

I am a man of my word, and I have strong convictions. You will not find a more honest and trustworthy employee anywhere. I murdered Jimmy with a kitchen knife, and I would do it again. He did wrong by me, and it made me so crazy. It still makes me crazy. I stabbed him again and again in the face, and I used the knife to carve a small poem about my feelings on his back. "I went to rent a movie / but they said I had fines / so many fines / I couldn't / rent again / until I paid / you said / you took that movie / back / I trusted / you."

I look forward to speaking with you again about this position.

Yours,
Joseph Comeau

Dear *The Herald*,

I'm writing to apply for a job with the *Herald*. You're looking for a Freelance Journalist to cover events in Antigonish, whatever that is, and I am including my resume for your review.

My major publication credits include small pieces in the *New York Times* and the *Observer*. I worked as an intern with *Forbes* magazine for whatever you consider an impressive amount of time. I just recently finished a brief stint working as copy editor of [THE BIGGEST NEWSPAPER I CAN THINK OF — the *Wall Street Journal*? Will they believe that?]

I have long been a fan of the *Herald*, and I have always dreamed of writing for you. When I was working at [WHATEVER MAGAZINE I SAID] I decided that I would pursue that dream, so I quit my prestigious copy editing job in the big leagues and decided to come work for you. The *Herald* is my chance to open up a little more, to enjoy the slightly looser restrictions on my writing.

Don't get me wrong, I like it in the big city. I love riding the subways to work, I love the way it lights up at night. I love those clubs you can go to, where they pull back the little window and ask for the password so you can go inside and have dirty sex with ugly women and ugly men. My friends think that it's disgusting. They ask, "Don't you worry about diseases?" and "Haven't you got any self-respect?" and what can I say to that?

Of course I worry about diseases. Of course I have self-respect. I have a steady girl that I see every Friday for a movie. We drink root beer together at the A&W, and we hold hands while we wait for her bus. We haven't kissed yet, but I know we will. She's so perfect for me, you know? She wants to be a lawyer, just like in the movies. I think that's so great.

My friends tell me that I'm using her, that I'm living a lie, and that it's unfair. I ask them, what's so wrong about what I'm doing? I love her and she loves me. When I go to those sex clubs, I tell the women there, "I don't hold hands with anyone but my girlfriend." I tell the men, "I hope you don't expect to share laughter over a root beer with me, because I am in love with a nice girl who wants to be a lawyer so she can put criminals away for what they did, and not let them get off on a technicality."

I don't know what an Antigonish is, but I'm more than willing to learn. I'm more than willing to learn anything you want if you'll let me write for your paper. My girl, my steady girl, she's moved to that small town there, Halifax, and I'm going to come with her. That's the real reason I left [WHAT-EVER MAGAZINE I SAID I WAS WORKING FOR], but don't tell her that. She said, "It isn't right for you to uproot everything for me, Joe, we haven't even kissed yet." Maybe we haven't, but we will. And I hope that when we do, she'll be kissing a newspaperman for the *Herald*!

Yours,
Joseph Comeau

Dear Double Fine Productions,

I saw your job posting for an Environmental Art Designer, and I was intrigued. What could be the connection between a video game company and the art form to which I have devoted my life? I am including my resume for your review.

I have been involved in the world's largest Environmental Art projects of the last decades, and I am certain that my planning skills, coupled with my ability to direct large-scale projects, will make me an asset to your company. But for a moment I would like to look beyond my job experience, beyond my technical skills. I would like to talk about why I believe in this life so strongly. And it is a life. It is a calling. I would like to talk about why I've devoted myself to environmental art in all its forms.

I was first recruited out of the Chemical Engineering program at MIT (with a minor in art history), and I had no idea what was going on. I thought it was a simple project, melding art and science. Something fun. When I finally did start to suspect the magnitude of what they were planning, I wanted to run.

Among our members were dozens of men and women from the highest positions of power in industry and government. And they all seemed bent on the destruction of the environment. It was terrifying.

Each member of the group had their companies emitting large quantities of greenhouse gases. These gases were to

sit in our atmosphere and allow less of the sun's radiation
to escape back into space. As more radiation is retained, the
earth would begin to heat up. The climate would begin to
change.

I tried to run. I packed my clothes in the middle of the night.
But when I opened my door, I came face to face with the man
who had recruited me. He sat me down on the couch. We had
the talk that changed my life.

"Art is a reflection of human nature," he said. "It is beautiful,
and awful. It is simple, and it is incomprehensible. Art is the
process of taking things apart to see how they work, and it
is the process of breaking things to remind us how fragile
they are."

He sat on the edge of my couch, drinking a glass of water,
and he said that we were creating an atmosphere that
would retain the radiation reflecting off the surface of the
earth. We were melting the edges of the ice caps, cooling
down the northern seas. We were slowing the Gulf Stream,
dramatically changing the way the environment behaved. He
grabbed my shoulder and said, "Isn't art supposed to move
you? Isn't it supposed to shake you by the hair and say, 'Aren't
you afraid?'"

He said art isn't just for your benefit, or mine. Art can be a
lesson that we leave behind, a horrible warning instead of a
shining example. Art, he said, isn't your little paintings and

comic books. Art is the meteor that wiped out the dinosaurs.

And I looked back on my life, at how empty it was. At how little I had done before now. This is how I will make a difference. A real difference.

Yours,
Joey Comeau

Dear Abrasion Enterprises,

I am forwarding you my resume because I believe that I would be a valuable addition to the Abrasion Enterprises sales team. My outstanding sales record speaks for itself, and I am ready to turn my skills to your needs in the abrasive industry. I am enthusiastic about the world of Abrasion!

As you will discover upon reading through my resume, I was first employed promoting the Cottonelle Brand in establishments across the continent. My responsibilities included all manners of persuasion, but in the end it all came down to two factors: the cottony softness of the product and my skill as a salesman. I believe that both of these factors are equally important, and I cannot do my best if I am not representing a product that I truly believe in. And I believed in the wonderful gentleness of Cottonelle's bathroom products.

After Cottonelle your eye will be drawn to the fact that I spent five years with Kraft, promoting their wondrously spongy and warm Kraft Dinner product line. My job with Kraft started off as sales, but over time drifted into marketing. In the end it mainly consisted of approaching the authors of children's books and convincing them to include Kraft Dinner in their work, helping to promote the Kraft Brand and its association with warmth and spongy security. I am proud of the work I did at Kraft, but it is in sales where I am happiest, where I am the most productive.

After Kraft I spent a number of years working with the Royal-Pedic mattress company of Los Angeles. It was around this time that I began to notice that whenever I would visit my brother and his family, things would be different. I was pleased that they were using Cottonelle in their bathroom, and that we would sit down to talk over a bowl of Kraft Dinner, but it worried me that they wrapped the corners of their furniture in blankets. It worried me that they would only give me a spoon to eat with (though of course it is one of the selling points of Kraft Dinner that it doesn't require the child to use a fork). Above all, I was worried by the way the children looked at me: with pity in their eyes.

I began to suspect that I had a problem.

I HAD A PROBLEM.

This, of course, explains the year-long gap between my last day at Royal-Pedic and the date of this application. At first, I was wary of the dangers of therapy to my sense of self-worth, but by proactively selling myself on the long-term benefits, I was able to enlist the aid of a therapist and begin my year-long struggle with fear. I will admit it. I was afraid. I was so afraid that I had to surround myself with comfort, with softness in all its forms. But now things are different. Now I feel I am ready to face a world with sharp corners and all. I feel I am ready to come to work for Abrasion Enterprises.

Yours,
Joey Comeau

Dear Neopost,

I am responding to your job posting for a Credit and Collections Manager. I am currently in the market for a job in this field, and on one of my daily visits to your site I was thrilled to discover that Neopost was hiring. I have waited a long time for this opportunity, and I am including my resume for your review.

My resume details my fifteen years of extensive experience in Credit and Collections Management. It sometimes feels like I have worked in Credit and Collections Management all my life. Do you ever feel that way, Neopost? Anyway. If you have any questions, please don't hesitate to call me. This opportunity is once in a lifetime, and I assure you that I believe in what your company is doing one hundred percent. And I have certainly been watching closely.

My first encounter with Neopost came two years ago, while I was on the internet looking for alternatives to the traditional postal system (which had previously caused the death of my entire family). I found Neopost's website to be pleasantly designed and informative, and I immediately saved the address in my "Bookmarks." On a subsequent visit, I began to realize the full implications of the existence of services such as yours.

Using equipment purchased on your website, I have begun to construct my own post office in the basement of my house. Your company has provided me with the finest in mailroom furniture and high-volume sorting and folding machines. The newest addition is, of course, a 30-kg digital scale, for weighing mail and determining the rate. It's interfaced with the mail machine, and I have named it Maggie because that was my youngest daughter's name.

The chance to put my Credit and Collections Management experience to work for your company is something I am willing to die for. My post office is almost finished, but I know that I will need to build one in every town before I can fully replace the postal service. The employee discount that you will hopefully provide should make a helpful dent in the costs associated with that as well.

The depression and suicidal fantasies of three years ago are nothing but a memory to me now. I am a man consumed with passion, and your products have given a new meaning to my life. Without you I do not know where I would be, and I do not want to know. I am happy now, pursuing my goal.

My dead family and I are in your debt, and I long to help you in any way I can. I feel I could make a real difference at your company.

Thank you for taking the time to consider my resume. I am willing to relocate to anywhere in Canada.

Yours,
Joey Comeau

Dearest Eastlink,

I'm responding to your job posting regarding a
Communications Manager. I am not including my resume
for your review, because (though impressive) my resume
would only distract you from the opportunity I am
about to offer you.

Since its emergence, I have been impressed with the potential
of Eastlink Communications. You're the new blood here in
the Maritimes. The fresh face. You stand poised on the edge
of greatness now, and all it takes is one small push to send you
down that path to glory. I am here to offer that push.

Let's not beat around the bush. I could include my resume
with this email. I could be like every pimply faced university
graduate who graces your inbox with desperate pleas to
be taken seriously. I could list the companies that I've sent
soaring with my PR skills. I could list the endorsement deals
until I'm blue in the face, and in the end what will I have said?

Nothing.

Instead, let me talk about what I see for your company's
future. A glory that can be summed up in three words: the
Eastlink Party.

I'm not talking about a wine and cheese here, I'm talking
about making a play for power, right now while the iron
is hot, while the voters and their high-speed internet

connections are still in the honeymoon period. With my experience, and the massive popularity you've achieved due to the brilliance and convenience of your Service Bundles, we could take a real shot at making this government ours.

Imagine the delight of the voting public. Here is a party without some political agenda, interested only in the wonders of capitalism. A party with no difficult speeches and no complex ideologies. Imagine the benefits of being a Corporate Government!

Eastlink digital cable, high-speed internet, and local and long distance telephone services, these would be utilities. The resources of a country would be yours to call upon. Aliant Telecom would fall before you, weak before your strength. Maybe you won't be able to just shut them down, but you will certainly be able to manipulate laws and taxes to cripple them quickly. With the resources of an entire government at your hands, you will be able to undercut their prices with ease.

I'll be honest here. I have no experience with the duties and responsibilities involved in running a government. I'm not sure what is legal and illegal for you to do once you have taken office, but it is a simple matter for you to find people with these skills once you have power, and it is I who will get you there.

I've taken the liberty of contacting various agencies on your behalf, and I've been testing the waters with some very broad, vague polls. Things look good, right now, but make no mistake: satisfaction with your fantastic bundles, with your amazing high-speed internet service, will soon begin to peter out. Even with your terrific services, they will begin to expect more. Pirated movies will seem to take too long to download, long distance won't cost few enough pennies a minute, bundled service packs won't save them enough money a month.

This is your chance to leave all of the inconveniences of the free market behind.

You may call upon me, night or day.

Joey Comeau

Dear Leisureworld Fitness,

I was excited to learn that the Leisureworld Fitness Centre was seeking an Activation Assistant. I am an up-and-coming Activation enthusiast who wishes to make my hobby into a career. I have experience activating all manner of electronic devices and private property alarm systems ranging from vehicular ones to those designed for the home.

I feel that an assistant-level position will give me time to acclimatize myself to the professional world of Activation, as well as allow me to judge my skill set by industry standards. I am certain that I will not remain at the assistant level for long, but I am more than aware of the necessity of beginning there. I have enclosed my resume, which lists these skills, as well as my experience.

Unfortunately I do not have a diploma in Activation, though you state that you require one. Please understand that this is due to my overwhelming skill at activating, and not because of any lacking. You see, the Activation college down the street from my house uses a number of different security systems, and my attempt to break in and print myself up an Activation diploma was foiled by my almost innate ability to activate those alarms.

Shaken by the high-pitched screeching, I was driven from the building into the cold, cold night, where I promptly activated the hood on my jacket and headed for my home. On the way,

I reflected on Activation in general, and it was while I walked past your fine establishment that I finally decided to go for it.

You were my inspiration.

Watching unhappy, ever-forward-looking people climb electric stairs through your plate-glass window made me wonder. Am I climbing a set of stairs that goes nowhere because it's not actually stairs, but in fact just an electronic gizmo designed to simulate stairs? Am I going to be an Activation hobbyist for the rest of my life, or am I going to go right home and draft my resume?

At the age of forty, will I activate an electric radio in my bathtub, after reflecting on my sad, failed life? Or will I activate my memory and a bottle of expensive wine, and recall the night I sat down and finally activated my ambition, turning its fantastical powers to a career with your fantastical company?

Thank you,
Joey Comeau

Dear RCA Healthcare,

I am responding to your job posting seeking a Medical Dictatypist with two or more years of experience. I have been a professional Dictatypist in the medical field for fifteen years, and I have published several successful guides to modern Dictatyping through Random House Publishing. I am including my resume for your review.

The majority of my resume, you will notice, is made up of Dictatypist positions where I made much more than the $12 to $14 an hour that you advertise, but please be assured my salary expectations are much lower with the current depressed market for Dictatyping services. I am well aware that as demand for our services has gone down, so too have the salaries we command.

If I don't get this job, something will have to change.

That might be for the best, actually.

Tomorrow I will wake up and my dream of sustaining myself with Dictatyping will be dead. I will stand in front of the mirror and I will tell myself, "Today you can start over. You can throw away all your old hopes. Why are you still wishing on that same old star? That was somebody else's star. You're brand new today! Dream a new dream, dipshit!"

Joey Comeau

Dear MetLife,

I am writing in response to the Life Insurance Information Verification job posting on monster.ca. I believe that I am well suited to this job, and I feel that you would agree. Please take a moment to read what I have to say. I will try to keep it to the point.

I have, for a number of years now, been living next door to a man named Christopher Sullivan. Last summer I went over and introduced myself to him, and we became fast friends.

JOB SKILL: I HAVE AN EXCELLENT CUSTOMER SERVICE MANNER.

I think it goes without saying that I was only acting. I had no honest interest in becoming his friend. My interests were in Life Insurance Information Verification (and so they remain). I could tell from Sullivan's not-quite-decent attitude that he was clearly involved in fraud of some kind. It became my goal to discover more.

JOB SKILL: I SHOW INITIATIVE.

As Christopher (Chris, to his "friends") sat drinking beer on his couch, I rummaged through his medicine cabinets. Row upon row of pill bottles. Levsin, read one. Modulon, read another. But inside those bottles I found only Percocets, Oxycocets. Painkillers.

JOB SKILL: I AM FAMILIAR WITH PAINKILLERS.

"You better not get any on the walls," he laughed drunkenly, believing my ruse about bowel problems. Yet my heart raced as the doorknob jiggled. The lock held, I laughed heartily, and he went away. But from then on I was more careful.

JOB SKILL: I AM CAREFUL.

Yet time wore on, and I could find out nothing more. I had occasion to check every room in his house. Every room except the bedroom, that is. But Christopher is a very private man. How could I expect him to let me into his room? After much soul-searching, and asking myself whether I am really committed to Life Insurance Information Verification, I came to realize how I would proceed. I began sleeping with him.

JOB SKILL: I AM DEDICATED TO MY WORK.

Sleeping with Mr. Sullivan was not altogether unpleasant. Ultimately, though, it left me wanting. It did, however, lead me to the discovery that I had long searched for. His filing cabinet. As he snored loudly on the bed, I plied through his files to discover his life-insurance records. It was as I suspected: Christopher Sullivan had claimed to have no health problems and no addictions. I knew what I had to do.

JOB SKILL: I KNOW WHAT I HAVE TO DO. I KNOW WHEN I HAVE TO DO IT.

I feel that I am ready to move up in the world of Life Insurance InformationVerification, and I am choosing your company as my vehicle. I am not sure what your company's name is, but I am sure it is very nice. You may contact me by email or the telephone.

Yours,
Joey Comeau

Dear Chicken Farmers of Nova Scotia,

I am writing to you in response to your posting of December 11, seeking an individual with strong administrative background for the position of General Manager with the Chicken Farmers of Nova Scotia. I am enclosing my resume, and I am certain that you will agree that I am more than qualified for this job.

As my resume shows, I have been working in the chicken farming industry since June 26, 1971. Back then I was a clean-faced boy of seventeen, with a passion in my heart and a purpose in my step. I didn't know a thing about chicken farming, and being young and foolish, I didn't believe that I needed to.

I thought that my revenge would come easily, and so at first I learned only from my mistakes. I understand WHY I made the mistakes I did. I was hurt. I was angry. I was filled with the fires of fantasy, and I fancied myself a chicken apocalypse that would wash the surface of the globe, leaving behind only carnage. I blundered from farm to farm, and it wasn't long before they knew I was coming. It was only through the faking of my own death that I escaped their wrath. And it made them wary.

So (as my resume indicates) following my "death," I moved from chicken farm to chicken farm, often staying for no more than a few months. I can imagine that from your perspective this job history must make me seem unreliable. That is why

I feel I must be frank with you. I cannot promise that I will stay with your company for longer than a month. In the past, I have stayed as long as a year, but I want you to be aware that there have been instances where I have been forced to tender my resignation much sooner. The chickens seem to get smarter every year, and often I find myself in the awkward position of leaving employers in the lurch.

It is important that you understand. These chickens cannot know what I am up to. It is only through infiltrating the chicken farms of the world that I can truly hope to discover their plans. It has taken me a long time to come to this conclusion. At first I was content to work at hatchet jobs, taking my revenge on one feathered throat at a time. But they are innumerable, and there are chicken farms in every province. I can't kill them all, and no amount of wishing will change that.

But maybe I can stop them all. So I move from farm to farm, learning more about their plans, putting the pieces together. I stay only until the chickens begin to suspect me, and then I must move on.

I am not a monster. There have been chickens along the way that have earned my respect, that have seemed almost decent to my foolish heart. But my heart is indeed foolish and blind, and I have long ago learned that its advice is useless in the real world. It is only common sense, cold and hard, that can possibly see me through this. It is only my intelligence that can save our planet. Even if it is too late to save my own soul.

I hope that my honesty has aroused something like trust in you, and I hope that you will provide me with employment on your farm. You may contact me by email or telephone, night or day.

Respectfully,
Joey Comeau

Dear Workers' Compensation Board,

I am a recent graduate from a doctorate program in Nursing, and I am enclosing my resume for your review. It details the numerous internships and volunteer work that I have performed in the satisfying field of Adjudication, and I hope that it reflects my complete and utter devotion to the field. I have long admired the severe and final adjudication handed down by the Workers' Compensation Board of Nova Scotia, and I think that I will be happy working for you.

Though you will find that none of my previous jobs have been directly related to Adjudication responsibilities, I think I can show that I do not lack experience. I have often taken the initiative upon myself, adjudicating with neither the knowledge nor the thanks of my superiors.

A recent example might help to demonstrate my dedication to the true justice that is Adjudication.

While working as an intern at the Victoria General Hospital, my job was to process dozens of applications every day for one of our hospital's more expensive procedures. These applications were filed and eventually passed on to the hospital adjudication board. In order to lessen their load, and to help them in the sorting process, I made it my personal mission to dispose of those proposals that were clearly unsuitable and constituted a waste of their time. In this way, I worked as a sort of unofficial Adjudication Screener.

While there, for example, I averted an awkward situation where the adjudication staff would have had to decide between two patients, both in dire need of treatment. The first patient was an elderly man of ill repute. Let me be perfectly clear when I tell you that he was a vagrant. He signed his name with an X, and he stared openly at the breasts of female patients. I had often seen him while Saturday shopping, sitting on the side of the road jingling his change jar at people as though he deserved their money. As though it were owed him!

The other patient was a young man from the local university. An upstanding citizen with his entire life ahead of him. He smiled at me with genuine charm, and I wondered if he might not one day be walking those halls as a doctor himself. He was a lovely young man. I wouldn't be able to consider myself a human being if I were to pass both applications on to the adjudication board, where both men would be reduced to their names, where they might be considered as equals.

Adjudication of that sort should be handled by the people who actually deal with the patients, by those of us who have seen these vagrants spitting on the ground. It should be the responsibility of people who are more equipped to decide where the money would be better spent. You can imagine which of the two I chose, and it is upon this faultless sense of adjudication that you will be able to rely when I am your employee.

Thank you for taking the time to consider my resume, and I look forward to hearing from you in the future.

You may contact me by email or phone.

Yours,
Joey Comeau

Dear Lung Association,

I'm applying for a job as Arts and Crafts Director for the Lung Association, as advertised on the internet. Enclosed, you'll be happy to find my resume, which is a document detailing my previous work experience and my skill set. I had my secretary put it together.

The first thing you will notice is that I am slightly overqualified for this position. Please don't let this deter you from considering me. I assure you that I am applying for this job because I believe very strongly in what you do at the Lung Association, and I believe that my talents would be of use to you. You've done so much for me, and I just want to give back.

I feel that I have a lot to give, and I think you'll agree that I'm the sort of handsome creative person you are looking for.

While I was CFO at Maritime Life, I ran an underground newsletter in our office entitled "Peggy's got a wart," which was a forum for the more creative of our employees to vent about their frustrations with office life. We published everyone from the Vice-President down to Mailroom Clerks, and everyone remained anonymous.

Often I would be called upon to write short-notice pieces to fill space when someone did not meet their deadline, and I published some of my best work under a tight schedule, including my one-act play *Revolution's fine, but give me the high fives and the hugs and I'm happy.* This magazine was an eye-opening experience for me, and since then I have actively looked for high-pressure situations, as I believe that I work best under pressure.

The magazine was a critical success, too. We published six issues in the year I was CFO, and we were featured in the corporate issue of the zine-review magazine *Broken Pencil*, not to mention the advertising interest we garnered from the Xerox corporation and Timex. But the life of a CFO was not for me. I have a facility with finance but no passion for it, and so I moved on.

Next, I put my self-publishing skills to good use during a brief stint as CTO of Microsoft Canada, where I published a collection of my personal comics using the company's in-house printing services. The machines were designed for perfect-binding user manuals, which do not normally run below sixty pages, but I was able to produce enough material to fill these extra pages.

My comic is titled "The Demon in Joey," and it deals with the profound changes I went through after having a lung replaced. I anthropomorphized my lung with big silly eyes, and I tried to explore the confusion and anger that I went through as part of my body turned against me. At times, the comic is dark, dealing with betrayal and fear, but in the end there is a feeling of redemption. A redemption courtesy of the Lung Association of Nova Scotia, I might add.

As you can see, I'm a very creative person, and I am quite dedicated to giving something back to the Lung Association of Nova Scotia. Arts and crafts sounds fun! And I could easily deal with working with children, if I had to. I look forward to hearing from you regarding this position.

Yours truly,
Joey Comeau

Dear Maritime Beauty,

I read your recent posting on some internet or other, seeking someone for a shipping and receiving position at Maritime Beauty, and I am absolutely positive that I am the man for the job.

I know that my background may not seem to lend itself to shipping and receiving. I've got no experience in shipping, none in receiving. Instead I have certificates in Welding and Practical Engineering, as well as my Silver Scissors from the school of cosmetology. I guess you could say I've been having trouble finding my calling.

But shipping and receiving seems so perfect. I can already picture myself behind the wheel of the greasy yellow forklift, the warehouse filled with the sounds of crashing and hollering, the air hot and thick with machines working. I've always felt an affinity for machines. They're strong and built for hard work. Sometimes I see myself as a sort of machine, and that's when I like myself the most. But I have always known that there was another side to my personality.

The delicacy of hairdressing has always been embarrassing to the part of me in love with machines, but I love the creative process with my whole being. I cannot slide my finger and thumb into those scissors without feeling the rush of fear, knowing what my welding buddies would think of me, what they might say. But it is also true that once my forefinger and thumb have slid into place I feel a rush of another kind.

Excitement.

So why hire me? Well, ideally I see myself as a jack of all trades in your company, prepared to toss aside my dirty smock and step into the front room of your salon. I'm confident in my ability to advise your customers on which beauty products would best suit their colouring and hair type, and which hair cuts are in style for their professions and their lifestyles.

I wear my own hair cropped short, the simple look favoured by working men, though I would never admit to them that I left the bangs a half-inch longer and took the shears to them for that naturally messy look that's so popular this season.

And imagine the looks on the faces of my old cosmetics-school friends if they found out that I've been giving my jeans that beat-up look by lodging them in the treads of a CAT bulldozer! But it works!

It's frustrating to be torn between these two obsessions, and I am certain that this shipping and receiving job is my answer. I know that I have a lot to offer. More than most.

I look forward to hearing from you, and you may contact me by email or telephone.

Thanks, always,
Joey Comeau

Dear Priszm Brands,

I am enclosing my resume in the hopes that you will consider me for the position available at the Dartmouth Pizza Hut. I do not have any experience in fast food, but I do believe that circumstance is strongly in my favour.

I have long been a fan of the Priszm Brands family of franchise outlets, and it would make me unhappy to see the company go bankrupt over something as silly and avoidable as not hiring me. But, due to circumstances beyond my control, that may well happen.

A company in Denver refused to make me Vice-President of their acquisitions department, and in the next quarter their stock price fell drastically. I believed this to be nothing more than a satisfying coincidence, until one week later that same company's offices collapsed into rubble. They literally just fell over. Still a coincidence? Maybe.

I was wary of applying to another job, but then I heard of a computer programming position with an Oakland, CA, firm that I had long respected. I applied in person, flying down to Oakland only to learn that the position had already been filled. Three weeks later, that company was being investigated for massive stock fraud. Perhaps you've read about them in the news? Still, I tried to convince myself that it was another coincidence.

But then I had an experience that refused to be ignored. I decided to apply for a job with Future Shop through their website. On their site, there is a map of Canada with small red dots representing their office locations across the country. When I first visited the website, that map was almost solid red. There were dots everywhere.

After my interview, I waited three weeks for them to respond. They didn't. They didn't even have the decency to let me know why I was unsuitable. Monday of the third week of waiting, I brought up their website on my screen. It was then that I knew something was wrong. The page informed me that massive losses had forced Future Shop to close hundreds of their offices. There on the map, right on the front page, the remaining offices spelled something out in little red dots:

HIRE JOEY COMEAU OR YOU ARE DOOMED

I began to realize that while this was a curse in some ways, it was also a blessing. Who would be foolish enough to not hire me now?

Please let me know as soon as possible whether you're going to hire me, because I don't know how long you have before the curse assumes that you aren't and dooms you.

Yours,
Joey Comeau

Dear SouthSea Child Care,

I'm writing to apply for the position of Preschool Teacher
with SouthSea Child Care, as advertised on the internet.
Attached, you will find my resume.

I am returning to Mount Saint Vincent University in the
fall, where I will enter my third year of the Early Childhood
Education program. I have been away from school, recently,
on a two-year hiatus. I believe that this hiatus has done me
nothing but good. It has opened my eyes, and I am returning
to my child care studies with a completely new perspective.
And I have your child care centre to thank for that.

Your dedication to the care and education of our nation's
youth has been an inspiration to me. I was on the devil's road
before you. Without the guiding force of your example, I
have no idea how I may have ended up. I can tell you that it
may not have been a pretty sight. My life was forever changed
when I first discovered you, when I heard about the good that
you and your people do.

That was years ago now, but it seems like yesterday. I first
learned about your child care centre when I saw the beautiful
millennium flag your children designed, which flew at the
Tall Ships 2000. This flag was one of the last things I saw
before I began the two years of my correctional sentence and
the image really stuck with me. It represented the promise of
the future, and the ability to leave our past mistakes behind.
During the course of my sentence, I realized where my life

had gone wrong, and that I had been pursuing Childhood Education for all the wrong reasons.

As my resume indicates, I have extensive experience working with children. I've worked in daycares and after-school programs for as long as I can remember. But more important than my experience with teaching children is my volunteer experience in prison. I have never felt more at home than when I was helping my fellow inmates with literacy problems. It was there that I really learned the satisfaction that comes from helping someone to discover their full potential.

It was a difficult two years, but I wouldn't trade them for anything. They helped me to find a genuine love of teaching within myself, and it has since replaced the aimlessness that first led me to early childhood care. I would have pursued my degree in Early Childhood Education only because an ex-girlfriend once told me that I was good with kids. That isn't something that a career should be based on, and I'm not proud of that, but I feel that I have so much more to offer now.

I want to help children to discover their talents, I want to instil in them a sense of honour, and by my example, I want to reinforce that tired old adage "Crime does not pay." I want to do this at SouthSea.

I look forward to hearing from you about this position.

Sincerely,
Joey Comeau

To: [REDACTED]

Re: Barista/cashier

I am responding to your job posting looking for a "Barista / Cashier," which I clicked on initially because it sounded like you might be hiring a Barista/Cashier. Reading further into your ad, though, painted a slightly different picture. It turns out, for instance, that you aren't a coffee shop, but instead a "people and standards driven" company which aims to "consistently deliver excellent service to our business client base."

"Currently recruiting for a well-presented, committed, and dedicated worker who is a proactive thoughtful team player and looking for a long-term role." REALLY? You can't just say, "Clean and reliable?"

I wish I was dead. I wake up in the morning, not dead, and I think, "UGH."

And, because I am not dead, I have to find a job. That's how it works. But at least finding a job is something that can be done in a straightforward, self-respecting manner, right?

"All applicants must be used to working within a fast-paced environment whilst delivering exceptional customer service. Initiative, extremely high attention to detail, and the ability to interact courteously and efficiently with customers without being intrusive is also crucial."

80

EXTREMELY HIGH ATTENTION TO DETAIL, you say? Well you're in luck, because I'm Sherlock Holmes. Here's your coffee, sir. I'm sorry that your wife left you three nights ago, and you've been sleeping on the couch with your cat. Maybe your college roommate who you once had a fling with would be willing to take you in.

"Our staff members are expected to take pride in their role, and to work above and beyond their job remit, continually ensuring complete customer satisfaction and [. . .]"

Go fuck yourself.

Joey Comeau

Joey Comeau wrote the comic *A Softer World*, which has appeared in the *Guardian* and been profiled in *Rolling Stone*, and which *Publishers Weekly* called "subtle and dramatic." He is the author of a number of books, including *Overqualified*, *The Complete Lockpick Pornography*, and *One Bloody Thing After Another*, and the *Bravest World* comic book series. Joey lives in Toronto, Ontario.